Captive
In the Dark

CJ Roberts

Neurotica Books
ISBN-13: 978-0615429502
ISBN-10: 0615429505

Photo credit: Kurt Paris
Cover design: Amanda Simpson

Printed in the United States of America.

This book is dedicated to:

My mom, for loving me no matter what, even when I followed you around the grocery store with a pack of adult diapers until you bought me chips. I love you!

My husband, for believing in me more than I believe in myself. I've never laughed with someone so hard. We may never agree on a thing, but there's no one I would rather spend my life arguing with.

R. Robinson who has read this story in its many incarnations and continued to thirst for more. No doubt – you're my number one fan. Thank you for always being so open and honest – and for never making apologies.

K. Ekvall and A. Mennie who ushered me through the Dark (ahahahah) so that I might emerge on the other side. Without your words of wisdom, critical observations, keen editing eyes, plethora of emails, and metaphorical kicks to the ass I would never have gotten this done. Thank you for not letting me give up.

S. Davis for reading my work when it was horrible and still believing in my talent.

A. Simpson for her incredible design talent. QAF Forever. Team Justin.

My Girls (you know who you are), meet me on the 13th floor with a bottle of wine; I have stories. I love U!

PROLOGUE

Revenge, Caleb reminded himself. That was the purpose of all this. Revenge, twelve years in the planning and only a few months away in its execution.

As a slave trainer, he had trained at least a score of girls. Some were willing, offering themselves as pleasure slaves to escape destitution, sacrificing freedom for security. Others came to him as the coerced daughters of impoverished farmers looking to off load their burden in exchange for a dowry. Some were the fourth or fifth wives of sheikhs and bankers sent by their husbands to learn to satisfy their distinct appetites. But this particular slave, the one he eyed from across the busy street—she was different. She was neither willing, nor coerced, nor sent to him. She was pure conquest.

Caleb had tried to convince Rafiq he could train any one of the other types of girls. That they would best be prepared for such a serious, potentially dangerous task, but Rafiq would not be moved. He too had waited a long time to achieve his revenge, and he refused to leave anything to chance. The girl had to be someone truly special. She had to be a gift so valuable she and her trainer alike would be talked about by everyone.

After years of being the sole apprentice to Muhammad Rafiq, Caleb's reputation had slowly built, establishing him as a man both efficient and single-minded in whatever tasks were entrusted to him. He'd never failed. And now, all those years had been spent preparing for this moment. The time had come to prove his worth to a man he owed everything to as much as himself. There was only one obstacle remaining between him and vengeance. The last true test of his soullessness—willfully stripping someone of their freedom.

He'd trained so many he no longer remembered their names. He could train this one too, for Rafiq.

The plan was a simple one. Caleb would return to America and seek out a candidate for the *Flower Sale*, what the Arabs called, the *Zahra Bay'*. The auction would take place in his adopted country of Pakistan in a little over four months. It was sure to be littered with beauties from the typical male-run countries, where acquiring such women was limited only by supply and demand. But a girl from a first world country – that would be considered an accomplishment. Girls from Europe were highly sought after, though American girls were the crown jewels of the pleasure trade. Such a slave would solidify Caleb's standing as a true player in the pleasure trade and gain him access to the most powerful inner circle in the world.

His goal was to find someone similar to what he was used to: someone exquisitely beautiful, poor, likely inexperienced, and predisposed to submit. Once he made his selection, Rafiq would send four men to assist Caleb in smuggling the girl out of the country and into Mexico.

Rafiq had contacted an ally who would provide safe haven in Madera during the first six weeks Caleb would need to help his captive acclimate. Once she was reasonably compliant, they would make the two-day trip to Tuxtepec and board the private plane. Eventually landing in Pakistan, where Rafiq would assist Caleb in the final weeks of training prior to the *Zahra Bay'.*

Too easy, Caleb thought. Though for a moment, it felt like anything but.

Caleb, from his vantage point diagonally across the street, glanced at the girl he'd been observing for the last thirty minutes. Her hair was pulled away from her face, and a heavy frown played across her mouth as she stared intently at the ground before her feet. She fidgeted sometimes, alluding to a sense of restlessness she was unable to hide. He wondered why she seemed so anxious.

Caleb was both close enough to see and hidden away so the only thing noticeable was a dark vehicle, heavily tinted, but non-descript. He was almost as invisible as the girl tried to be.

Could she sense her life as she knew it hanging precariously in the balance? Could she feel his eyes on her? Did she have a sixth sense for monsters? The thought of it made him smile. Perversely, there was a part of him that hoped the girl did possess a sixth sense for spotting monsters in broad daylight. But he'd been watching her for weeks; she was completely oblivious to his presence. Caleb let out a sigh. He was the monster no one thought to look for in the light of day. It was a common mistake. People often believed they were safer in the light, thinking monsters only came out at night.

But safety—like light—was a façade. Underneath, the whole world was drenched in darkness. Caleb knew that. He also knew the only way to truly be safer was to accept the dark, to walk in it with eyes wide open, to be a part of it. To keep your enemies close. And so that's what Caleb did. He kept his enemies close, very close, so he could no longer discern where they ended and he began. Because there was no safety; monsters lurked everywhere.

He looked down at his watch and back up to the girl. The bus was late. Seemingly frustrated, the girl sat on the dirt with her backpack on her knees. Had this been a regular bus stop, there would be others meandering behind her or sitting by a bench, but it wasn't. So every day Caleb could observe her sitting alone under the same tree near the busy street.

Her family was poor, the next most important factor after being beautiful. It was easier for poor people to disappear, even in America. Especially when the person missing was old enough to have simply ran away. It was the typical excuse given by authorities when they couldn't find someone. They must have ran away.

The girl made no move to leave the bus-stop, despite the fact her bus was running forty-five minutes late, and Caleb thought it was interesting for some reason. Did she enjoy school so much? Or did she hate home so much? If she hated home, it would make things easier. Perhaps she'd view her kidnapping as a rescue. He almost laughed—*right*.

He eyed the girl's shapeless, unflattering attire: loose fitting jeans, gray hoodie, headphones and a backpack. It was her consistent outfit, at least until she got to school. There, she would usually change into something more feminine, flirty even. But at the end of the day, she'd change back. He thought about her hating her home life again. Did she dress that way because her home life was restrictive or unstable? Or to prevent unwanted attention from a dangerous neighborhood to and from school? He didn't know. But he wanted to.

There was something interesting about her that made Caleb want to jump to the conclusion she was the girl he'd been looking for, someone with the ability to blend-in. Someone with the good sense to do as they're told when faced with authority, or do as they must when faced with danger. A survivor.

Across the street the girl fidgeted with her headphones. Her eyes stared dispassionately at the ground. She was pretty, very pretty. He didn't want to do this to her, but what choice did he have? He'd resigned himself to the fact that she was a means to an end. If not her, then someone else, either way his plight would be the same.

He continued to stare at this girl, his potential slave, wondering how she would appeal to the target in mind. It was rumored that among the attendees at the auction this year would be Vladek Rostrovich, one of the wealthiest men in the world, and most assuredly one of the most dangerous. It was to this man the slave would be entrusted for however long it took Caleb to get close and destroy everything the man held dear to him. Then kill him.

Still, Caleb wondered, not for the first time, why he was drawn to her. Perhaps it was her eyes. Even from a distance he could see how dark, how mysterious and sad they were. How old they seemed.

He shook his head, clearing his thoughts, when he heard the cough and squealing gears of the school bus approaching from down the street. He watched closely as the girl's face relaxed in relief. It seemed to include more than just the arrival of the bus, but of escape, maybe even freedom. At last, the bus arrived, in perfect synchonicity with the sun as it finally rose to its full strength. The girl glanced up with a frown, but she lingered, letting the light touch her face before disappearing inside.

***

A week later, Caleb sat in his usual spot, waiting for the girl. The bus had come and gone. The girl wasn't on board, so he'd figured he'd wait and see if she showed up.

He was about to leave when he saw her round the corner at a dead run toward the bus-stop. She arrived out of breath, almost frantic. She was an emotional thing. Again he wondered why she was so desperate to make it to school.

Caleb looked out through his car window at the girl. She was pacing now, perhaps with the realization she had missed her bus. It seemed unjust that just last week the girl had waited for nearly an hour for the bus to arrive, but this week the driver had not waited at all. No girl, no stopping. He wondered if she would wait another hour, just to be sure there was no hope. He shook his head. Such actions would only reveal a desperate nature. He both hoped she would and wouldn't wait.

His fractured thoughts gave him pause. He

shouldn't have hopes at all. He had orders, his own agendas. Plain. Simple. Clear-cut. Morals had no place when it came to revenge.

Morals were for descent people, and he was as far from descent as a person could get. Caleb didn't believe in the existence of any higher being or an afterlife, though he knew a lot about religion from growing up in the Middle East. But if there *was* an afterlife where a person reaped what they'd sown on earth, then he was already damned. He'd go to hell happily—after Vladek was dead.

Besides, if God or gods existed, none of them knew Caleb did; otherwise, they hadn't given a shit about him when it mattered. No one had given a shit about him, no one except Rafiq. And in the absence of an all-punishing afterlife, Caleb needed to make sure Vladek Rostrovich paid for his sins right here on earth.

Twenty minutes later, the girl started to cry, right there on the sidewalk, right in front of him. Caleb couldn't look away. Tears had always been mystifying to him. He liked looking at them, tasting them. Truth be told, they made him hard. He once abhorred this conditioned response, but he was long over self-loathing. These responses, these reactions, were a part of him now, for better or worse. *Mostly worse* he admitted with a smile and adjusted his erection.

What was it about such displays of emotion that just dug into his gut without letting go? Pure lust rolled through him like a heavy ache bringing with it a strong desire to possess her, to have power over her tears. Each day, he thought of her more as a slave than a riddle. Though she maintained an alluring type of mystery locked away with downcast eyes.

His mind flashed with images of her sweetly innocent face awash with tears as he held her over his knee. He could almost feel the softness of her naked bottom under his hand, the surety of her weight pressed against his erection while he spanked her.

The fantasy was short-lived.

Abruptly, a car pulled up in front of the girl. *Shit.* He groaned as he willed the images away. He almost couldn't believe this was happening. Some asshole was trying to move in on his prey.

He watched as the girl shook her head, declining the driver's invitation to get into his car. It didn't seem like the guy was listening. She was walking away from the bus-stop, but he was following in his car.

There was only one thing to do.

Caleb stepped out onto the corner, fairly certain the girl hadn't taken notice of how long his car had been parked. For the moment, she seemed too terrified to notice anything but the pavement in front of her downcast eyes. She was walking very fast, backpack in front of her, like a shield. He crossed the street and slowly walked in her direction. He casually scanned the scene, while moving directly in front of her, their paths set for a head-on collision.

It all happened so quickly, unexpectedly. Before he had the chance to execute a simple strategy to remove the external threat, she suddenly flung herself into his arms, the backpack making a loud thud on the concrete. He looked at the car, the shadow and incongruent shape of a man. Another predator.

"Oh my god," she whispered into the cotton of his t-shirt. "Just play along okay?" Her arms were steel around his ribcage, her voice a frantic plea.

Caleb was stunned for a moment. What an interesting turn of events. Was he the hero of this scenario? He nearly smiled.

"I see him," He said, catching the other hunter's gaze. Stupid ass, he was still sitting there, looking confused. Caleb placed his arms around the girl as if he knew her. He supposed in a way he did. On a playful impulse he ran his hands down the sides of her body. She tensed, breath caught in her throat.

The car and competition finally sped away in a cloud of smog and squealing tires. No longer requiring his protection, the girl's arms released him quickly.

"I'm sorry," she said in a rush, "but that guy wouldn't leave me alone." She sounded relieved but still shaken by the incident.

Caleb looked into her eyes, up close this time. They were just as dark, beguiling, and cheerless as he had imagined they would be. He found himself wanting to take her then, to bring her to some secret place where he could explore the depths of those eyes, unlock the mystery they held. But not now, this was not the time or place.

"This is L.A.; danger, intrigue and movie stars. Isn't that what it says under the Hollywood sign?" He tried to lighten the mood.

Confused, the girl shook her head. She was apparently not ready for humor yet. But as she stooped to pick up her backpack she mumbled, "Um…actually, I think it's— *'That's so L.A.'* But it's not under the Hollywood sign. Nothing's under the Hollywood sign."

Caleb suppressed a wide grin. She wasn't trying to be funny. It was more like she was searching for comfortable ground. "Should I call the police?" he feigned concern.

Now that the girl felt safer, she appeared to take real notice of him, an unfortunate, yet completely unavoidable moment. "Um..." Her eyes darted back and forth from his eyes, lingering on his mouth a bit too long before they darted back to her sneakered feet. "I don't think that's necessary. They won't do anything anyway, creeps like that are all over the place here. Plus," she added sheepishly, "I didn't even get his plate."

She looked at him again, eyes roving his face before she bit her lower lip and looked down at the ground. Caleb tried to keep the look of concern on his face when all he really wanted was to smile. *So the girl finds me attractive.*

He supposed most women did, even if they realized later, or too late, what the attraction really meant. Still, these sorts of naïve, almost innocent reactions always amused him. He watched her, this girl, opting to look at the ground while she shuffled from side to side.

As she stood there, looking blissfully unawareher coy, submissive behavior was sealing her fate, Caleb wanted to kiss her.

He had to remove himself from this situation.

"You're probably right," he sighed, flashing an empathizing smile, "the police wouldn't be worth a damn."

She nodded slightly, still shifting from foot to foot nervously, even shyly now. "Hey, could you—"

"I guess I should be—" This time he allowed his smile to take over his face.

"Sorry, you first," she whispered as her face flushed beautifully. Her performance as the cute, shy girl was intoxicating. It was as if there were a sign hanging from her neck that read, "I promise, I'll do whatever you say."

He knew he should get going. Immediately. Oh, but it was too much fun. He looked up and down the street. People would arrive soon, but not yet.

"No, please, you were saying?" He regarded her jet black hair as she incessantly fiddled with it between her fingers. It was long, wavy and framed her face. The ends curled over the mound of her breasts. Breasts that would fill his palms quite nicely. He put an end to his line of thinking before his body rendered a response.

She looked up at him. The sun in her face, she squinted when she met his eyes. "Oh...um...I know this is weird, considering what just happened...but, I missed my bus and," flustered she tried to get the words out in a rush, "You seem like a nice guy. I mean, I have projects due today, and I guess I was wondering... Could you give me a ride to school?"

His smile was nothing short of nefarious. And hers so big he could see all of her pretty white teeth. "School? How old are you?" She blushed a deeper shade of pink.

"Eighteen! I'm a senior, you know, graduating this summer." She smiled up at him. The sun was still in her face and she squinted whenever she made eye contact. "Why?"

"Nothing," he lied and played upon the naivety of

11

her youth, "you just seem older is all." Another big smile—even more pretty white teeth.

It was time to put an end to this.

"Listen, I'd love to give you a ride, but I'm meeting a friend of mine just up the street. We usually carpool, and it's her turn to brave traffic on the 405." He checked his watch. "And, I'm already running late." Inside, he felt a wave of satisfaction as her face crumpled. At the word *no*, at the word *her*. Not getting what you wanted was always the first lesson.

"Yeah, no, sure—I get it." She recovered coolly, but still blushed. She gave an unaffected shrug and her gaze moved away from him. "I'll just ask my mom to take me. No biggie." Before he had a chance to offer any further condolences, she stepped around him and put her earphones in. "Thanks for helping me out with that guy. See you around."

As she hurried away, he could faintly hear the music blaring in her ear. He wondered if it was loud enough to drown out her embarrassment.

"See you around," he whispered.

He waited until she rounded the corner before he walked back to his car, and then he slid behind the wheel while opening his cell phone. Arrangements for his new arrival would have to be made.

ONE

I woke with a really bad headache and noticed two things simultaneously: it was dark and I wasn't alone. Were we moving? Vision hazy, my eyes rolled around, almost out of instinct, to gain a semblance of balance, recognition of something familiar. I was in a van, my body strewn haphazardly across the floor.

Startled, I attempted to move all at once, only to find my movements sluggish and ineffectual. My hands had been tied behind my back, my legs free but decidedly heavy.

Again, I tried to focus my eyes in the dark. Both back windows were heavily tinted, but even in the gloomy darkness I could make out four distinct shapes. Their voices told me they were men. They spoke to each other in a language I didn't understand. Listening, it was a torrent of fast-speech, clipped tones. Something rich, very foreign…Middle Eastern maybe. Did it matter? My brain said yes, it was information. Then that small comfort slipped away. Seeing the iceberg hadn't stopped the *Titanic* from sinking.

My first instinct was to scream. That's what you do when you find out your worst nightmare is playing out in front of you. But I clenched my jaw on the impulse. Did I really want them to know I was awake? No.

I am not inherently stupid. I'd seen enough movies, read enough books, and lived in a shitty neighborhood long enough to know drawing attention to myself was the worst thing I could do – in almost any situation. A voice inside my head yelled sarcastically, "Then why the hell are you here?" I winced.

This was the worst of all my fears, being dragged off by some sick fuck in a van, raped, left for dead. From the first day I realized my body was changing, there had been no shortage of perverts on the streets, telling me exactly what they'd like to do to me, *all* of me. I'd been careful. I followed all the rules in becoming invisible. I kept my head down, I walked fast, and I dressed sensibly. And still, my nightmare had found me. *Again.* I could almost hear my mother's voice in my head asking me what I'd done.

There were four of them. Tears flooded my eyes and a whimper escaped my chest. I couldn't help it.

Abruptly, conversation around me halted. Though I struggled to not make a single sound or movement, my lungs heaved for breath, rising and falling in the rhythm of my panic. They knew I was awake. My tongue laid heavy and thick inside my mouth. Impulsively, I screamed, "Let me go," as loud as I could, as though I were dying, because for all I knew I was. I screamed as though someone out there would listen, hear me, and *do* something. My head throbbed. "Help! Somebody help!"

I thrashed wildly, my legs careening in every direction as one of the men tried to capture them with his hands. As the van rocked, my captors' Arabic voices grew louder and angrier. Finally, my foot connected solidly with the man's face. He fell back against the side of the van.

"Help!" I screamed again.

Incensed, the same man came at me again and this time struck me very hard across my left cheek. My consciousness faded away, but not before I acknowledged my body, now inert and at the mercy of four men I didn't know. Men I never wanted to know.

The next time I came around, rough hands dug into my underarms while another man held my legs. I was being dragged out of the van, into the night air. I must have been out for hours. My head throbbed so hard I couldn't speak. The left side of my face felt like a soccer ball had smacked it and I could hardly see out of my left eye. Dizzy and with practically no warning, I vomited. They dropped me and I simply rolled onto my side. As I lay there dry heaving, my captors yelled amongst them, meaningless voices, in and out, broken and jarring. My vision flashed, clear then hazy. This continued, one action triggering another. Too weak to resist, I lay my head next to my vomit and passed out again.

***

Sometime later I regained consciousness, or some state of being, similar to consciousness. I jerked. I felt pain everywhere. My head throbbed, my neck was stiff to the point of searing pain, and worse, when I tried to open my eyes I discovered I couldn't. There was a blindfold over them.

It came to me in flashes. Screeching tires. Grinding metal. Footsteps. Running. Musk. Dirt. Dark. Vomit. Hostage.

Summoning every ounce of strength and resolve, I attempted to lift myself. Why couldn't I move? My limbs wouldn't budge. My mind was telling my body to move, but my body wasn't responding. A new wave of panic rushed through me.

Tears burned behind my closed lids. Fearing the worst, I attempted to remove the blindfold by moving my head. Pain shot down my neck, but my head barely moved. What did they do to me? I stopped trying to move. Just think, I told myself, *feel*.

I took a mental assessment of my person. My head rest on a pillow, and my entire body lay on something soft, so I was probably on a bed. A shiver ran through me. I still felt clothes against my skin – that was good. Fabric around my wrists, fabric around my ankles, it wasn't difficult to figure out I was tied to the bed. *Oh god!* I bit at my lip, holding in my sobs as I acknowledged the fabric of my ankle-length skirt lay high up on my thighs. My legs were open. Had they touched me? *Keep it together!* Exhaling a deep breath, I stopped the thought before it could grow.

I felt intact, no missing fingers. Mechanically, I focused on here, now. Knowing my faculties were in order, I expelled a small sigh of relief that sounded more like a sob.

That's when I heard his voice.

"Good. You're finally awake. I was beginning to think you'd been seriously injured." My body froze at the sound of a male voice. Suddenly, I had to instruct myself to breathe. The voice was eerily gentle, concerned…*familiar?* The accent, what I could comprehend over the sound of the ringing in my head was American, yet there was something off about it.

I should have screamed, afraid as I was, but I just froze. He had been sitting in the room; he had been watching me panic.

After a few moments, my voice trembled, "Who are you?" No response. "Where am I?" My words and voice seemed to be on some sort of delay, almost sluggish, like I was drunk.

Silence. The creak of a chair. Footsteps. My heart hammering in my chest.

"I am your master." A cold hand pressed against my sweat-slick forehead. Again, a nagging sense of familiarity. But it was stupid. I didn't know anyone with an accent. "You are where I want you to be."

"Do I know you?" My voice was raw, stripped of anything but my emotion.

"Not yet."

Behind my eyelids the world exploded into violent streams of red; my dark vision drowned in adrenaline. Acid fear ate down my synapses carrying *Danger. Danger. Run. Run!* to my limbs. My mind howled for every muscle fiber to contract. I willed everything to fight all of the constraints: I twitched.

I gave way to fits of hysterical crying. "Please...let me go," I whimpered. "I promise I won't tell anyone. I just want to go home."

"I'm afraid I can't do that." Just like that a sea of despair dragged me under its crushing waves. His voice was devoid of so many things: compassion, inflection, emotion, but there was one thing that wasn't missing and that was certainty. I couldn't accept it, his certainty.

He smoothed my hair back from my forehead, an intimate gesture that filled me with foreboding. Was he attempting to soothe me? Why?

"Please," I cried as he continued petting me. I felt his weight on the bed, and my heart stuttered.

"I can't," he whispered, "and more than that...I don't want to."

For a moment, only my crying and deep, anguished sobs punctuated the silence that followed his statement. The darkness made it all the more unbearable.

His breathing, my breathing, together, in empty space.

"Tell you what I *will* do, I'll untie you and get these bumps and bruises cleaned up. I didn't want you to wake up in a pool of water. I'm really sorry about the hit to the face," he stroked his fingers across my cheekbone, "but that's what happens when you fight without thinking of the consequences."

"A pool of water?" I jittered. "I don't want to get in any water. Please," I begged, "just let me go." His voice was too calm, too refined, too matter-of-fact, and too... reminiscent of Hannibal Lector in *The Silence of the Lambs*.

"You need a bath, Pet." Was his terrifying response. *Hello Clarice....*

All I could do was cry as he untied me. My arms and legs were stiff and numb; they felt too large, too heavy, too far away to be a part of me. Was my entire body asleep? Again I tried to move, I tried to hit him, to kick him. And again my efforts reflected in twitching, jerky movements. Frustrated, I lay inert. I wanted to wake up. I wanted to run away. I wanted to fight. I wanted to hurt him. And I couldn't.

He kept the blindfold on and lifted me off the bed, carefully. I felt myself rise and become suspended within the dark. My heavy head draped over his arm. I could feel his arms. Feel his clothes against my skin.

"Why can't I move?" I sobbed.

"I gave you a little something. Don't worry, it'll wear off." Scared, blind in the dark, his limbs wrapped

18

around mine, his voice took on texture, shape.

He shifted my weight in his arms until my head lolled against the fabric of his shirt.

"Stop struggling." There was amusement on the surface of his voice.

Halting my struggle, I tried to focus on details about him. He was perceptibly strong and he hoisted my weight without so much as a strained breath. Beneath my cheek I could feel the hard expanse of his chest. He smelled faintly of soap, perhaps a light sweat too, a masculine scent that was both distinct anddistantly familiar.

We didn't walk far, only a few steps, but for me each moment seemed like an eternity in an alternate universe, one where I inhabited someone else's body. But my own reality came crashing back to me the moment he set me down inside something smooth and cold.

Panic gripped me. "What the hell are you doing?"

There was a pause, then his amused voice. "I told you, getting you cleaned up."

I opened my mouth to speak when the initial burst of cold water hit my feet. Startled, I let out a skittish yelp. As I pathetically attempted to crawl out of the tub by rolling my body toward the edge, the water turned warmer and my captor hoisted me back against the tub.

"I don't want to take a bath. Let me go." I tried to remove the blindfold, repeatedly smacking my own face as my lethargic arms countered my purpose. My captor did a horrible job of stifling his laugh.

"I don't care if you want one, you need one."

I felt his hands on my shoulders and mustered my

strength to attack. My arms flew back haphazardly landing somewhere, I think, on his face or neck. His fingers speared through my hair to force my head back at an odd angle.

"Do you want me to play rough too?" he growled against my ear. When I didn't answer he squeezed his fingers tight enough to make my scalp tingle. "Answer my question."

"No." I whispered on a frightened sob.

Without delay he loosened his grip. Before removing his fingers from my hair, his fingers massaged my scalp. I shivered at the utter creepiness of it.

"I'm going to cut your clothes off with some scissors," he said flatly. "Don't be alarmed." The rush of the water and the beat of my heart thundered in my ears as I thought about him stripping me down and drowning me.

"Why?" I let out frantically.

His fingers caressed the column of my tense throat. I shivered in my fear. I hated not being able to see what was happening, it forced me to *feel* everything.

His lips were suddenly at my ear, soft, full, and unwelcome. He nuzzled in further when I attempted to bend my neck and twist away. "I could strip you slowly, take my time, but this is simply more efficient."

"Stay away from me you asshole!" *Was that my voice?* This ballsy version of me really needed to shut up. She was going to get me killed.

I braced for some act of revenge, but it never came. Instead, I heard a small burst of sound, like he was laughing. *Creepy son of a bitch.*

He cut my shirt off slowly, carefully, and it made

me wonder if he was savoring my panic. The thought took me places in my mind I willed myself not to go. Next, he removed my skirt. Though I struggled, my attempts were pathetic. If my arms were in the way, he held them away with little effort. If I lifted my knees, he simply pressed them back down.

He hadn't put the drain stop into the tub yet, the water hadn't been rising. Cold overwhelmed me as I sat there in my underwear. He reached for my bra and I stopped breathing, just shaking uncontrollably.

"Relax," he said soothingly.

"Please," I managed to say through sobs. "Please—whatever it is you think you need to do, you don't. Please, just let me go and I won't tell, I swear...I swear it."

He didn't answer me. He pressed the scissors up between my breasts and cut my bra open. I felt my breasts slide out and I started another fit of crying.

"No-no, don't *touch* me!" Immediately he grabbed my nipples and pinched them. I screamed in shock and surprise, sensations flooding me.

He leaned in close to my ear and whispered, "You want me to let go?"

I nodded, unable to form words.

"Yes, please?" he pinched my nipples harder.

"Yes! Please!" I sobbed.

"Are you going to be a good little girl?" came his voice, once again imbued with a cold indifference that was contrary to the gentleness he tried to convey earlier.

"Yes." I whined through clenched teeth and managed to place my hands over his. His hands were

21

huge and they held me firmly. I didn't even attempt to tug his hands away. There was no way he was letting go.

"Good girl." He replied with sarcasm. But before he let my poor nipples go, he rubbed the sensitized and tender buds with his palms.

There was seemingly no end to my tears, as I forced myself to succumb to his more merciful side. I sat quietly and tried not to earn another dose of punishment. As he removed what remained of my bra and cut off my panties, I could feel the cold metal slide against my skin, the sharpness cutting through cloth, and maybe even me if I pushed too far.

After spraying my body with what could only be a detachable showerhead, he finally put the stop in the tub. The water was warm enough, better than the air against my exposed skin, but I was too terrified to feel any relief that I was still in one piece, relatively untouched. Each time the water got to a cut or some area I hadn't realized was damaged, it stung, making me wince.

I tried to control my crying and speak calmly. "Can you please just take off the blindfold? I'd feel better if I could just see what's going on." I swallowed, throat dry. "You're not going to hurt me…are…you?" My teeth chattered as I waited for a response, still blind, still trapped.

He was quiet for a moment, but then he said, "You have to leave the blindfold on. As for hurting you, I'd only planned to clean you up for now. But understand there are consequences to your behavior, that when you do wrong, you will be punished." He didn't wait for my answer. "So keep still and I won't have to hurt you."

He set about washing my body with a soft liquid soap that smelled of mint leaves and lavender. The darkness bloomed with the scent; it filled the room, wrapped around my skin. Like his voice. I'd once enjoyed the smell of lavender. Not anymore, now I *loathed* it.

When he passed over my breasts, I couldn't resist the compulsion to once again try to trap his hands in mine. Without a word, he slipped one soapy hand free and squeezed my wrist until I released the other.

Later, he slapped my thigh when I kept closing my legs and wouldn't let him wash between them. This part of me was private. No one had seen it but me, not since I'd been a child. No one had touched it; even I had not explored it fully. And now a stranger, someone who had done me harm was acquainting himself with…me. I felt violated and the feeling was reminiscent of a past I had tried long and hard to forget. I fought, but with every touch, with every invasion, my body belonged a little more to him than it did to me. I couldn't stop shaking.

And then it ended. He pulled the stop out of the bath, pulled me out, dried my skin, combed my hair, rubbed ointment on my scrapes and gave me a bathrobe to wear. I was terrified, embarrassed, exhausted, and blind, but was still glad to feel clean—on the outside at least.

His voice was a soft breeze against my neck as I stood without assistance in front of him. "Come with me."

Unable to do otherwise, I allowed him to take my hand and guide me blindly out of the bathroom.

TWO

Caleb led his beautiful captive toward the center of the room. Her steps were hesitant, frightened, as if she expected him to push her off a precipice. He urged her forward only to have her push back against him. That was fine with him. She could push back against him all night as far as he was concerned. Offering no resistance, he let her collide against him, barely subduing a laugh when she let out a gasp and sprang forward like a cat avoiding water. Or in this case, his hard-on.

Caleb reached out to gently grasp her arms, she stilled, obviously too frightened to move forward or back. Lust rolled through him. He finally had her—here—between his fingers, under his control. He closed his eyes, heady for a moment.

She had arrived over three hours ago, slung over the shoulder of that waste of a human being, Jair. She was bruised, dirty, and reeking of bile and sweat, but that hadn't been the worst of it. One of them, and he didn't have to wonder at whom, had struck her across the face. Heat crawled down his spine the moment he saw the blood on her lip, and the purpling bruise swelling her left eye and cheek. He resisted the urge to kill that motherfucker on the spot. He doubted he had marred her as a last resort. She was a woman, how difficult could it be to pacify her?

At least she had managed to kick his face. He would have paid to see that.

The sound of soft but deep breaths returned his

thoughts to the present. The desire that had settled warmly in his stomach sunk heavily to his balls. His cock became painfully engorged. He trailed his fingers across her shoulders while shifting to her left side. He wanted a better look at her. Her pink lips were parted just slightly, whispers of breath rushing through them.

Caleb wanted nothing more than to remove her blindfold, to stare into those bewildering eyes of hers, and kiss her until she melted beneath him—but they were a long way from there.

Like a falcon, she needed the dark to understand who her master was. She would learn to trust him, to rely upon him, to anticipate what he wanted from her. And like any master worth his salt, he would reward her for her obedience. He would be exceedingly firm, but he would also be as fair as he could be. He had not chosen the instrument of his revenge at random. He had chosen a beautiful submissive. And what was a submissive if not adaptable—if not a survivor?

He leaned in close, inhaling the light scent of her skin beneath the lavender. "Would you like some ice for your face?" he asked. She tensed sharply at the sound of his voice: soft and low.

For a moment, it was comical. She shifted around from foot to foot, nervous, blind, and incapable of choosing a direction. Her hand floated up to her face and he knew she itched to remove the blindfold. He made a sound of disapproval, and her curious fingers went back to clutching her robe instantly.

Caleb, feeling what passed for pity, sought to guide her once again toward the bed. She gasped the moment his fingers curled around the lapel of her robe grazing

25

hers in the process. "Easy, Pet, there's something behind you, and I'd hate for you to get hurt again."

"Don't call me pet." came the shaky, yet firm command.

Caleb went absolutely still. No one talked to him like that—least of all blindfolded, nearly naked women. Instantly, he pulled her forward until her soft cheek pressed roughly against his own. He growled, "I'll call you whatever the fuck I want - *Pet*. You belong to me. Do you understand?"

Against his cheek he felt her infinitesimal nod, and against his ear, heard her small squeak of capitulation.

"Good. Now, Pet," he urged her back a few inches, "answer my question. Ice for your face, or not?"

"Y-y-yes," she answered in a tremulous voice. Caleb thought that was better, but not yet settled.

"Y-y-yes?" he mocked. Caleb pressed into her assuredly, dominating her with his size. "Do you know how to say please?"

Her head craned, as if she could see him through her blindfold, and a grimace contorted her full mouth. He would have laughed, but the moment was abruptly no longer comical. Her knee collided with his groin, *hard*. What was it with women and kicking men in the nuts? Throbbing pain crept upward, knotted his intestines, hunching over his body. Whatever food he'd eaten threatened to come back up.

Above him, his captive continued to fight like a hellcat. Her fingernails dug into his hands as she tried to pry him loose from her robe. When that failed, her frantic elbows landed repeatedly between his shoulder blades. He managed to suck in a breath, though to her ears, it probably sounded like an animalistic growl.

"Let me go, you fucking asshole. Let go." She yelled between frantic sobs and screams. She twisted and turned in his grasp, weakening his hold on her robe. He had to get her under control, or she was going to run herself into a much worse situation than his retribution.

Thoroughly riled, Caleb forced himself to stand. Towering over her, his angry eyes met hers. She'd removed the blindfold and now she stood completely still, eyeing him with a mixture of horror and shock. She didn't blink, didn't speak, didn't breathe, she simply stared.

He stared back.

He spun her around and pinned her arms to her sides. Anger raced through him as he tightened his arms around her, forcing the air from her lungs.

"You?" The question slipped past her lips in a rush of expelled air. The single word seemed to ride on a wave of despair and an undercurrent of raw anger. He'd known this strange moment would come. He was no longer her hero. He never was. She struggled for air, panting like a dog, and the idea mildly amused him.

"Fuck!" he exclaimed as her head collided soundly with his nose. He released her on instinct, his fingers pressed to either side of his nose.

She moved quickly, a flutter of long dark hair and bathrobe flying toward the bedroom door.

Caleb growled deep in his chest. Lunging toward her, he snagged a fistful of her robe, but as he pulled back, she simply spilled out of the fabric. Nubile flesh assaulted his senses.

As her hands reached the bedroom door, finding it securely locked, his fingers speared into her hair and made a fist. He pulled back sharply, causing her to tumble backward onto the floor. No longer taking her vigor for granted and no longer amused by her flailing limbs, he sat squarely on top of her.

"No!" she screamed desperately, knees once again seeking his groin, nails fixated on digging into his face.

"You like to fight don't you?" He smiled. "I like to fight, too." With more effort than he would have thought necessary he wrapped his legs around hers and trapped her wrists above her head with his left hand.

"Fuck you," she panted, chest rising defiantly. Her entire body was tense beneath him; her muscles fought, unwilling to give up, but that burst of energy had cost her. Her eyes were wild, crazy, but she was weakening. He held her easily now.

Slowly, the realization of her warm, trembling body pressed so intimately against him flooded his senses, intoxicating him. Her delicate pussy was pressed against his belly, with only the soft fabric of his shirt separating him from her. Her full and decidedly warm breasts heaved under his chest. Just beneath them he felt the hammering of her heart. In her struggles, her heated skin moved against him with greater friction. It was almost more than he could stand. Almost.

Holding her wrists in his left hand, he reared up and slapped the underside of her right breast with his palm, then the underside of the left with the back of his hand. Instantly, choked sobs erupted from her throat.

"Do you like that?" Caleb barked. Again he slapped her breasts, and again, and again, and again until her entire body let go, until he felt every muscle beneath him slide loose, and she simply wept into the crook of her arm.

"Please. Please stop," she croaked, "Please."

She was warm, undone, and afraid beneath him. Her lips moved quickly, silently, spilling words not meant for him to hear. Caleb swallowed thickly, old memories gaining purchase. He blinked, pushed them back under lock and key. A reflex, usually quick and easily done after all these years. But he felt it this time, as her fear and his passion battled as much as mingled, congesting the air and filling the room. It seemed to create a new person, breathing along with them, and watching them, invading the moment.

His anger evaporated. He stared down at the girl's beautiful breasts; they were deeply pink where he had struck her, but it wouldn't leave a lasting mark. Gingerly, he released her wrists. His thumb unconsciously sought to smooth the red mark of his grip. He frowned down at her.

He hoped she was out of surprises.

The moment she felt his grip loosen from around her wrists, she crossed her palms over her breasts. At first he thought she was attempting modesty, but her kneading fingers suggested she was more concerned with alleviating the pain.

She kept her eyes closed too, unwilling to acknowledge him straddling her thighs. Most people didn't want to see the bad thing coming. The moment was perhaps unbearably worse because she recognized him. He had recognized the look of betrayal in her eyes. Well, she'd have to get over it—he had.

His captive subdued, Caleb slowly removed his weight and stood above her. He had to be firm, there could be no indication that such an act of clear defiance would be met with anything but swift and thorough punishment. He pushed the beautifully rounded and supple curve of her bottom with the tip of his boot. "Get up." His tone was commanding. It brooked no argument or misunderstanding. Her body recoiled at the sound of his voice, but she refused to move.

"Get up or I'll have to do it for you. Trust me, you don't want that." Her will to resist notwithstanding, she removed her right hand from her breast and attempted to push herself up. Slowly, she pushed her weight onto her arm, but her struggle was obvious as her arm shook under the strain causing her to collapse.

"Good girl, you can do it...get up."

He could help her, but the lesson would be lost. Four months was not a lot of time when it involved training a slave. He didn't have time to coddle her. The sooner those survival instincts kicked in, the better – and he didn't mean the kind where she kept trying to kick him in the nuts. They had six weeks together in this house. He wouldn't waste them on fending off childish antics.

She scowled at him, injecting as much loathing as was possible into a look. Caleb resisted the urge to smile. He guessed she no longer thought he was cute. Good. Cute was for pussies.

Summoning her strength, she pressed the heel of her hand into the carpet and straightened her elbow. Her breath was labored, her eyes winced with pain, but her tears had dried up. Forcing herself onto all fours, she attempted to stand. Fully upright, Caleb reached for her, ignoring her staunch protests. She tugged her arm loose from his grasp, but kept her eyes trained on the ground. He bristled, but let it pass and guided her, without touching, toward the bed.

She sat precariously on the edge of the bed, her hands covered her breasts and her head tilted forward, hiding her in a veil of tangled ebony waves. Caleb sat next to her. He resisted the urge to push her hair away from her face. She could hide from him for now, just until she calmed down.

"Now," he said pleasantly, "would you, or would you not, like some ice for your face?"

He could almost feel the chilling anger rolling off of her. Anger, not fear? He could barely reconcile it in his mind. While he expected some anger, he found it particularly odd that she had yet to acknowledge her stark nudity. Shouldn't she be more frightened than angry? Shouldn't she be begging her way into his good graces? Her reactions to him refused to fall between the usual and predictable lines. It was as bemusing as it was intriguing. "Well?"

Finally, between clenched teeth she forced herself to say the words, "Yes. *Please*."

He couldn't help himself, he laughed. "Now, was that so hard?"

Her jaw visibly ticked, but she remained silent, her eyes fixed on her bruised knees. Good, Caleb thought, he had made himself perfectly clear.

Standing, he turned toward the door, though no sooner had he taken a step than he heard her strained voice at his back.

"Why are you doing this?" she asked hollowly.

He turned, a wry smile playing across his lips. She wanted a reason. Serial killers had reasons. Reasons made no difference.

She continued, "Is it because of that day on the street? Is it because I…" She swallowed hard and Caleb knew it was because she was trying not to cry. "Because I flirted with you? Did I do this to myself?" Despite her noble effort, a fat tear slid down her right cheek.

In that moment, Caleb could not help but regard her as he would any strange creature—objective but insatiably curious.

"No," he lied, "it has nothing to do with that day." She needed him to lie; Caleb understood. Sometimes a gentle lie was enough to remove the weight of a harsh truth. *It's not your fault*. Perhaps he needed to lie to himself, too, because he remembered wanting her that day, and not for reasons having to do with his mission.

"I'll go get you some ice. And you could probably use some aspirin, too."

They both started at the sound of a key being turned in the lock.

Jair casually entered the room, and Caleb made no effort to disguise his anger. "What the fuck are you doing in here?" Jair was obviously drunk, and that made him more dangerous. Jair's eyes flashed with anger before striding toward the girl cowering on the bed. His eyes raked over her naked body and his lips curved in a covetous smile. "I see the little slut is awake."

The girl was scared, really scared. She'd huddled all the way to the top of bed, covering herself with her hands and hair—trying to pull the comforter up from under her body. He was struck by the fact she hadn't reacted to him that way while they were on the bed together.

She had seemed more pissed off than frightened of him, but only after the blindfold came off and she realized who he was. It could mean one of two things: one, she felt like she knew him based on their very brief encounter, or two, she didn't find him threatening. Either way, her thought process seemed asinine.

He glared at Jair, who was eyeing the girl as if he wanted to simultaneously kill her and fuck her. Given what Caleb knew of him, it was possible that's exactly what he wanted.

There was a test here.

Caleb forced himself to regard Jair as if he mattered, "Well, I'm not sure that's the name I'll go with, but yes, she's awake." Caleb glanced coolly at the girl over his shoulder, just the barest of looks. He quickly noticed her pleading expression, and added, "And quite spry." He smiled.

Need and lust were unchecked on Jair's face, and Caleb knew all too well what men like him fantasized about doing to scared girls. Without hesitation, Jair staggered toward the bed and wrapped his filthy hand around the girl's ankle and pulled. The girl screamed and clung to the bedpost.

Caleb turned swiftly, grabbing her around the waist as she was dragged across toward the foot of the bed. He pulled her into his arms and sat casually, his back against the headboard, his left foot planted on the ground. The girl scrambled into his lap and buried her face in his shirt. Against his chest, her frantic, pleading sobs vibrated his entire body. She was using him as protection? *Interesting*.

Caleb winced as her fingernails dug sharply into his

ribs. Swiftly, and deftly he pried her fingers from his shirt and captured her wrists.

"No, no, no, no, no…" tripped over her lips repeatedly while she attempted to once again gain sanctuary in his arms. Caleb, suddenly irritated by the thought, spun her in his arms using her own momentum. After securing the girl's wrist between her breasts, he held her tightly against him.

Jair made another grab for the girl's ankles.

"No," Caleb said calmly. "You're job was to get her for me, not to hit her *or* fuck her."

"This is *bullshit*, Caleb!" Jair shouted angrily, his thick accent made him sound barbaric. "That little bitch kicked my face, and I could have done more than slap her. I should get something for that."

At the sound of his name, Caleb's grip intensified to the point of strangling all the sobs out of the girl in his arms. The ensuing silence effectively punctuated the rage in Caleb's stare. It took Jair a moment to realize what he'd done. The glaze over Jair's eyes cleared in full realization, and the drunken stupor, for a fraction of a moment, cleared. And that was enough. Caleb could see the Arab understood his mistake at declaring his name to the girl.

Suddenly remembering the gasping girl in his arms, Caleb loosened his grip. She sucked in breath after breath, so concerned with getting air in her lungs it seemed, for the moment, she had forgotten to resume her crying. Within Caleb's tensed arm his captive made hoarse, mewling sounds, but he made no effort to reassure her of her safety.

With his free hand Caleb reached for her chin and tilted it up for Jair to see. "It could take weeks for this to heal." His fingers dug into the girl's face as his temper rose.

The room was filled with tension, and then the silence broke with the sound of the girl's sobs.

"Fuck," he sighed, "You're right." He paused, adding through clenched jaws, "Don't tell Rafiq. It won't happen again."

The man wasn't as stupid as he seemed. He knew hitting the girl was the least of his transgressions. He'd offered the girl his name. Names had power. Jair had to know what he'd done would cost him. If not, Caleb would have to make sure of it. As a mercenary available to the highest bidder, Jair's bread and butter were earned in the acquisition and safeguarding of high-end pleasure slaves. One word about these juvenile mistakes and his *contracts* would dry up. And one word about Jair fucking with Caleb, and Rafiq would see to it that *Jair* dried up, preferably in the desert somewhere. Still, the very idea Caleb needed protection from anyone was an insult he didn't take lightly. "I'm my own man, *Jair*," he spoke the name with venom, "Why fear Rafiq from thousands of miles, when I could kill you in just a few steps?"

Jair stiffened, but he kept his mouth shut.

Oh yeah, Caleb thought, you're my bitch. Caleb's voice was sugar laced with arsenic, "Now, *please*…go get our guest some aspirin and an icepack. It seems she's got quite the headache."

Jair left the room without another word, tension lined his body, and Caleb smiled.

Once alone, the girl in Caleb's arms broke down completely. "Please, please, I'm begging you, don't let him hurt me. I swear to God I won't fight anymore."

Exasperated, Caleb let out a wry laugh, "*Now*, you don't like to fight? What makes you think *I* won't hurt you?"

Through distorted sobs he heard, "You said you wouldn't. *Please* don't." She added emphasis to the word "please.'" Caleb hid a smile in her hair.

No longer willing to expose her beautiful curves to Jair, he leaned across his captive to retrieve the end of the comforter. In doing so, he pressed her face-down into the mattress and his unbelievably hard cock pressed against her bottom. She shook so fiercely, Caleb wondered how her body could endure it. He released her wrists and covered her body. "You need to calm down. I don't want you to go into shock." She only whimpered in response.

Caleb laughed and stroked her hair, "I promise you, if you do what I say, you will always come out better than you think."

Jair returned, holding the items Caleb asked for. His captive's shaking intensified.

Obviously still angry, Jair tossed Caleb the aspirin. "Anything else?" he said bitingly. Catching the bottle in one hand, Caleb shook his head and made a tsk-tsk sound. He removed one aspirin and another similar looking pill from his pocket. He made a gesture for Jair to come closer, and handed over the pills. He reached for the ice pack Jair held and set it aside.

"Don't be so sensitive, Jair. It only makes you more unattractive." Jair snarled. "But I'm sure our guest thinks you're lovely. She's agreed to play nice so long as you don't hurt her." Beneath the blanket she stopped shaking all together, her body suddenly tight as a bow.

36

He stood up from the bed. "Go on, make nice. Offer her the gifts you've brought."

Jair gave Caleb a suspicious look, but approached the bed and held out the glass of water. Her eyes were wide, filled with an anguish Caleb no longer understood.

"Go on, Pet." He made a point of using the moniker, not surprised to find, when her eyes shot to his, that her expression was no longer one of anger, but appropriate fear.

When he made no further comment, her trembling hand finally reached for the pills and glass. She was extremely mindful of not touching Jair. That was smart. The glass rattled against her teeth as she swallowed, but she managed not to spill any.

When the glass was empty, she handed it back to Jair, careful again not to make casual contact with his fingers. Her eyes stared past him toward Caleb. They were quite pitiful.

"Give thanks, you whore," Jair spat when she simply curled into the fetal position. Caleb frowned, but he let the remark pass.

Her eyes once again searching Caleb's for direction, she finally mumbled feebly, "Thank you," before pulling the comforter more tightly around herself.

Caleb approached the cotton covered mass on the bed carefully and sat.

At Caleb's dismissive look, Jair left the room. And once again, Caleb was left alone with his puzzling acquisition. "Your ice."

A slender arm reached through the folds of the comforter and took the offering.

"You're very proud," he whispered. "As kind as I have been, you've been a brat. But for the man who would rape you, you show nothing but obedience...that says a lot."

"Go fuck yourself," was her small, raspy reply.

He let out a burst of laughter. "Well, you're nothing if not interesting." And that was the truth. For some reason, he'd known that from the beginning, yet he had not expected this. His laughter ebbed away slowly and when next he spoke, his voice was cold but velvet, "But you know... I'd much rather fuck *you*."

The cotton mound twitched, and then contorted violently as she turned over and scurried backward, gripping the comforter to her chest as if it would be enough to stop him. He couldn't help but laugh. Her eyes shot daggers at him, but he could already see her pupils were dilated. Her stomach was empty and the drugs were working fast. Considering the dose he'd given her, she was high as a kite. But cute.

Her head drooped, but she picked it up quickly, catching herself in jerky movements. He found himself smiling, though briefly. "What's...wrong...with me?" she slurred. Her body was relaxing against her will. And she kept struggling, fighting the drug.

"You're going to sleep now, Pet," he said simply.

"What? Why?" Her eyes were comically wide with shock and she pulled at her lip. "My face is numb, numb, numb." She let out a strange giggle, but it soon faded away to heavy breathing.

He walked toward the door, the slow smiling curving upward despite himself.

THREE

I was seven the first time I was warned about being a whore. It was one of the very few times I spent time with my father, and I remember it vividly because he scared me.

We were watching *Return to the Blue Lagoon* and the character Lilli had just panicked over blood she found between her legs. I was too young to understand what was happening, so I asked my dad. He said, "Women are dirty whores and full of dirty blood, so every month they have to get rid of it."

I was stunned into fearful silence. I imagined myself being emptied of blood, my skin shrunken down the bone. "Am I a woman, Daddy?"

My father drank deeply from his rum and coke, "You will be someday."

My eyes misted over with tears as I imagined the horror of being exsanguinated, "How do I get more blood?"

My father smiled and hugged me. The smell of the liquor on his breath would always be a comfort to me, "You will baby girl…just don't be a whore."

I squeezed my father, "I won't!" I leaned back and looked in his drunken eyes, "But what's a whore?"

My father laughed outright, "Ask your mother."

I never did. I never told my mother about the things my father said, though she asked whenever he brought me home. Instinctually, I knew they would only fight if I did.

Two years later, on my ninth birthday I had my first period and cried pitifully for my mother to call a doctor. Instead, she burst into the bathroom and demanded to know what was wrong. I looked up at her, shame radiating throughout my body and whispered, "I'm a whore."

I was thirteen before I saw my dad again. And by then I had a deep understanding of what a "whore" was.

My mother had been a "whore" for falling in love young and becoming pregnant with me…and my brother…and my sister…and my other sister…and my other brother…and well—the rest. I was destined to become one because of her. Whoredom, it seemed, was in my blood, my dirty blood.

My grandparents believed it; my aunt's believed it, as did their husband's and their children. My mother had been the youngest of her siblings, and their opinion weighed heavily with her. So most importantly—*she* believed it. She made *me* believe it.

She dressed me in floor length dresses, forbade me make-up, earrings, or anything more exotic than a barrette for my hair. I could not play with my brothers or my male cousins. I could not sit on my father's lap. All this was to keep my inner whore at bay.

By the time I was thirteen, I was fed up with my families *Puta Manifesto*. I rebelled at every opportunity. I borrowed shorts, skirts and t-shirts from my friends. I saved money from birthday cards and the occasional stipend my mother gave me for babysitting, while she went out to search for her next boyfriend, to buy tinted lip gloss and fingernail polish.

My mother was thrown into fits of pure rage whenever she found these things in my room.

"Disgraciada!" she would yell while pitching my pilfered items at my head. I was a disgrace in her eyes. "Is this what you're doing behind my back? Wearing this...this...nothing! Showing your tits and your legs like street trash!"

I always cry when I'm angry, overwhelmed by emotion, I can't control my face leakage or my mouth, "Fuck you, Mom. Fuck you! You're the whore, not me. I just..." I sobbed, "I just want to dress like other girls my age. I'm sick of paying for your mistakes. I didn't do anything wrong."

My mother's eyes swam with tears and fury, "You know Livvie, you think you're so much better than me," she swallowed, "but you're not. We're more alike than you even know and...I'm telling you...act like a whore and you'll get treated like one."

I sobbed loudly as she gathered my things in a trash bag. "Those clothes belong to my friends!"

"Well, they're not your friends anymore. You don't need friends like that."

"I hate you!"

"Hmm, well...I hate you too right now. All I've sacrificed...for a brat like you."

***

I awoke, gasping and disoriented, the edges of the dream dissipating, but not the dread lingering inside me. The darkness was so complete, for a second, I thought I hadn't woken from my nightmare. Then slowly, frame by frame, it all came back to me. And as each frame was cataloged and stored away in my mental library, a faint but growing concept took hold, that this nightmare was reality, *my* reality. I suddenly found myself longing for the dream. Any nightmare would be better than this.My heart sank to new depths, eyes burning in the darkness. I looked around dispassionately, noticing familiar objects, but none of them mine. As the haze cleared, ever more steadily into cold hard reality, I thought, *I really have been kidnapped.* It hit, hard, those words in neon, in my head. I looked around again, surrounded by strangeness. Unfamiliar space. *I really am in some strange place.*

I wanted to cry.

I wanted to cry for not seeing this coming. I wanted to cry for the uncertainty of my future. I wanted to cry for wanting to cry. I wanted to cry because I was most likely going to die before I got to experience life. But mostly, I wanted to cry for being so horribly, tragically, stupidly female.

I'd had so many fantasies about that day he'd helped me on the sidewalk. I'd felt like a princess who'd stumbled across a knight in shining armor. Jesus Christ, I'd even asked him for a ride! I had been so disappointed when he said no, and when he mentioned meeting another woman, my heart had sunken into my stomach. I cursed myself for not wearing something cuter. Shamefully, I had fantasized about his perfect hair, his enigmatic smile, and the exact shade of his eyes almost every day since.

I closed my eyes.

What an idiot I'd been, a damned foolish little girl.

Had I learned nothing from my mother's mistakes? Apparently not. Somehow I'd still managed to go all retarded at the sight of some handsome asshole with a nice smile. And just like her, I'd gotten good and fucked by him, too. I'd let a man ruin my life. For some reason beyond my understanding, I hated my mother in that moment. It broke my heart even more.

I wiped angrily at the tears that threatened to escape my eyes. I had to focus on a way to get out of here, not on a way to feel sorry for myself.

The only light came from the dim glow coming off a nearby nightlight. The pain had subsided into an overall soreness, but my headache still raged. I was unbound, lying under the same thick comforter, covered from head to toe in a thin layer of sweat. I pushed the comforter away.

I expected to find my naked body under the comforter. Instead I found satin: a camisole and panties. I clutched frantically at the fabric. Who had dressed me? Dressing meant touching and touching could mean too many things. Caleb? Had he dressed me? The thought filled me with dread. And underneath that, something else entirely more horrible: unwelcome curiosity.

Fending off my conflicting emotions, I set about inspecting my body. I was sore all over, even my hair hurt, but between my legs I didn't feel noticeably different. No soreness on the inside to suggest what I couldn't bring myself to think might happen to me at some point. I was momentarily relieved, but one more look around my new prison and my relief evaporated. I had to get out of here. I slid out of bed.

The room appeared rundown, with yellowing wallpaper and thin, stained carpet. The bed, a huge wrought iron four-poster, was the only piece of furniture that appeared new. It hardly seemed like the kind of thing that belonged in a place like this. Not that

I knew much about places like this. The linen on the bed smelled of fabric softener. It was the same kind I washed my family's clothes in at home. My stomach clenched. I didn't hate my mother, I loved her. I should have told her more often, even if she didn't always tell me. Tears stung my eyes, but I couldn't fall apart right now. I had to think of a way to escape.

My first instinct was to try the door, but I dismissed that idea as stupid. For one, I remembered it being locked. For another, if it wasn't, the chances were good I'd run right into my captors. The look in that guy Jair's eyes flashed through my mind, and a violent shiver of fear ran down my spine.

Instead, I crept to a set of curtains and pulled them back. The window was boarded shut. I barely contained an exasperated scream. I slipped my fingers around the edges of the wood trying to pull it up, but it proved impossible. *Damn.*

The door opened behind me without warning. I spun around, slamming my back against the wall as if I could somehow manage to blend into the curtains. The door hadn't been locked. Had he been waiting for me?

Light, soft and low, filtered through, casting shadows across the floor. Caleb. My legs shook with fear as he shut the door and walked toward me. He looked like the Devil himself, dressed in black slacks and a black button up shirt, stepping slowly, deliberately. Still handsome enough to make my insides clench and my heart stutter. It was pure perversion.

In the fall of light from the door, his shadow loomed, long and dark. Unbidden, words once made ominous by Poe manifested as flesh in the man before me: *"Suddenly I heard a tapping, as of someone gently rapping, rapping at my chamber door."*

Crap, crap, crap. Okay, that last part was me.

Caleb raised his hand as if to hit me, and I threw my arms up to protect my face. His hand slammed against the wall. While I cringed, the bastard laughed. Slowly, I moved to bring my arms down and cover my breasts. Caleb grabbed both my wrists in his left hand and pressed them to the wall over my head. Pinned between him and the wall, I reacted like a frightened hamster. I froze, as if my stillness would discourage his predatory nature. Like a snake that only eats live mice.

"Are you hungry?" he asked.

I heard the question, but the words had no meaning. My brain ceased to function as it should. The only thing my mind could focus on was his closeness. The intense warmth of his firm fingers pressed into my wrists. The clean, wet smell of his skin in the air around me. The invisible pressure of his gaze upon me. What was this?

When I failed to respond, the fingers of his right hand trailed across the underside of my right breast, the fabric of my camisole made his fingers balmy satin against my flesh. Our earlier exchange forced its way into my consciousness. *"Go fuck yourself."*

"...I'd much rather fuck you."

My knees slightly buckled and my nipples hardened. I took a sharp breath and leaned away from his touch, forcing my tightly shut eyes into the skin of my upraised arm.

His lips caressed the shell of my ear, "Are you going to answer? Or must I force you again?"

Food? My stomach suddenly twisted sharply. A primal pain. Yes, there was my hunger, when he

45

reminded me of it. I was absolutely starving. I mustered up my courage by taking a deep breath. "Yes."

I felt his smile against my ear, and then his fingers held my chin. In my peripheral vision, I watched him lean into me. His breath was cool against my heated flesh.

"Yes," he repeated my response, "you're hungry? Yes, you're going to answer? Or yes, I have to force you again?"

My heart raced. I felt his breath on my cheek. There was suddenly not enough air, as if his proximity sucked it out of my lungs.

"Or is it just yes?"

My lips parted and my lungs pulled in deep, bringing in as much air as they could. It didn't seem like much. I forced myself to answer through my panic.

"Yes," I stammered, "I'm hungry."

I knew he smiled, though I couldn't see it. A shiver, so strong my body nearly jerked toward his, ran down my spine.

He kissed me softly on the cheek. I think I whimpered. Then he walked out of the room, leaving me paralyzed even after I heard the door shut.

Caleb returned shortly with a wheeled cart laden with food. My stomach gnawed as I smelled the meat and bread. It was difficult to control the urge to run toward the food. Then Jair followed him into the room carrying a chair.

Seeing Jair made me wish the floor would open up and swallow me. Earlier, when Jair had sought to rape me, I had—once again—tried to find protection in Caleb's arms. I suppose that, somewhere in my head, I'd clung to the hope that this man, this Caleb, would protect me. All I could see was that horrible, feral look in Jair's eyes. He wanted to *hurt* me.

The door shut and I looked up to find Caleb sitting next to the food. We were alone again. Fear and hunger tore at my insides.

"Come here," he said. His voice startled me, but I moved to walk toward him. "Stop. I want you to crawl over here."

My legs shook. *Crawl? Are you kidding me? Just run. Run right now.* He stood, looking straight at me. *Run where? See how quickly he slams you to the ground and drugs you again!* My knees hit the floor. What choice did I have? I put my head down but I could still feel his eyes on me like a weight that promised his hand. My knees and my palms moved across the ground until I reached the tops of his shoes.

I was trapped. I was nearly naked. Weak. Scared. I was his.

He bent and gathered my hair in both his hands. Slowly, he lifted my head until our eyes met. He looked at me intently; his brows were knit together, his mouth set in a hard line. "I wish he hadn't done this to you," he said while stroking the corner of my left eye. "You really are a very pretty girl; it's a shame."

My heart twisted. A memory, *the* memory ripped through my defenses and surfaced at the forefront of my mind. My stepfather had thought I was pretty, too. I was a pretty *thing*, and pretty things did not fare well in this world, not in the hands of men like him. Instinctively, my hands grabbed his wrists in an effort to guide his hands from my hair, but he held me firmly. Not roughly, just firmly. Without words, he made himself clear; he wasn't done looking at me yet. Incapable of holding his gaze, I averted my eyes to some point just beyond him.

The very air around me seemed to shift to accommodate him. His breath skated across my cheek, and beneath my trembling, sweaty hands, his forearms hinted at his immense strength. I shut my eyes and took a deep breath in the hopes of calming down. The smell of him mingled with the food and rushed into my lungs. The combination did strange primal things to me. I suddenly felt carnivorous. I wanted to tear the flesh from his bones with my teeth and drink his blood.

Unable to help myself, I whispered, "It's your fault he did it. All of this is your fault. You're no better than he is." It felt good to say the words. I felt I should have said them sooner.

A bead of sweat trickled down the side of my neck, its slow crawl over my collarbone, across my chest, and into the well of my breasts served to remind me of my body. My soft, breakable body.

He sighed deeply and let out a slow breath. I shivered, unable to discern whether the sigh meant he had calmed or he was about to slap me senseless.

His voice, thinly coated with civility, filled my head, "I'd watch what you say to me, Pet. There is a world of difference between me and *him*. One that I think you'll learn to appreciate, despite yourself. But make no mistake; I am still capable of things you can't imagine. Provoke me again and I'll prove it." He let me go.

I sank without thinking, back down to all fours, once again staring at his shoes. I was sure I'd completely break down if I tried to imagine all the things I wasn't capable of imagining, because I could imagine some pretty horrible things. In fact, I was imagining some of those horrible things when his voice interrupted my thoughts.

"You're entire life is going to change. You should try to accept that, because there's no possible way to avoid it. Like it or not, fight it or don't, your old life is over. It was over long before you woke up here."

There were no words, no me, no here. This was crazy. I had awoken with sweat and fear to this, this darkness. Fear, pain, hunger, this man—eating at me. I wanted to put my head to the tops of his shoes. To stop. The words hung in the air like a speech bubble, still clinging to his lips. How long before? Before that day on the street?

I thought about my mom again. She was far from perfect, but I loved her more than I loved anyone. He was telling me I'd never see her again, that I'd never see anyone I loved again. I should have expected those types of words. Every villain had a similar speech, "Don't try to get away, it's impossible," but until then, I hadn't realized how truly terrifying those words were.

And he stood above me, as if he were a god who had torn the sun away, not caring for my devastation. "Address me as *Master*. Every time you forget, I will be forced to remind you. So you can choose to obey or choose punishment. It's entirely up to you."

My head snapped up and my shocked, horrified, pissed off eyes met his. I wasn't going to call him *Master*. No. Fucking. Way. I was sure he could see the determination in my eyes. The unspoken challenge behind them that screamed, *Just try and make me asshole. Just try.*

He lifted a brow, and his eyes responded, *With pleasure, Pet. Just give me a reason.*

Rather than risk a fight I couldn't possibly win, I returned my eyes to the ground. I was going to get out of here. I just had to be smart.

"Do you understand?" he said smugly.

Yes, Master. The words remained unspoken, their absence duly noted.

"Do. You," he leaned forward, "Under. Stand?" He drew out each word, as if speaking to a child or someone who doesn't understand English.

My tongue pushed against my teeth. I stared at his legs, unable to answer him, unable to fight him. A lump began to form in my throat, and I swallowed hard to keep it down, but the tears eventually came. These were not the tears of pain or fear but of frustration.

"Very well then, I guess you're not hungry. But I am."

At the mention of food my mouth surged again with saliva. The smell of the food twisted my stomach into tight knots. While he tore off pieces of bread, my nails dug into the thin carpet where my tears now dripped onto the floor. What did he want from me that he couldn't just take? I sniffled, trying not to sob. He touched me again, stroking the back of my head.

"Look at me."

I wiped the tears from my face and looked up at him. He sat back in his chair, head cocked to one side. He appeared to be considering something. I hoped whatever *it* was wouldn't cause me more humiliation, but I doubted it. He picked up a piece of cut meat from his plate and slowly stuck it in his mouth, all the while looking at my face. Every tear that sprang from my eye I quickly wiped away with the back of my hand. Next, he picked up a piece of cubed beef. I swallowed hard. He leaned forward and held the delicious smelling morsel to my lips. With an almost unabashed relief I opened my mouth, but he snatched it away.

He offered again. And again. Each time I crawled closer and closer, until I was pressed between his legs, my hands on either side of his body. Suddenly I threw my arms up around his hand and wrapped my mouth around his fingers to get the food away from him. *Oh my god, so good.*

His fingers were thick and salty against my tongue, but I managed to wrest the meat from between them. He moved quickly, his fingers found my tongue and pinched viciously while his other hand dug into the sides of my neck. He squeezed, making me open my mouth in shock as pain cascaded down my throat. The food fell from between my lips to the floor and I howled around his fingers at the loss. He let go of my tongue, and his hands found control along the sides of my head as he tilted it up toward his. "I've been entirely too kind, and you're going to learn just how civil I've been. You're very proud and very spoiled, and I'm going to beat it out of you twice."

Then he stood up with enough force to push me backward onto the floor. He walked out of the room and shut the door. This time I heard the lock.

Beside me the food beckoned.

FOUR

My hunger was an angry, living thing, clawing and howling along the insides of my skin. I fell on the feast like a starving animal—forcing food and drink down my throat as fast as I could. I didn't even register what I shoved in my mouth as chicken or refried beans. It was food to fill the emptiness in my belly, and I ate until I couldn't. Until I was full.

Oil and salt and food chunks smeared my hands and my face as my throat constricted around the last of the buffet. My hunger no longer gripping me, I finally saw the single plastic fork amidst the empty paper plates. Frantically I clutched at it and ran to the boarded up window, stabbing uselessly at the boards. As my meal continued to make its way to my belly, the plastic fork shattered under my hands as I pried at the window. Breathing quickly and shallowly around the food, I finally threw the broken pieces across the room towards the closed door.

Tears once again blurred my vision as an overwhelming tide of fear and sadness dragged me under. *You're not going to get out of here. You're fucked. He's going to come back and he's going to do something awful. Really, really, fucking bad and there's nothing you can do to stop him. Please, please, please God, please get me out of this.*

I rushed toward the darkly lit bathroom, lifted the toilet lid and vomited everything I'd eaten. I screamed into the bowl between surges of spicy bile. My voice echoed against the porcelain, a strangled gurgling sound that finally gave way to weepy moans and heavy breathing. I flushed before the sight of my puke could make me sick all over again. I actually felt a little better after that. Hungry again, but calmer.

I tried to flip on the light, but apparently that too had been removed. In its place there was another nightlight. The bathroom was a work in progress, the new mixed in with the old. I carefully ignored the Jacuzzi tub where I'd been stripped down and man-handled. Just one glance and his hands were on me again. I looked away sharply, focusing instead on washing my face and rinsing my mouth in the pedestal sink. I had to get the taste and smell of puke out of my head.

Above the sink, there was a circular metal plate. Inspired, I dug my fingers around the shallow lip, trying to pry it off but it was embedded into the wall. Dully, I stared at it. It was so shiny and flawless it was almost like glass. In it, I saw my face for the first time since I'd been taken. The skin around my eye had taken on a light purplish-green color; it felt puffy to the touch. I could now open it enough to see out of, but it looked disfigured when compared to my right eye. I touched it with my fingers, surprised it hurt less than it did earlier. I looked terrible. Aside from my swollen and bruised eye, my hair was a tangled mess. Strangely, I found myself trying to arrange my hair. I felt like an idiot the moment the absurdity of it hit me. *Yeah Livvie, don't forget to look cute for the handsome kidnapper. Stupid!*

I didn't know what was happening to me, but Caleb was at the center of it. He was the source of all this pain and confusion. Whatever had befallen me or would befall me, it would be on account of his distorted and perverted appetite. Defeated, I turned around and began walking out.

The bedroom door swung open, making me jump. Frantically, I searched around the bathroom for a way to escape or somewhere to hide. It was irrational, as I'd already established there was no escape. Nevertheless, instinct was instinct. My instincts said to hide, even for the few seconds it would take for him to find me.

Caleb walked directly to the bathroom, humming. As he reached the doorway, I hid under the sink. In plain sight.

He approached me calmly, without the malice he exhibited before and called for me in a calm voice. "I want you to get up."

He stretched out his hand toward me. Weary, I stared at it for what seemed a long time, thinking of the damage waiting to be done by that hand. His calm and my fear hung between us in a thick and heavy coil. He was going to hurt me, something in me knew it. That certainty nearly numbed me. Searching to work my way into his good graces, I reached out tentatively, waiting for the snake to strike. I touched his out-stretched hand, wanting to recoil and shrink back. But I didn't. He smiled. It was a smile that struck me instantly as both beautiful and evil.

He wrapped his fingers around my wrist, and from his touch, an electrical energy trickled into me. I was utterly petrified. He pulled me up slowly, and soon I stood staring at him with wide eyes and anxious breath. He held the palm of my hand up to his face so I could feel his skin for the first time. The intimacy of this single act forced my eyes to the floor, and I abruptly feared his kindness more than his cruelty.

He ran my fingers across his face, holding my hand firmly when I tried to shrink away. He was clean-shaven, soft, but undeniably masculine. His touch was simple, but specific, meant to show me he could be like a lover, gentle, intimate, but also he was a man unaccustomed to hearing the word no. Yes. I understood. He was a man, and I? I was nothing but a girl, not even a woman. I was meant to fall at his feet and worship at the altar of his masculinity, grateful he'd deigned to acknowledge me. All this from a simple touch.

He raised his right hand, pushing my hair off my shoulder, and then caressed the back of my arm. A violent shiver ran down my spine, causing me to move back. The cold porcelain of the sink grazed my skin. As if it were a dance, he stepped forward. His fingers speared into my hair, possessive, cradling my head as I continued to stare at the floor. He kissed my fingers, nibbling at them with his teeth. The slightly sharpened canine, once part of his boyish charm, now imbued him with a sinister obscurity.

My heartbeat pulsated in my ears, my breathing became labored. Anxiety coursed through my body only to settle in my stomach, making me feel nauseous.

Do I fight him?

Do I risk his temper?

My instincts didn't say run, or hide; they said, stay still. They said...obey? *Please stop.*

He dropped my hand, setting off alarms; not knowing what to do with my hands, I put my arms around myself. I felt as though he were burning a hole through me with his eyes. The intensity with which he stared at me bordered on obscene. What was he doing to me in his mind?

A very strange thing was happening inside me: an awareness as basic and simplistic as male and female, masculine and feminine, hard and soft, predator and prey. Yes, I was terrified. But there was also this undercurrent of something very vaguely familiar. *Lust?* Maybe. My eyes darted off his face. I had fantasized about this guy, dreamed about him touching me. I had hungered for his eyes on my naked skin. Imagined his soft mouth on my breasts. And now here he was, *touching me*. It was nothing like I had imagined.

This was unlike any fantasy I'd ever had, even the really morbid ones. I admit, I'd dreamed of being ravaged by Anne Rice's vampires. I'd seen it on the big screen in my head. It's the eighteenth century, and I'm standing in an alley, the handsome, questionably evil Lestat is between my thighs. I'm a whore and he's just another patron. I sense how dangerous he is, how predatory, but one kiss and I don't give a damn. I know he'll sink his fangs into me, but I throw myself at his mercy in the hopes that death won't be the end of me.

This was nothing like my dreams. In a dream you can't really feel. Every touch is subject to your imagination: what you think a kiss feels like, what you think being fucked feels like, what you think real fear feels like. If you've never truly felt it, then your mind can't truly recreate it. I knew about kissing, had an inkling about petting, but I lacked all knowledge of intent. When my boyfriend touched me, I knew he'd stop the second I asked, conversely, I knew this man wouldn't. Intent made all the difference. This was real. Real touching, real intimidation, real man, real fear.

He caressed my face, running his fingers over my earlobe, down the column of my throat, the back of his fingers brushing across my collarbone. My breathing became broken, heavy. This was wrong, yet it didn't feel so bad. My fear sat heavily and low in my belly, but farther down a different kind of weight was taking shape. I made a sound of protest, begging him in my wordless way to stop. He paused long enough to breathe me in before he continued. I shook my head slowly, trying to pull back but he held my head firmly in his other hand.

"Look at me," he said, his voice controlled, but wavering. I shut my eyes tight, slowly shaking my head again. He sighed. "I want you to look at me."

I didn't obey, frozen with trepidation. *This can't be happening. Not to me.* But it was happening, and I was unable to stop it. I whined, pulling my head back against his hand. He grew further agitated when I drew my hands up, touching his wrists.

"No-o-o," he said softly, as if reproving a child. My hands shook badly and my knees felt as though they might buckle. He tightened his grip in my hair, forcing my head up. I closed my eyes even tighter as soft, tearless sobs broke past my lips. I was treading the thin line of his patience while falling off the thin line of my sanity. He leaned in, kissed my cheek, then the nape of my neck. I sighed fretfully, pulled away, but I wasn't getting anywhere. He touched my lips with his thumb, trying to hush my sobs and whimpers.

"Where is all your bravery now, Pet? No clawing, no hissing? Where's my tough girl?"

My heart sank into my stomach. I had no idea where my bravery had gone. Had I ever really been brave? I don't think so. I never had to be brave. I settled for being invisible, the person behind the camera. How I wished I could be invisible now.

My voice was gone, strangled by the magnitude of the moment. I was in the grips of a panic attack when he let me go. I slid to the floor, covering my face with my hands as I told myself repeatedly, *I am not here. This is a dream, a horribly fantastic dream. Any moment now, I'm going to wake up.* I brought my knees to my chest and rocked back and forth. The mantra just made it seem more real.

I didn't cry when he picked me up. I knew it was coming. I felt hollow, as if my body were merely a shell holding my broken soul inside it. He carried me toward the bed, effortlessly standing me in front of it. Slowly, my eyes lost focus, as if my brain had begun shut down procedures. I simply stood, waiting. He swept my hair over my left shoulder, standing close behind me. I could feel his cock against me, hard, foreboding. He kissed my neck again.

"No," I pleaded, voice cracking. So this was what I sounded like, completely desolate. "Please...no."

His soft laugh fluttered against my neck. "That's the first polite thing you've said." He wrapped his arms around me as he spoke in my ear, "It's only a pity you haven't learned to speak properly. Feel free to try again. This time say, 'Please no, *Master.*' Can you do that?"

I wanted to cry, I wanted to scream, I wanted to do anything but what he asked. I stayed silent.

"Or maybe," he licked my ear, "you need a push."

He stepped away from me abruptly, leaving my back open to the chilled air. I sunk to the floor, balling the comforter into knots as I pressed my forehead against it. He crouched behind me, rubbing my back. The will to fight him swelled inside me and, although I knew what I was getting into, I couldn't stop myself. I threw my elbow back, hitting him in the shins. Pain shot through my elbow, and I couldn't move for a few seconds. *Shins of steel.*

"There's my tough girl," he said coldly. Grabbing a handful of my hair, he dragged me from the bed. I screamed wildly, digging my nails into his hand trying to get loose, but all my struggling was for naught. It was over before it began as he rolled me over onto my face and dug his knee between my shoulder blades. I was pinned. Defeated.

"I hate you!" I roared. "I hate you, you horrible son of a bitch!"

"I suppose it's lucky for me that I don't care," he said, pitilessly, "I'll tell you what does bother me; you still haven't learned any manners. You could've gone easy, Pet, but I must confess..." I felt his breath on the side of my face, "I like it better this way." He reached for something on the bed above us. I strained to see what it was, but his knee dug into me savagely.

He labored to grab hold of my wrists, but quickly caught them both firmly in his left hand as he tied them together with soft cord, almost like silk. I cried as I struggled under him, still trying vainly to get away.

I shut out any idea of the pain, of him tearing through my innocence, decimating my body. The eventual degradation, the afterglow of shame. This was better I supposed. I preferred him sick, twisted, and sadistic. It made it easier to define how I felt toward him. Gone were the images of the gorgeous angel sent down to save me. I had no business dreaming of his blue-green eyes, or the way his golden hair would feel in my hands. Even the smell of him would make me sick now. At least this way we would both recognize this for what it was: rape, not seduction, not the fantasy. There was no confusion. He was only the monster now. Just another monster.

He pulled me off the floor by my wrists and, in one quick movement, hoisted my wrists over one of the bedposts until I stood precariously on tiptoe. I hung there on display; my body stretched tightly—everything exposed, my breath short. He grabbed my face roughly, "You know what your problem is, Pet? You haven't learned to choose wisely. Dinner could have gone differently, but you chose this."

I had some smart-ass comment on the tip of my tongue. They were words meant to make him as angry as I was terrified, but then he kissed me. The kiss was violent, possessive, meant to lay waste to my comment where it crouched, ready to attack.. There was no tongue; he was too smart for that, just the hard press of his full lips against mine. It was over before I had a chance to react.

He went to the cart where the food had been and riffled through a black bag. My eyes widened. *Where the hell did that come from?* Nothing in life is as ominous as a black bag; a black bag meant business. A black bag meant planning, preparation, thoughtful packing. I suddenly felt very light headed.

He returned with several items, smiling at me as though all this were normal. He set the items on the bed with care and due diligence. A leather collar was lifted for me to see; a wide leather band with a metal loop on each end, one of which had a small lock attached to it and a key. The collar also featured a little loop in the front. He put the collar around my neck quickly. Once secured, it put pressure on my throat. He dangled the key in front of my eyes before placing it on the nightstand. There was a long chain, similar to one used to walk a dog, but with a clasp on each end. He placed the chain over the bedpost making a loud clanking sound that startled me into screaming, and then fixed both clasps to the loop at the front of the collar. I had to look up at the ceiling to keep from feeling strangled. It became difficult to breathe the harder I cried, so I stopped, but the tears continued to fall down my face, making puddles in the crevasse of my ear.

Please. Don't. Don't do this. I wanted to say the words out loud. To beg him. But I couldn't form words anymore. I was too scared, and too angry, and too… prideful. All the things I should have done came all at once. More sobs.

He ran his hands down my arms and massaged my breasts in his hands; my body trembled, my nipples peaked. Two thick leather wrist straps replaced the ribbon, fashioned very similarly to the collar around my neck, small chain links dangling on each end that could be locked together. He unhooked the chain from my collar to turn me around. I was relieved to be able to breathe. I didn't much care that it was now being attached to the links of the wristbands. I had more freedom to move now, the chain had more slack and I could put my feet squarely on the ground. My forearms were pushed together, and then tied to the bedpost in front of me. This position made it completely impossible for me to move away from him, my arm muscles tensed under the strain. I was really scared now; I couldn't hide it. He had me and only he knew what that meant.

He stood back, presumably to assess me, or perhaps he was just admiring his work. Either way, his actions filled me with a sense of impending finality. I had challenged him and he had accepted. I stood facing the bed, my arms laced to the bedpost from wrist to elbow. I wore nothing but the mockingly sexy under things he had picked out.

"Spread your legs," he said evenly. When I didn't, he came up close behind me insinuating himself between my legs. I let out a stunned yelp when his left hand cupped me between my legs. I tried to pull away. Useless.

"If you don't start doing what I say, I'm going to open up that little pussy of yours with my entire hand. You understand?" His voice was level but firm. His question was not a question at all, but a reinforcement of his threat.

I whimpered loudly, but I nodded my head.

"Good, Pet, now let's have what I asked for."

He stood back once more and waited. Slowly I opened my legs, wider and wider, until he told me to stop. "Now move your hips back toward me."

As I did as he instructed, I rested my head in the crook of my bound arms.

"Are you ready?" he asked, pausing for the desired effect.

"Fuck you," I whispered, trying to hide my fear.

The first blow struck me on the calves, flashing through my mind as a blinding white light. My mouth opened in a scream that was devoid of sound. I was most certainly *not* fucking ready for that! Frantically, I tried to look behind me. There was a belt in his hand. The scream that had been struggling to come out of my chest finally burst out.

The second lick of the belt overlapped the first, coming so fast I couldn't have expected it. My knees buckled, swinging my body toward the bedpost in front of me. My pubic bone struck the post. I wailed in pain, choking on my tears.

"Straighten your legs," he boomed. "If you black out, I'll only revive you."

When I simply hung there by my arms, he continued. I heard the next blow before I felt it; the belt cut the air with a whistling sound before landing across my thighs. I struggled to get away. I moved this way and that, nearly pulling my arms out of the sockets as I twisted away from the blows. But time and again they landed on my skin. I screamed so hard, for so long, that I was unable to take in air.

He brought the strap down with impossible force as he whipped my ankle. I immediately straightened my legs to rub my ankle with my other foot. He whipped at my calves as I jumped up and down trying to alleviate the pain. I picked up my feet, attempting desperately to rub away the sting. I never felt pain like this. I never dreamed pain like this was possible. My entire body tingled and throbbed and itched with pain.

"Please, God, stop!" I shrieked. He hit me across my lower back. I thought I might faint.

"No...not God. Try again." A torrent of blows came crashing across my body. I wailed and shook. I writhed as I pulled on the bed trying to get loose from my bonds.

"Master," I yelled, "Master!" It hit me then, like the lashes he dealt out, as I screamed that hideous word, Master. He had finally won. I'd been wrong, the pain wasn't better. Oh God, anything but the pain.

"Finally," he said grimly. "But don't think you're done, not even close. You have plenty to atone for."

I cried harder than I ever had in my life. Tears got sucked into my lungs, sobs caught in my chest. *More? I can't take any more.*

"Please, Master. Please, no more." He paused long enough to pull my panties down. They were so drenched with sweat they stuck to my burning skin. I panted against my forearms, he had to stop. He had to. Was he trying to kill me? He cast the panties aside and pressed his fingertips to the welts across my backside. I moaned. He stood up, and brought the belt down across my buttocks, making a wet slapping sound.

"Much better," he said. "Every time you feel my belt I want you to tell me why you deserve it." The belt landed with so much force across my butt that it wrapped around to strike between my legs. I clutched the bedpost in my hands pressing my face against my forearms, biting down against the pain. I could not search my mind fast enough to answer him, all I could do was scream and beg him to stop.

"Do better," he said and whipped me behind my knee.

"I'm sorry I hit you!" I screamed; it was the only thing I could think of.

"I hit you...*what*?" he growled. The slaps came so fast I lost track of how many. I bucked and screamed under the strap that beat me.

"That I hit you, Master. I'm sorry." It was a game, I knew that now. If I forgot to say 'master', he hit me several times; otherwise, he only hit me once.

By the time it ended, my throat was raw, my body burned, and the word "Master" came easier to me than crying. My hair was strewn everywhere, sticking to the sweat that covered me from head to toe. My knees had given out on me during the beating. I hung by my arms, panting for breath. He was panting, too. He grabbed a brush from his bag and I whimpered.

"Please, no more...Master, please, no more." My voice rasped weakly, but he heard me.

"Shhh, Pet." He brushed my hair back gathering it in a bun on the back of my head. He gave me water as well, as much as I wanted. Most of the water dribbled down my body but it felt so good I found myself spilling it on purpose.

I shook violently as I was untied. It was only a matter of unclasping the chain from the straps and untying my forearms, but as he unleashed me, he also unleashed an all new pain. I collapsed onto the floor and rolled onto my face. The prickling of the carpet tortured my skin. I yelped at the feel of his fingers digging into my abraded flesh as he lifted me.

The comforter was much different. It felt cool, inviting, and I writhed against it, lifting my backside into the air. I didn't care about what I looked like anymore. I had no decency or shame. He misted my body down with water and all I could do was moan.

"This is going to hurt a little but I promise you'll feel better when I'm done."

My body tensed. I pressed my buttocks together, afraid he wasn't done with his belt yet. I flinched when his hands made contact with my wounded flesh. He rubbed me down with cold cream, the feel of it so delicious I leaned into his hands as he put it on. I was sure he broke skin in some places.

I wanted to cry when he stopped, but didn't. He lay down next to me, his face close to mine, but I did not turn away. I stared him directly in the eyes. But when he smiled, it was warm, inviting, kind even. Somehow, and against all odds, it still reminded me of the first time I met him. I shut my eyes.

Exhausted, I fell asleep again. This time I did not dream.

FIVE

Caleb shut the girl's door behind him and locked it, putting the key in his pocket. He put his forehead to the closed door. He saw her body again, laying face down on the mattress, welts crisscrossing the back of her body from shoulder to ankle. He wanted to trace each one with the tip of his tongue, leaving no part of her untouched. Through the door he could hear her muffled crying, and a strange shiver ran through him.

Tension coiled inside him, manifesting in his entire body, his muscles tight. He stretched his hands and then fisted them tightly, knuckles popping then relaxing. He loosened his body further, forcing himself to unwind. It was three in the morning. He was wired, sweaty, and in need of something, anything — a woman maybe. He looked away, the soft hue of the lights muted but illuminating enough.

He liked this house. He liked it more with each passing week he spent inside it. From what he was told, it was once a sugar plantation until the Mexican revolution put an end to slave labor. The land was barren now, but the house still stood. The owner had spent hundreds of thousands remodeling the home, allowing for electricity throughout, though many things were still incomplete. The large, square kitchen still looked like it was falling apart, but you could see flashes of the new and modern. It had a fire stove, but a state-of-the-art microwave. The ceramic tile under his feet was probably original, but the fireplace was

67

electric. In fact, the only room in the house that was completely finished was the one he currently occupied — the master suite.

In the background the girl continued to cry, and the sound of her sobs seemed amplified to his ears. When he shut his eyes his brain immediately sought the memory of her flushed body tied to the bedpost — open, at his complete mercy.

Caleb let out a sigh and adjusted himself. Perhaps he'd visit the bar up the street and find a more than hospitable woman to take his mind off the girl behind the locked door. He raked his fingers through his hair and expelled another rush of air as he made his way across the kitchen. He opened the fridge door; the cool, swampy air felt good against his skin, too good. Every nerve ending in his body was alert at the moment. Even the clothes he wore added a friction when he moved. Propping his elbow on the refrigerator door, Caleb leaned in and wrapped his fingers around a bottle of *Dos Equis.* The condensation on the bottle instantly reminded him of sweat. He thought of the girl again, and other girls, past slaves; he never tired of their salty taste, and sweet smelling sweat. Only women could boast of such a thing. Only women were capable of being so fucking sexy you wanted to lick them clean when they considered themselves dirty. He shut his eyes, leaning his forehead against the freezer as he indulged in the base sensations that coursed through him. He smiled, faintly to himself, before it slipped away. He opened his eyes and pushed away from the fridge, shutting it softly. He had conquered and she had submitted. A small victory, but it was a start.

Caleb popped off the cap on the bottle, letting the

metal skid across the granite counter. He brought the beer to his lips. Strong, cold, carbonated fluid rushed down his throat dissipating some of the heat in his body. There was no denying how good he felt. He felt powerful, and nothing was more important than power. Even the girl seemed to know it, or she wouldn't have tried to defy him at every turn.

Caleb leaned against the counter, drink in hand but not drinking. *The girl is absolutely crazy.* His mouth tilted up at the corners, the smirk threatening to become a full blown smile. If she knew who she was dealing with, she wouldn't try to provoke him so much. She was downright adversarial. He winced, remembering how her knee had collided with his balls. *Fuck!* She was lucky he hadn't put a belt to her ass right then. Yet, if he had, perhaps the food incident might not have happened.

A short burst of laughter escaped his lips as he recalled the look on her face when he told her to call him Master. Her eyes had said it all in that moment. He was going to have to break her down to her foundation before he'd have any chance of building her back up. The challenge was intriguing to say the very least, truly, unexpected.

Abruptly, Caleb's smile faded. He stared down at the drain as drops of water fell slowly from his bottle. Some of the drops hung from his fingers for dear life before falling and slipping toward the drain. He stood up, taking a long pull from his bottle. Yes, he would break her down and build her up—for Vladek.

She was his and Rafiq's instrument of revenge. Through her, they'd get close enough to kill that motherfucker. He needed to put a swift end to her rebellious nature, not admire it. He needed to bring out the Submissive he'd observed. Submissives were survivors.

Caleb had underestimated the girl in some regard. For weeks he had observed her, and for weeks she had played the would-be chameleon. She had made it a habit to wear masculine, shapeless clothing when walking in her own neighborhood. At first, he'd thought it was simply a fashion choice, but it hadn't taken long before he'd become less convinced of his original assessment, especially when he observed her wearing flirty skirts and bright colored shirts through the fence of her school. After that, he pegged her as woman who understood how important it was to adapt to her surroundings. She knew she lived in a man's world, and she reacted accordingly.

It was important for girls in her position, in this kind of situation. To her parents she might have been the teenage daughter they didn't need to worry about, because she didn't wear provocative outfits to entice the young horny boys. In her neighborhood, she was the invisible girl, no one of interest. But inside, she was still her—whoever she was. And whoever she was, she'd appealed to him under her camouflage.

It had felt unavoidable at the time, selecting her. She had been the only one to command his attention, though he didn't completely understand why. Then, that day on the sidewalk, during their strange encounter, he'd known he had to have her. She had made an impression on him; she would make an impression on others. Perhaps he'd made a mistake in that regard, choosing someone he had found indefinably appealing.

Instead, the mystery had drawn him nearer, and now he found himself only further confused, further drawn in. It suddenly seemed such a waste that such a gift was meant for Vladek.

He turned around, leaning against the counter, the edge digging into his spine. One hand gripped the edge of the counter, the other holding the bottle, quickly cooling as veins of water cascaded down his arm. He drank. A lot rested on the girl, and in turn, him. Aside from his own vengeance, he could not fail Rafiq. Vladek Rostrovich had to die. In this, Rafiq and he had never disagreed. Upon how to execute each step, that was something else. He took another mouthful, rolling the liquid in his mouth before swallowing and feeling it fill him.

Destroying lives was something he was good at, this was no different, of course. Or was it? He drained the bottle, tasting little, but wanting more. He turned around and rinsed it out, watching the water rush out.

The girl was genuinely terrified of him, that much he was sure of. He had to use it to his advantage. Under his tutelage, she would become whatever she needed to be in order to survive. She would accept the hand she was dealt and make the best of things. She would find whatever good there was in the bad, for however long it'd last. She would fight him, that was a given, but he would convince her despite herself.

He finished his bottle, which had done nothing for him. He was still restless. He walked over to the fridge again, cracked open another. Repeat. Another taste, another gulp, the thirst just growing.

New thoughts distracted him. What would he do

71

with the girl when this was all said and done? He stood still, listening to the house, listening for signs of the girl, but there was nothing, no clamor from behind the locked door. No desperate shrieking, just a girl, plotting her time. He walked to the table and noiselessly pulled out a chair. Another long pull of beer, his gaze passed around the room. He sat. What would he do with a girl who'd never trust him? Caleb drank, set his bottle down on the table then sat deeper in his seat, head back and breathing in through his nose, eyes closed.

Caleb knew nothing about caring for a woman long term. He'd heard a lot about love in the last twelve years, but he never felt the things people talked about. He ran his fingertips up and down the neck of the bottle absentmindedly. The only person he felt any type of affection for was Rafiq, but he doubted it could be called love. Caleb understood Rafiq, understood his anger and his need for revenge. He trusted Rafiq with his life. Without that man to give him purpose, Caleb would have been lost, and for that he respected him. Did understanding, trust and respect equate to love? Caleb didn't know. Rafiq had taught him to read and write, to speak five languages, to seduce a woman, to hide in plain sight, and to kill, but never to love.

He leaned back again, drank, and then set the bottle in a different spot. He stared at the ring of water on the smooth lacquered surface of the table. Leaning forward, he dragged his other hand through it, creating two long translucent trails. They traveled along the surface of the table, slick and solitary, before colliding into one another when his fingers came together.

A few years ago, Rafiq met a woman. The woman was his wife now and had given Rafiq two sons. Caleb had never met them, nor would he and he'd never expected it. He fully understood his role with Rafiq. While afforded great respect and appropriate affection as someone Rafiq had raised into manhood, Caleb was not family. It was not a confusing situation for him, the boundaries clearly defined and consistent early on.

Perhaps there had been moments when Caleb had felt something akin to jealousy toward Rafiq's family. However, he consoled himself with the knowledge that what Rafiq and he shared ran deeper. They shared a thirst for vengeance. They were equal partners in the settling of old scores. It suited him fine since he knew nothing of family. He could scarcely remember his.

There were a lot of things Caleb couldn't remember: his birthday, his age, what his name used to be. It didn't bother him to not remember, though he sometimes wished he knew where he'd grown up so he could avoid it. This small detail had the ability to put him on edge whenever he was forced to visit America for one reason or another. What if he had a mother who thought he was dead? It was his secret horror to fathom a mother elated at the sight of him. Because whoever her stolen boy had been, he was most certainly dead, and Caleb wanted him to stay that way.

The bottle, somehow drained again, rested in his hand, still cool to the touch. He got up as quietly as he'd sat, and silently moved through the kitchen. He rinsed the bottle, listening to the soft *glug-glug* of the water going down the drain. Then took a soft towel and wiped away any evidence of his presence. It wasn't the forgetting Caleb didn't like, it was the remembering.

He needed a shower and a lot more beers. He'd

miss beer when it was time to return to dry, spiritless, Pakistan. It was an excellent aid in the forgetting process. He just hoped the bar in this piece of shit town was still open.

Once inside his room, Caleb removed his clothes and walked into the bathroom to take a shower. Setting the temperature of the water, he let the room steam up before he finally stepped inside to put his face under the jets. The water washed over his nakedness, scalding him slightly, but Caleb welcomed the slight pain. He would never admit it, but from time to time, he needed to feel pain as much as he needed to dole it out.

Once again, Caleb envisioned the girl, face down on the mattress, welts crisscrossing the back of her body from shoulder to ankle. It was perverse the way this particular image affected him. It made him aroused instead of sick. It was ironic.

Unable to fight it, Caleb thought of the past and of Rafiq.

***

Vladek had not always been rich and powerful. Once upon a time, the seedy Russian had been a mercenary and a trafficker of anything that would sell —drugs, guns, people, it didn't matter. He traveled throughout Russia, India, Poland, Ukraine, Turkey, Africa, Mongolia, Afghanistan, and one fateful day, Pakistan.

Muhammad Rafiq was a young man then, a captain in the Pakistan Army under the direction of a zealous Brigadier. The war against Saddam Hussein dubbed by the Americans as *Desert Storm* was well under way and Rafiq had been called to assist the coalition forces on the ground.

74

Rafiq, whose father had just passed, preferred to remain close to home until he could make arrangements for his mother and sister, but it was not to be. The Brigadier was thirsty for rank, and nothing elevated rank like a war. Rafiq's absence was unavoidable and ultimately disastrous, for it was during his two year absence that Vladek set his eyes on Rafiq's sister, A'noud. By the time Rafiq returned with the happy news that he had earned the rank of Lieutenant Colonel, his mother had already been murdered six months earlier and his sister was missing.

Assuming responsibility, Rafiq devoted what resources were available to him to discovering the identity of his mother's murderer. He followed every lead, chased every rumor trying to ascertain if his sister might still be alive.

It took Rafiq three years to hear the name Vladek Rostrovich. After murdering Rafiq's mother, he'd taken A'noud, but apparently, he'd tired of her after a short while. He had retired her to a brothel, established by him in Tehran.

Rafiq went to Tehran, but like his mother, A'noud had been dead long before he had arrived to rescue her. With his hope of finding her alive scattered like ashes in the wind, his fervor for vengeance only grew. He was going to burn the brothel to the ground, kill every patron and save the proprietor for last. If he was later court-martialed and put to death, it was a risk he was willing to take.

But then, he heard a sound, so unspeakably horrible it gave voice to his own suffering. He followed the screaming to a door that would change everything:

huddled in blood and filth, darkness pulled tight around his small, shaking, angry form, was a boy in desperate need of a doctor. A boy the proprietor called *kéleb—dog.*

Pained, disgusted, and mourning his sister, Rafiq recognized the look in the *kéleb*'s eyes. They were eyes that knew the anguish of being unspeakably wronged. They longed for a death that could not come too soon. Rafiq offered to purchase the boy from the proprietor who warned him the boy was likely near death and he would not offer a refund. Rafiq accepted the terms and carefully wrapped the wounded, mewling *dog* in linen so he could take him to the hospital.

Kéleb had been incredibly mistrusting at first, unconvinced that Rafiq did not desire from him all the things as the rest. He attacked Rafiq repeatedly, punching, scratching, and kicking wildly with no concern for how he injured himself in the process. Rafiq had felt for him, but he was also impatient and unwilling to suffer the repeated attacks of an angry teenager. Rafiq used force to calm him down, until he could be reasoned with.

It wasn't until Rafiq offered him a taste of something he thirsted for that *Kéleb* became something more than his fear. Under cover of darkness, *Kéleb* had learned to kill for the very first time. It was too easy, over too fast. While Rafiq stood guard at the door, *Kéleb* shot and killed the man who had tormented him for most of his life. He had stood over the body, admiring the large hole that was once Narweh's face. In his hand, he held the .44 Magnum Rafiq had let him borrow for the auspicious occasion.

The gun had been given to him by an American

officer as a show of gratitude for Rafiq saving his life. Rafiq said it was "Dirty Harry's" gun, but *Kéleb* did not know this man. He only knew the damn thing had thrown him backward onto the ground when he fired it. He'd missed the spectacle of Narweh's face exploding, only appreciated the damage afterward. Whoever Dirty Harry was, *Kéleb* admired his weaponry.

Later that evening, Rafiq had relinquished ownership of Dirty Harry's gun to *Kéleb* and confided in him the story of how he'd come to find him that day in Tehran. Rafiq spoke about his mother and sister, of the futility of his search for Vladek, but mostly, his passion for revenge.

When he was finished, an alliance was formed, a pact so solid, it made everything else irrelevant. That night, after the boy confessed to having no recollection of any name but *dog*, Rafiq renamed the boy *Caleb* – the loyal disciple.

***

Caleb blinked; the water had grown cold against his skin. He stepped out of the shower, feeling as though it had been useless. It had been twelve years since that night in Tehran. *Twelve* years. Five since he had last questioned why he was doing one thing or another.

In the beginning, when he'd been a young man shadowing a powerful Pakistani military officer, speculation about their relationship and Caleb's past had run rampant. Life's lessons came in ways that were unexpected, though, as a man, he knew some of them had been inevitable. Like the day Rafiq had taught Caleb to mitigate rumors by putting the loudest voice to rest—permanently. It had been harder than killing Narweh, but easier than he'd thought it would be. The men who spoke of such things were not good men and it made them easier to kill. But regardless, the hushed whispers, the condescending smiles and speculative gazes told him there were still those whom doubted his motives and authenticity in their world.

Respect came at a very high price in the criminal world, even more so in the Middle East, and especially for a Westerner like Caleb. There could be no half way, Rafiq would remind him; it was all in, or nothing. If Caleb stood any chance of finding Vladek, he would have to venture into his world. Thus began his journey into the world of training pleasure slaves.

He tossed the towel aside, walking from the far side of his bedroom, past his bed to the large windows. He pulled the curtain aside, staring out. Stars, a dark horizon; the black veil of night and a moon unwilling to show itself.

The journey had not been an easy one. It was easier to kill guilty men than sell innocent women. It was an education in callousness and single-mindedness, and choosing a path that promised obliteration of the soul. Despite all this, Caleb had ventured forward.

He trained them with Rafiq's help at first, then on his own. And with every slave Caleb brought to auction he gained recognition in the seedy world of sex for sale. With every wealthy, well-to-do, duplicitous business man that boasted of Caleb's prowess, he gained more footing among the underworld elite. With every success, he delved deeper into the dark and closer, he had hoped, to finding Vladek.

But years went by, and Vladek had remained

elusive. Meanwhile, Caleb had become more involved in the world he wanted to destroy. With each act, he traveled toward the center of that world, until one day, when he looked back, he found he could no longer see the way he'd come. He had wanted out. It had been so long, years with no word of Vladek Rostrovich, of where he'd gone or what had happened to him. Rafiq's thirst for revenge had seemingly never waned, but Caleb had, at times, wondered if that too had become little more than habit. Caleb had begun to formulate his plan, to let Rafiq know of all the turmoil inside him.

As fate would have it, it was in those very days, seven years after Rafiq had pulled him out of that brothel, that someone recognized the twenty-sixth richest man in the world, Demitri Balk, as the former gangster Vladek Rostrovich.

In seven years, Vladek had risen in wealth, privilege, and power. He had used the wealth gained from his underground activities to fund his legitimate business aspirations. He now owned most of the steel and a good amount of oil-rich land in Russia, diamond mines in Africa, and enough stock in large European companies to make the world forget his less than humble beginnings. He was heavily guarded and widely mistrusting.

If Caleb had had any chance of leaving the life he'd created, it evaporated in that moment. He and Rafiq were once again of a single mind, a single objective. They would make whatever sacrifice was necessary to achieve their critical goal. Caleb had gone far, he was now resolved to see it through. He owed Rafiq at least that much, if not more. But after twelve years of waiting, it wasn't only vengeance that kept Caleb moving forward into the dark. It was the inane hope that there truly was some metaphorical light waiting at the end of all this.

He let the curtain fall back into place, the view uninteresting as his thoughts turned to the girl sequestered in the room across the wide living area, and down the corridor from his room. Her role was more important than she could ever guess. He'd owe her too, one day. But for now, he needed her. Vladek had not been an easy man to get to, especially masquerading as Demitri Balk, billionaire. It had taken five years for him to return to his roots, to return to the slave trade.

Caleb rolled his head, wincing as a muscle in his shoulder contracted and coiled back into its tense position. He went through his closet. After twelve years of planning, maneuvering, and infiltrating, the moment Rafiq and Caleb had been waiting for was finally approaching. In four months the *Zahra Bay'* would take place in Pakistan.

The first phase of the plan was complete. As it stood, he was not yet certain of the girl's virginity, but he'd find out. It would be a small setback if he brought a slave with no 'flower' to a flower auction, but Rafiq had maintained that her nationality, coupled with her beauty, as far as Caleb had described it, would secure her status as the most desired slave at the auction.

Caleb, half dressed, pulled on his Armani shirt and began buttoning with deft fingers. At first, he had not agreed with Rafiq, had not seen the purpose in seeking an American, with their loose morals and trademark willfulness. However, having the girl in such close proximity and expericing her allure first hand, he had to

80

admit Rafiq had been right. The girl was somehow different, unique.

He raised his arms and finished buttoning his shirt, leaving his throat exposed. He reached for his cuffs.

When, not *if*, Vladek bid on the girl, he would have to inquire about her trainer. Then, however the moment unveiled itself, Caleb would offer Vladek the girl as a gift, a token of his admiration, his way of requesting an audience. From there, it was all about the impression he made. Vladek would have to be very impressed, not just with the girl, but with him. Impressed enough to grant him access to his tightly-knit life.

He would get access; he would find the best way to take from Vladek, all that he loved and cherished before killing him. Vladek's death would not be as quick as Narweh's. There would be no .44 Magnum to the face to end it hastily. Rafiq and Caleb had waited twelve years to taste revenge, and they'd savor it accordingly.

In the meantime, Caleb expected the girl to behave as the survivor she was. Then, when it was all said and done, they would each—Caleb, Rafiq, and the girl— find a way to move on. Alone.

Fully dressed, he grabbed the key from the back pocket of his other pants and put it into his current pair. Then Caleb ran his fingers through his hair as he assessed his reflection. His lashes were too long, his mouth too full, his entire visage was contrary to his unquestionable masculinity. He was too damn…pretty and that had always been his problem. Had he some physical defect, however small, his entire life would have turned out differently.

Heading out the door, he took Dirty Harry's gun

with him; he needed the cold, heavy metal to remind him he wasn't "pretty" anymore. He grabbed his jacket, pulling it on and situating his holster. Without looking back, he closed the door silently behind him. He made his way down the corridor, past the antique sofa, toward the front door.

The dim setting of the lights in the house, at this time of night, was functional and for precaution. No one knew they were here, except those who had traveled with him, but Caleb trusted them less than he did strangers. Approaching the exit, his eyes once again locked onto the girl's bedroom door.

He had six weeks with her. Six weeks to make her understand all that would be required of her. Then, it was on to Pakistan to meet Rafiq. Given his unyielding nature, he would be less than kind to her if she did not obey the moment he ordered. Vladek even less so. She had to be ready to conform, to survive.

Caleb sauntered through the foyer, his shoes making soft whispers across the ceramic floor. As he opened the door, the night passed through him. He paused on the threshold. Suddenly he wasn't restless, thirsty or horny. For a moment, he didn't want to leave. But he knew he needed to, so he did.

The night was warm, but comfortable and some of Caleb's uneasiness began to subside. The unpaved, dirt streets of the village appeared all but deserted. No sounds could be heard from inside the small, concrete or wood homes of the villagers. As Caleb walked, he paid close attention to the soft, nearly indiscernible thud of his steps meeting the packed dirt. Against the stillness of the night, the sound of the crickets rubbing their legs together furiously seemed a thundering sound, but a nice accompaniment to his steps.

The farther Caleb progressed down the road, the less he heard the crickets and his steps, until finally they were completely drowned out by music and noise. The bar in this piece of shit town was indeed open. Caleb's mouth tilted up in the corners.

SIX

It was raining outside. I could hear it. Taking a deep breath, I slowly opened my eyes, forgetting for a moment where I was, but then the sadness set in. I didn't exactly know what day it was. He kept me in the dark, always, with only the nightlights to guide my way around the room. I didn't know why he did things this way. If it was to disorient me, it was working. I never realized how the inability to account for time could wreak havoc on ones grasp of reality. It was easy to get lost in the endless dark and passing hours.

I thought a lot about home, about my mother and what she may or may not be going through. Perhaps she was sorry for all the times she never told me she loved me. Perhaps she regretted never giving me those hugs I had needed so desperately. Now it was too late. I wondered if they had any idea where I might be or if the police had already told my mother hopes of finding me were gone. I counted the days by inspecting my meals. I had eaten six breakfasts so far. I wanted to go home.

The day, hours, whatever length of time had passed after that first beating had created a shift in the relationship between my captor and me. While I slept, he had made himself the master of my fate, and I could do nothing but allow it. I opened my eyes that next day and he was just coming into my room with the jar of cold cream he had used on me after my punishment. His face had been more serious. Devoid of the constant hint of his smile. I had known instantly not to test his patience.

I had slept on my stomach, exactly as he had left me, without the strength or desire to move. My skin, from shoulder to ankle, and across my backside especially, felt painfully tight and itchy. Whenever I moved my head, my shoulders burned and ached. It was a pain that extended all the way down my legs.

He had stood above me next to the bed, breathing deeply and exhaling slowly. I wondered if he felt any shame over what he had done to me. "Can you get up?" he inquired. His voice sounded detached, unconcerned with my answer.

"I don't think so," I'd croaked, eyes stinging with tears. "But I hurt, Master." I'd kept my head down, hoping he understood how difficult it had just been for me to address him as he wished.

His voice had lowered, grown softer, "I bet it does, but look what it's done for your manners." I'd clenched my jaw, saying nothing.

Now, all these days later, I both dreaded and eagerly anticipated his company, if for no other reason than I loathed my solitude and the dark.

I slid out of bed and, for the first time in a few days, didn't feel that horrible stinging pain. I stood up carefully, muscles contracting tightly and resisting. I winced, pain echoing through me.

The days, I don't know exactly how many, perhaps three, following that first horrid encounter, I'd spent lying on my stomach with Caleb at my side. He had helped me get up when I needed to use the restroom, denying me privacy under the guise of helpfulness. He'd bathed me, fed me, and placed each piece of food on my lips for me to take carefully from his hand. I felt like a doll at times. When I resisted or showed hesitation, his bare palm slapping against my raw backside became encouragement enough to obey. Surrendering my will, that was the price I paid.

Cold cream was applied to my skin at least twice a day and it always stirred the strangest emotions in me. He touched me while he rubbed the cream in. Though he tried to make it seem casual, to me it felt specific, calculated. He would start at my ankles, which usually made me bite my lip from the pure ecstasy of it. I'd never had anyone massage me before and I had never known my ankles to need so much attention. When he touched me, he made things feel better that I wasn't aware felt so bad. I lay perfectly still, trying as hard as I could not to give him any indication his ministrations made me heady. Then he would grab hold of my calves and knead his fingers into my flesh until I let out a long, low, sigh into my pillow. He always somehow managed to pry my legs ever so slightly apart, rubbing so close to my nether regions I struggled not to yell, "Stop!" He did, however, speak to me whenever he massaged my buttocks. I think it thrilled him to absolutely no end to make me uncomfortable. One day, it was made all the worse because of his incessant questioning.

"So you've never been with a man." This was more of a statement and less of a question, as if he were speaking of things he already knew. I wondered how I made the fact so obvious.

"No, Master."

"Women?"

I shook my head quickly. "No, Master." But I had lied.

I had been with a woman before, well, a girl anyway. I don't know if I would define it as sex, mostly she let me touch her, kiss her. Nicole and I had never been with a boy before. I guess we were experimenting with things. Her skin was so soft, pink, and she always smelled mildly of vanilla. I loved the feel of her small nipples getting hard on my tongue as I sucked on her gently, occasionally nibbling at her with my teeth. She wasn't fully developed yet. Her breasts were much smaller than mine, but they were no less beautiful. Her mouth was very different than my boyfriend's. It was softer, smoother, and more delicate. It had been strange to be thinking of her while he rubbed me. A little knot of pressure formed between my legs, and for just a moment, while my skin yielded to his hands and my mind delved into fantasies, I wanted him to touch me *there*.

"Have you ever touched yourself?" Face burning I looked away and hid my face in my hands as well as my pillow. He let out that taunting laugh of his, but didn't force me to answer. I was becoming accustomed to his ministrations, believing them more routine than intimate. Other things still made me uncomfortable. The nakedness was definitely something to get used to. I became thankful that no one but Caleb came in and out of my room, but even he made me incredibly shamefaced. Clothes of any sort were far too uncomfortable to wear. Even the comforter, at once so soft against my skin, felt abrasive now that I was healing. I hated sitting on it when I took my meals.

I went into the bathroom, still bare and prison-like, and looked into the mirror. My bruise had faded some, but the shade was indeterminable. I was relived the puffiness had disappeared. My hair was a tragic mess. I stared for a long moment at myself. Who was this girl looking back out? I lifted my hair to stare at the collar around my neck. I had to admit, the effect was arresting. I looked like some exotic creature captured in the rainforests of Brazil. I asked myself for the millionth time what Caleb's motives were for keeping me prisoner. I was naked around him daily, yet he made no move to take full advantage of how vulnerable I was. I was at his complete mercy. There were times when it seemed as though he struggled to restrain himself, but he did, always. I slipped my index finger through the loop in front, tugged on it, very secure.

The wrist-straps were also a part of my permanent attire as they too were secured with locks. I might have tried to cut them off, but there wasn't anything in the room to do it with. The restraints made me feel more naked somehow; they drew attention to the fact I had nothing *else* on. I turned around, surveying, as I did daily, the wide array of fading belt marks.

The door opened. The "master" came in with breakfast. I stepped into the doorway of the bathroom, staring at him as he shut the door with his foot. I swear, the man never slept. I wasn't sure what time it was, but either way it struck me as too early for him to be showered and dressed. He always dressed as though he was at a party or going out for the evening, never casual or comfortable. Except, of course, the day we met. I jumped when he spoke.

"Why are you covering yourself?" I immediately looked down at the ground but did not move my hands away from my breasts.

"I'm naked, Master," I replied in a tremulous voice.

He set the tray down on the bed. "You've been naked in front of me before. Why are you suddenly so modest? Drop your hands and come here." I dropped my hands, clasping them in front of me as I slowly made my way toward him. He sighed when I reached him, brushing my hands away from my sex. "Don't cover yourself in front of me. It's ridiculous." I bit into my lip.

"Yes, Master." I said, just above a whisper. I was in a very strange sort of mood. It's true, I was pretty depressed, and who wouldn't be? Angry, scared, confused, lonely—all had become customary emotions. Yet today, I felt something else in addition to all these, and against all logic I wanted Caleb to understand. I wanted him to say nice things to me, maybe even hold me. *Strange* did not begin to define my mood. I suddenly wanted to cry but instead stared at the floor, trying not to think.

He sighed deeply, taking my face in his hands, "I don't have a wealth of time to teach you how to behave." I frowned at the cryptic words. *What the hell does that mean?*

"I'm feeling better," I whispered. Though I was sure my face said otherwise. My heart picked up its pace as his soft, warm hands held me still. His face, those lips, were too close for comfort, or not close enough. "There isn't any reason I can't wear clothes again."

A few seconds passed, his blue eyes searching my brown ones. His mouth quirked, a slight mean-spirited smile tilting up one side of his mouth. It was a smile I had come to know well. I'd forgotten to address him as

89

master. I'd issued what might have sounded like a command. I think I cringed, and I think it was what he had been waiting for.

I pulled away from him, instantly kneeling at his feet, hoping he would take pity on me and grant my request. He reached for his belt buckle and my heart kicked into overdrive. I shook my head furiously as I reached for his hands to hold them firmly in mine. "Please don't hit me," I said in a hoarse whisper. I wiped my face as tears fell. "I'm sorry, Master. Please don't hit me."

He made a sound not unlike a laugh, but closer to an annoyed grunt and slapped my hands away. "Stand up," he said in a calm voice, but I only clung to his leg and wept. He sighed heavily, just before he jerked his shirt out from his pants roughly, making quick work of the buttons. I don't know what frightened me more, the thought of him beating me again or his undressing. He pulled me up by my hair as a sea of dread washed over me. "Take off my shirt." I opened my eyes slowly, taking in the moment piece by piece. I think I was stunned. His height brought me to eye level with his smooth, sun kissed chest. His breathing, like mine, had picked up. Perhaps it had been a mistake to tell him I felt better. Perhaps it had been the only thing keeping him at bay the last few days. Unable to do anything but comply, I rested my hands on his shoulders, gently pulling the fabric back until it slid off of him. It fell to the floor.

He took my face in his hands, wiping the tears from my face. "You still think having some scrap of fabric between us will protect you from me?" I stared at him, imploring him with my eyes. "Pick up the shirt," he said. I knelt down slowly, still looking up at him as he held my face. I picked up the shirt with my fingertips. "Put it on." He gave me a huge smile as I put on his shirt. It hung down to my knee, the sleeves hung just a little bit above that. "We'll see," he whispered against my ear. I shivered.

While he turned to leave the room—to get another shirt, I assumed—I let relief at not being punished wash over me. I set about buttoning the shirt he'd given me, surprised to acknowledge the way his smell made my stomach flutter. His shirt, his scent, surrounded me. It was the first time since I'd arrived that his presence, pressed against me, brought me comfort. I indulged by raising both cuffs to my nose and inhaling deeply. It wasn't a hug, but it was comfort just the same. I needed to get the hell out of here before I lost my mind.

He returned sooner than I expected and without his shirt. My eyes were unable to look away from all of his lean, well-muscled flesh, his tapered waist, the small trail of hair leading from his belly button to beyond the waistband of his tailored pants. He set the wheeled cart and chair he'd brought with him near the door. My face crumpled, memories of that horrible night setting my entire body on edge. I had no desire to reenact any of the events that transpired that evening.

But I said nothing and silently obeyed as he turned me around, locking my wrists together behind my back. This time he'd made sure I couldn't wrestle food away from him, not that I had any desire to. I wasn't very hungry actually, just sad.

It was difficult to pretend I was hungry while still preoccupied by our earlier conversation. He fed me breakfast as I knelt on the floor in front of him, my wrists locked behind my back. He smiled a lot, but didn't he always? He was very cool, premeditated. I never doubted that everything he did served some darker purpose, right down to that smile. I thought back to when he said he didn't have a lot of time to teach me things. What was I supposed to be learning? When were we going to start? Did he ever plan to let me go? Was I even going to live through this? He was a handsome man, no one could deny that, so why? Why take women when he could obviously have them willingly? This was all very *Kiss the Girls*. I turned my head when he tried to feed me more eggs.

"Not hungry?"

I shook my head. "No, Master."

"Fine. I'll finish it for you."

I wanted to talk to him. I wanted to ask him important questions I knew he wouldn't answer. Each question crouched on the tip of my tongue, trying to burst out of my mouth. I licked my lips, getting ready to ask, when he spoke.

"Lie down." My eyebrows knit together. "What is so difficult to understand? Lie down." He put his hand on my left shoulder as he lowered me to the ground by the chain he'd attached to my collar.

I was slightly uncomfortable in this position. My bound hands put pressure on my tailbone and the soles of my feet touched my buttocks. I struggled a little, but managed to pull my legs out from under me to close them.

"Do you have any idea how sexy that is?" he said. I gritted my teeth and looked away. "White looks very good on you, I'll have to make a note of it. I'm glad you suggested clothes. Seeing you dressed makes me think of undressing you. However, I think this is a very good opportunity to make you comfortable being naked around me, and it will afford me a pleasant view while I eat."

I pressed my knees tightly together but opened them when he pried. I still remembered my beating quite well and had no desire to upset him. The room was silent with the exception of my heavy breathing. I had never felt so exposed.

"That's lovely," he inhaled sharply and when next he spoke his voice was thick, slightly hoarse, "I bet you're just the right shade of pink. Now...keep your legs open. Don't provoke me."

I shut my eyes against the inevitable flow of tears. Dread and embarrassment flared into anger, slowly churning in my chest. I focused on breathing slowly. I stared at the wall, perfectly still as he ate. It felt strange having my legs open to his gaze. The air touched every part of me. At times, my sex seemed to open on its own, like a hungry little mouth. I wondered if he saw it and prayed he didn't. I tried to imagine what I looked like. Was I beautiful? Was I disgustingly vulgar? Why on earth did I care? I was wondering about all sorts of things when I was jolted into reality by the sudden touch of cold metal between my thighs. He had lowered the chain between my legs, moving it back and forth between my lips.

I looked at him with narrowed eyes, wishing more than anything I could kick his face to wipe that smile off.

"Not to make you arrogant, because you're that

already, but you're very pretty."

Pride overwhelmed my fear and I couldn't help taking his bait. "That's funny," I tried to close my legs, "you of all people calling someone arrogant." He could barely contain his laugh.

"Touché, but I'm not the one on the floor with my legs open." I started to cry, frustration and anger bubbling out of me as tears—a show of weakness.

"I *hate* you."

"You don't hate me," He said it like it was fact, like he knew me. He knelt between my open legs and leaned over me with his hands on the carpet. I turned my head to the side. He kissed me, first behind my ear, then down my neck. "But you wish you did."

"Stop," I whispered.

"Why?" he whispered just as softly. "Is my shirt suddenly too warm?"

A small gasp escaped my lips as his warm hand palmed my breast through soft fabric. I opened my mouth to tell him not to flatter himself when his other hand darted down to touch me between my thighs. I lay frozen in place, paralyzed by my fear. Through the fabric of his shirt, he stroked me with his fingers, all the while keeping his eyes locked onto mine. He didn't enter me, couldn't with his shirt in the way, but still his fingers invaded every fiber of me. I felt him everywhere. Then, against any form of logic, I felt myself flush with warmth. Pleasure, desire, not pain. My entire body suddenly focused in on Caleb's fingers and what they were doing. My heart raced, I held back my urge to moan. Caleb's mouth turned into a knowing smile, and then he took his hands away slowly, leaving me gasping on the floor.

"Now. Tell me you don't hate me."

"*No.*"

His naked chest pressed against me; the heat of it sent shivers through my body. He kissed my neck while running his hand down my thigh. His breath drew in deeply, then out in a whisper across my skin. His erection warmed me through his pants. He pushed it against me, as if he could somehow come into me. I struggled with my wrist-straps, trying to free my hands. He slowed, calmingly caressing me in a gentle, loving way. He rocked back and forth on top of me, kissing me, rubbing me, breathing on my skin.

Something in my body changed, but I didn't want it to. I got hot, very hot. My breathing got faster, and all I could do was smell him, all over me, breathing him in, his scent inside me. He kissed down my chest, holding my knees apart.

"Stop...stop." The first objection was real, the second one...I wasn't sure.

His mouth latched onto my nipple through the fabric of his shirt, somehow more excruciating because he couldn't quite get to me. He sucked harder, making my nipple hard, wet and hot. I half sighed and groaned, unable to resist tilting my head back against the carpet, eyes closed, falling into sensations I'd never felt before.

"You don't hate me at all, I think you like me just fine." I was crying, but it wasn't for the right reasons. "I think I know something else you might like." His hands and his mouth trailed down my body, and though I knew I should, I couldn't bring myself to say anything against it. He was going to do what he wanted whether I protested or not. Would it be so horrible if I did nothing? Could I be held to blame?

My eyes shot open and I sat up as soon as his hot mouth covered my sex. He looked up and grabbed the collar around my neck, kissing me with fury before pushing me back down. Shocked, I twisted from side to side, crying and grunting. I tasted myself on my lips; I was on his lips. He moaned against me as he slid his tongue up and down my secret flesh, drawing moans and screams from my chest. I squeezed my legs as hard as I could, his fingers digging into the inside of my thighs. I felt nothing but his mouth on me. My body became an extension of that small, pink mouth between my legs. No conscience, no shame, it wanted what it wanted and it didn't care who did its bidding. My own body had betrayed me. My muscles tensed, all sensations running through my body concentrated to that one spot Caleb licked. My head swam, and in one blinding moment it seemed that my body exploded. I arched my back, biting into my lip, writhing against his face until the harsh spasm coursed through me and into him. I lay on the floor panting, moaning softly to myself as a gentle tingle spread throughout my body. He rested his body on top of mine. He kissed my neck.

"I told you you'd like it," he whispered.

I had no words for that. I turned my head and looked at him through half-mast lids.

"You shouldn't bite your lip so hard, next time just let it out," he said, wiping my lip with his thumb. His lips were wet, either with sweat or me, *please let it be sweat*. He smiled and kissed my mouth...it *was* me. Humiliation.

"I do hate you," I said softly, looking up at the ceiling, detached, satiated and emptied of something.

He pushed the hair off of my face and kissed me again.

His fingers pressed against my wet flesh and I couldn't help but whimper as my body pulsed harshly. "But your pussy doesn't...and that's the important thing." He smiled, and I closed my eyes, turning away. "As a matter of fact, that's what I'll call you...Kitten."

My heart suddenly hurt. I *have* a name. *Olivia. Livvie.* It occurred to me he'd never asked for my name, not even that day on the street, and it struck me also that it meant he had never seen me as a person – not once. My throat was thick with pain. Was there anyone on the planet who cared about who I was? I thought about Nicole, my best friend. She cared. She'd never give up hope of finding me.

When my eyes finally refocused, Caleb was staring at me with the strangest expression on his face. He was smiling still, not brightly, just curiously, as if he somehow knew I had just been a hundred miles away. We stared at each other for a few seconds, though I couldn't say what either of us was thinking just then. We just couldn't look away. My chest shook with a sob I wouldn't let loose.

Spell broken, he slowly untangled himself from me and then gripped my arm to haul me up. My head swam and my legs shook. I was about to jerk my arm from his steadying hand when I suddenly felt a rush of wet heat run onto my thighs. Instinctively I pressed my legs together and looked down, at once mortified to discover a bead of my wetness trying to run down my thigh. Caleb looked too and I couldn't keep the burn of embarrassment or fresh tears from my face.

Caleb let out a sound somewhere between a sigh

and a moan before he reached down to trace his fingertips along the source. He held up his fingers, rubbing the obvious moisture along the pads of his fingers with his thumb. To my absolute horror, he licked two of his fingers, closing his eyes, fucking savoring my humiliation. I sobbed. Out loud this time.

"What's wrong, Kitten?" he pressed toward me, "Is there something wrong with enjoying the pleasure I give you?" He watched me with obvious satisfaction, even as my tears rolled down my cheeks before falling to the floor. "Answer me." he insisted, some of the headiness leaving his voice. I couldn't give him a response.

Purposefully, he took hold of both my bound arms and led me over to the bed. He sat first, frightening me by pulling me onto his lap. I let out a surprised yelp, but quickly went silent. What fresh hell did he have planned?

"Why are you crying, Kitten?" he pried, "Have I hurt you today?" he gently kissed my shoulder.

"Yes," I answered in a sob. Today the pain was emotional, the worst kind. He drew back from my shoulder with a surprised expression, but quickly donned his mask of indifference. His lips once again found their way to my shoulder, this time trailing up toward the nape of my neck. I tensed, seeking some way to get away from his caresses but knowing there was none.

"Answer me properly please," he murmured, "Have I fucked you?" I gasped, frozen with overwhelming fear.

"No, Master," I said in a voice scarcely above a whisper. He wrapped his left arm around me tightly, pulling me closer to his chest, forcing my head onto his shoulder. Excluding my fear, humiliation and our semi-nudity, this had been exactly what I had wanted not an hour before. I had wanted him to hold me. *Careful what you wish for....*

"Did you come?" he whispered in the same soft voice. I shut my eyes and struggled not to shudder in my silent sobbing. "It's okay, Kitten; you can tell me the truth. Go on, say 'thank you, Master, for letting me come.'" With his right hand he forced my legs open over his thighs, fighting me as I vainly tried to close them. I struggled with tears as my mind reeled. "You're making me angry, Kitten; answer the question."

I snapped. "My name isn't Kitten!" I yelled, finally succumbing to hysteria.

Almost immediately, Caleb bent me over his left knee, holding my legs down with his right and delivered a swift torrent of blows that had me screaming. As my mind scattered in every direction, searching for my wits, the blows continued to fall on my naked bottom.

"Please stop," I begged. "Please stop, I'm so sorry. I swear to God, I'm sorry." Mercy seemed to be the last thing Caleb had on his mind. He buckled down on my squirming body and placed his weight on my shoulders so that he could spank me in earnest while I struggled in frantic terror. "Please...please, Master," I cried endlessly in long guttural moans. I wanted so badly to rub my backside, but he held my straps.

"Is it the pain that makes it easier for you *Kitten*? Does your pride require you be beaten into obedience?" His voice was low, raw—aroused. Beneath my belly his erection throbbed. Or was it only my heart? He spanked me once more, demanding an answer I refused to give. He spanked me again and I suddenly realized that after each spank, he rubbed away the sting. I wondered why, even as more slaps landed.

My thoughts were beginning to fracture as I searched for a way to escape what was happening to me. *Just give him what he wants. He'll stop.* What had I done to deserve this? *"Act like a whore and get treated like one…"* Always those words, always haunting me and punishing me. It was suddenly a comfort to know that once Caleb was done punishing me he would forgive me, too. He wouldn't hold on to imaginary transgressions. He would forgive me. I wanted to be forgiven.

Something interesting happened then. A shiver ran down my body and my mind was suddenly blank. I thought of nothing. Literally nothing. No pain, or shame, or longing, or sadness. There was only the sound of Caleb's palm landing across my bottom, my cries, his controlled breathing. His blows were no longer painful; my backside was numb, warm. I slowly went limp in his lap. It was strange, but I felt…at peace.

Caleb let up on me then, still bracing me firmly though I could feel his body relax against me. The moment was quiet, only our breathing. Mine harsh and fast, his deep and slow. He stroked my back silently, rubbing me as one would a horse, but I didn't mind. I needed it, craved it. I relaxed further. After several minutes, he gently broke the silence, "What is your name?"

"Kitten," I replied from some place outside myself. Gently, he rubbed my sore and swollen buttocks. My breathing slowed, my body hummed.

"It's so much easier when you give in Kitten," he said softly, "so much easier." He was answered only by a shallow whimper. Taking advantage of my lassitude, he slowly hoisted me upright into his lap. Tangled hair stuck to my face, neck and back. Caleb pushed it back.

Normal, rational thought still hadn't returned. I was grateful. Normal, rational thought dictated I be frightened, angry or some variation thereof. It was nice to be devoid of such things. Caleb's eyes wandered to my lips, then back up to meet my far off stare. He took a small key out of his pocket and undid the lock that held my arms behind my back. I gently placed them in my lap, awareness beginning to creep back in. I didn't like it.

"Kiss me," he said. "And before you say no..." I cut him off by touching my salty lips to his soft, supple mouth. He pulled back slightly at my impulsive boldness. But then I heard him sigh and he leaned back in. I inhaled deeply, ignoring the press of all manner of emotion trying to infiltrate my numbness.

I struggled to make the kiss seem natural, fighting the impulse to turn my face away. His demeanor gentled. He was never gentle when he kissed me. It seemed awkward, but I felt something within him changing. He moaned ever so slightly, a sound I hadn't really heard from him before. He reached for my breast, but then withdrew his fingers. Again, restraining himself. Without warning, I felt the tiniest surge of something similar to control. I'd been powerless in every encounter with him, but in this moment I knew what he wanted. He wanted *me*. Not just my body, but *me*. And although, he ruled me for the moment, while he dictated my future, in this one kiss…I owned him. Abruptly, he pushed me away.

"Good girl," he said softly, but the waver in his voice betrayed a hint of confusion. He stood up, looking down to find me staring directly at him. He smiled and grabbed a handful of my hair. "You shouldn't look at me unless I tell you to, Kitten. You'll only do yourself harm."

The moment was over. He was in control again, but angry. At having lost himself, even for a fraction of a second? I couldn't help but smile and didn't hide it fast enough. With a sneer, he led me by my hair into the bathroom and bathed me quickly in silence.

After he toweled me down and brushed my hair, he again joined my wrists together, this time in front. "Raise your arms," he said sternly. The sudden power in his voice made me jump. He placed his hands around my waist and hoisted my bound wrists over the bedpost. I was slightly distressed in this position, my body stretched tightly on tiptoe. I shivered in my nervousness, waiting for another savage beating to commence. My anxiety rose to a pinnacle as he placed a thick leather blindfold over my eyes.

"Please no, Master, please. It hurts too much." He ran his hands over my breasts, squeezing my nipples until they became hard little stones between his fingers. I winced and shifted my weight trying to get free.

"I like to hurt you, Kitten…it's what gets me off."

I froze, said nothing, waiting for the worst. "I'm not going to gag you, but if you don't keep quiet, I'll put a gag in your mouth so big, you'll forget any pain before it." I bit my bottom lip. I was still standing there, mind

102

blank, long after he'd left the room.

SEVEN

If I concentrated, I could stay on my tiptoes, which lessened the unbearable strain from my shoulders and back. I was my pain and nothing else. No thoughts, no emotions, only a body screaming to be released. My calves twitched with pain and a cramp formed. I pushed all my weight toward the floor, to alleviate the fire in my legs. I twisted this way and that, hoping to find a position that hurt a little less than the one before it. The minutes dragged into endless hours. Pain saturated every muscle in my tautly stretched body. I began to whimper softly, which merely grew louder with every breath. Panic in, panic out. I had been afraid of being beaten. Now I'd let him beat me if only he'd let me go.

A horrifying thought broke through to me. *What if he isn't even here? What if he doesn't come back for a long time?* How could I stand this kind of torture for another hour, let alone a full night? *If it was even nighttime.*

I tried to stop being the pain, tried to let my mind conquer my body. I honed in on the sound of my leather bound wrists creaking against the post of the bed. My breathing. The way my body heat had warmed the wrought iron of the bed at my back. I tried to find the peace just beyond the pain, beyond my suffering. Just as I had when he'd spanked me—but the trick didn't work for me this time.

Every breath I took seemed to make my bonds tighter. I cried. Quietly at first, then in loud mewling groans. My stomach turned, and I suddenly understood

104

why he didn't gag me…I was going to vomit. I
struggled to keep breathing, and thinking soothing
thoughts that managed to keep the stomach cramps at
bay. The story of my life—keeping the inevitable at
bay.

Droplets of sweat ran down the well of my breasts
and gathered in my belly button. It agitated me, this
feeling of sticky sweat all over. My hair clung to my
face, back and sides. It was driving me toward delirium.
I shook violently with frustration, every muscle turning
to molten pain. Then I heard the last thing I expected.

For a moment, I shook it off as a figment of my
imagination. I couldn't remember how often in the past
I had woken in the dark thinking I'd heard something.
I'm imagining things. I stood silently and focused
intently on the sounds around me. Not being able to see
sharpened my hearing, but I couldn't pinpoint the
source of the noise. It was everywhere. I kept my breath
shallow unwilling to let the sound of my own breath
distract from my search. I heard it again. Definitely a
woman. Crying? No, something else. There were
screams, yes, some of them reminiscent of pain, but
they rode on the wave of something much more primal
sounding. Sweat beaded on my overheated skin only to
grow fat and race across the contours of my body. I
strained to hear, but strove not to feel. I listened harder
and caught the distinctly loud thud of something hitting
what could only be a wall or some other hard,
stationary object repeatedly.

I stood still, taking rapid breaths while trying to take
in all that surrounded me.

Someone was having sex.

Was that…Caleb? With her, that woman? Even as I asked myself, I knew the answer. Of course. Caleb was having sex.

Mother. Fucker. Heat bloomed across my body. I couldn't breathe. I couldn't scream. But emotion had returned. He had tied me—naked—to a bedpost. To suffer. And he was somewhere in the house fucking some whore's brains out. He wasn't thinking of me. Of the pain I was in because of him. He simply did. Not. Care. Hot tears streamed down my face.

I couldn't help but wonder if he was being kind to her. Was his face buried between her legs as he had done to me? The thought did unusual things to me. I had never had an orgasm before. Never. But he had forced it out of me. What did that mean? I panicked, frantic and trying with all my remaining strength to pull myself loose…nothing.

The other woman's cries had become louder and more guttural. In fact, as I listened—hard, her sounds alternated between soft, low purrs and loud, piercing cries. Soft, then loud, without ceasing. I forgot about the pain for a moment, transfixed by the woman's sounds. The harder I listened, the more I seemed able to discern. She seemed to be enjoying it. Suddenly, an undercurrent of deeper, heavier moans prevailed.

I remembered those moans from earlier as he lapped at me with his tongue. Heat burst throughout my body at the memory— more sweat, more dizziness, more whimpers. Shame, pleasure, and I hadn't stopped thinking about it. I closed my eyes. Why couldn't I just fucking black out? His sounds became a little different, angrier and more labored, a runner trying to finish a race. I grit my teeth and leaned forward for reasons

106

unbeknownst to me. My shoulders burned. My struggling hadn't helped.

The woman screamed, hoarse, rasping screams that seemed to come from deep in her throat. She was yelling something. I wondered if it might be his name. The thought thoroughly irritated me for some reason. Here I was, here, in this place, tied to a fucking bedpost like a *thing* while some other *woman* screamed his name. No doubt during intense orgasms. Meanwhile, I had to call him Master. I wasn't allowed to say his name. Not even when I came, not that I would anyway, that wasn't the point.

She yelled again and this time I couldn't help whining his name out loud, not in ecstasy like her, but in agony. I'd never said his name before, and I hadn't realized until now. I'd thought of every day since I'd arrived here. He was Caleb in my head, always, but I'd never let his name slip past my lips. I said it again, daring myself to call his name a little louder, willing myself to outdo the competition. New aches assailed me, heavy, warm, and wet between my legs. I pressed them together.

"Caleb." I groaned.

"Caleb!" she screamed.

I pushed forward in my straps, ignoring the pain, ignoring the burning in my legs, anything that distracted me from listening intently. I could hear him. "Caleb..." I pressed forward. He was panting, low and hard. His sounds picking up pace even as the strange woman's moans became elongated and alien. Panic swelled inside me. The sweat. The fucking sweat, sticking to me, irritating me, driving me toward frenzy I

107

had never felt. If I thought I might be the least bit successful, I may have tried to chew through my arm like a coyote to get free.

"Let me go!" I screamed. "Let me go!" I cried piteously, panting and sucking in air as fast and hard as I could. I whispered his name. My muscles spasmed. My screams mingled with hers, with his, all of us together in a symphony of pleasure and pain. I heard her peak in one shrill scream that faintly outdid my own. I fainted. Finally.

I don't know how long I remained there, vulnerable as I hung, gone to the world.

What I do remember is waking to the feeling of warm and dense weight straddling my thighs. I didn't even feel a twinge of panic. My hair was wet, but clean, smelling of familiar lavender. Strong hands pressed my shoulders into the soft mattress beneath me and unable to resist I both moaned with relief and whimpered at the memory of the pain. I knew they were his hands, no matter who touched me in the future, I would always know his hands. What I didn't know, was what to make of it.

His thumbs pressed on either side of my spine between my shoulders and rode my flesh to the base of my neck. His fingers speared through my wet hair and tugged gently. My scalp tingled, my body followed.

I felt I should say something, do something. Rail at him, punch him, kick him, yell at him, do something violent to inflict unimaginable pain upon *his* person, but his hands felt too good and my aching body needed them too badly. Besides, I never won against him anyway. His large hands pressed against both shoulders. I exhaled a long breath. No. No fighting him.

Then, because I just couldn't help myself, I asked, "Why are you doing this? Why me?" He inhaled sharply then exhaled. He never stopped rubbing me, nor did he pretend he didn't know what I was asking.

"Why not you, Kitten? Would you choose someone else to take your place?" Gentle began to transition to rough. "If I agreed to let you go in exchange for some other girl, would that be better?" I wanted to scream yes.

Silence.

Only his hands kneading my flesh.

"What's going to happen to me?" I asked quietly, almost hoping he hadn't heard. I wasn't sure I wanted an answer.

There was no answer—then, "Whatever I wish." Before I could speak again, his fingers were doing that thing in my hair again. Only this time he gently tilted my head, pressing his thumb along the curve behind my ear. My mouth went slack. I closed my eyes, unable to think of anything else but the sensations coursing through me. Had I always been this starved for touch? The answer eluded me.

"Who was that woman you were with?" His fingers stilled and I cursed myself for being so…me. And yet, my heart sped up as I waited more than eagerly for his reply.

I narrowly avoided purring and stretching under him like a cat when his fingers once again trailed along my scalp and behind my ear. "My, my, Kitten, what big ears you have." He laughed and the sound of it sent an obscure thrill through me.

"Hey!" I said indignantly, "My ears are *not* big. Not

even a little bit." And they're not, really! His laughter spurred me on, "It's not like she was trying to be quiet. 'Caleb! Oh, Caleb!'" His laughter abruptly died and his grip in my hair became less than pleasant, though the reaction seemed involuntary. I stilled, biting the hell out of my lip. Would my stupidity never cease? "I'm sorry, Master," I whispered.

It was over too quickly, no more talking it seemed. Unexpectedly he went to the bathroom and returned with a bucket of water and a sponge which he set on the floor. He lifted me without a word as to his intent. I didn't speak either, too frightened of provoking him into some other form of torture. He set me on the ground. Next to a big wet spot.

"You pissed the floor," he said, his emotions masked behind a placid expression. I looked away, both embarrassed and scared. He walked toward the door and stopped, his hand grasping the knob. With his back to me he said, "Don't ever call me by that name again, Kitten. You don't know me. Not like that." He left and shut the door behind him. As I stared at the large stain in front of me, I heard the door lock. My face burned with the heat of my embarrassment. Why did my chest hurt? I blinked away the threat of tears.

I didn't know what to make of Caleb, at times so kind and gentle and at others, I feared him down to my soul. Who the hell was that woman? *Why does she get to call him Caleb?*

***

Time went on, and on. I never heard the woman again, but I often wondered what happened to her. My life became monotonous, filled only with Caleb, my punishments, my occasional orgasms, and the endless dark. It'd been so long since I'd seen the sun, or the moon, or any other light that didn't come from candles or nightlights. I lost track of the days. I used to be able to tell by the food that he brought for me, not anymore. Now I knew Caleb fed me whatever he felt I should eat, whenever he thought I should eat. I was losing it. If only I had some sense of time, I could...I don't know... something.

Finally, I became so angry I pulled the nightlight out of the wall and threw it as hard as I could, hearing it break. I spent what felt like several hours crying in the pitch black darkness, afraid to unplug the nightlight in the bathroom and move it, because I probably wouldn't be able to find the plug. I put my eyes near the bottom of the door, hoping I could see something, but all I saw was dark. I banged on the door with all my strength, screaming and crying, but no one came...no one cared. I stared into the dark wondering if death felt like this. I lay on my back, imagining myself in a coffin staring into nothingness, utterly forgotten. I think I even slept with my eyes open.

Though I couldn't know for sure, it seemed as though Caleb's visits to my room became more and more infrequent. Meanwhile, I became less and less unnerved by his presence—in fact, it became more soothing by the day. But he, on the other hand, seemed increasingly aggravated with me. More troubling, his anger often became my punishment, and I was obsessed with avoiding them both. When he touched me, I strained to remain immobile. When he spoke to me, I said not a word. When I could not help but resist, I immediately begged his forgiveness. But the more I gave in, the crueler he became. I didn't understand.

"Surrender," he had said.

"I don't know what you mean," I had insisted.

I turned my head slightly, hearing something familiar. My hearing had gotten better, and it only took another second for me to know. Dishes. I sat up quickly, banging on the door. There was no response. I lay on my back, pressed the soles of my feet against the door and proceeded to do something I knew was stupid. I kicked at the door wildly, demanding he acknowledge me. Again, there was no response. I started to panic in earnest. "Please!" I yelled. "It's dark in here and I want to come out!" When I heard only silence I cried out in despair. "Caleb! Caleb…please open the door." Nothing. That is, until someone kicked the door so hard I saw a flash of color. I scrambled backward, scared out of my mind. For once relieved the door was heavy, sturdy, and locked.

I had never been filled with more foreboding than when I heard the sound of a key turning in the lock. For the first time, I considered the dark an ally. I scrambled beneath the bed. It was an incredibly tight fit that left me pinned snugly, unable to turn my head between the floor and the box spring at my back. I held my breath as the door opened. The beat of my heart literally moved my entire body. I shut my eyes tightly, willing myself to another place. A voice in my head chastised me. *Under the bed? Stupid. Just fucking stupid.*

"What the fuck?" I heard him whisper. Relief was short lived as I realized it was Caleb who had entered my room. "Oh Kitten, what have we done now?" he taunted.

"I'm sorry," I said, but I don't think he heard me.

The door shut. I listened...only my heartbeat.

There was rustling. I knew he moved about the room but I couldn't discern where exactly he was until I heard his shoes against the tile of the bathroom floor. I bit into my lip so hard I tasted blood in my mouth. His voice filled the room. "Tell me something, Kitten..."

His steps felt nearby.

"When exactly did you imagine yourself as..." he seemed to be searching for a word, "my lover?" My heartbeat vibrated my skull. "Was it the first time I made you come with my mouth? Or one of the many times since that I've put you over my knee? You seem to like that." I felt the bed dip above me with his weight. Unfortunately, it was on the side I wasn't facing. I was openly crying now. He knew where I was and he was toying with me.

"I'm sorry, Master," I whispered.

He scoffed, mocking my pathetic nature without a word. "If I drag you out it'll be very painful. It's best you manage on your own." he crooned.

Sobbing, I told him I was going to come out, begging him already not to hurt me. I felt ridiculous, crawling on my belly like an animal. Crying, begging, unable to show any emotion but fear. And frustrated because once again, I had pretty much brought it on myself.

Once I was out he stood me up and pressed my head to his chest, rocking me back and forth gently. I gripped him tightly, both arms holding fast to his waist. It had become natural for me to seek shelter in his arms, even if he had just used them to hold me down to spank me. I told him repeatedly I would never to it again. I told him

113

I was sorry. He sighed and held me closer, his lips against the shell of my ear, "You will be, Kitten." In a flash he pushed me face down onto the bed. I whimpered but didn't struggle. I wanted to show him how obedient I could be, how sincere I was in my promise to never say his name again. To never assume we had that level of intimacy between us.

With deft fingers he managed to lock my wrists together between the bars of the headboard. My body tensed, bracing itself. His weight left the bed. Then I heard him undressing. This was different. Very different.

I pulled against my restraints. "Please no." I couldn't resist saying.

He was slow in his preparation. I stared into the pitch black of surroundings, trying to catch a clear glimpse of him. My blood pounded in my ears and my fear was almost tangible in the air around me. His weight shifted the bed and I instantly knew there was no avoiding what was about to happen.

He laid his naked chest against my bare back, his weight all but crushing me. "Do you want to be my lover, Kitten? Is that why you called to me by name?" I bucked wildly, trying to throw him off my back and pulling at my wrist straps. It was less than useless. I felt him grow hard between my thighs. I lay motionless. He was completely naked. He'd never been completely naked before. I sobbed into the sheets. He didn't sound the least bit out of breath as he continued speaking against my ear. "I've made you come so many times, but not once have I made you return the favor. You have to earn the right to call me by name."

"Master, please." I cried out into the dark.

He pressed into me, his erection impossibly hot and hard between my trembling legs. "No, don't call me that, not tonight. Call me by my name since you're about to earn it." I only cried harder.

He sighed, harsh, angry—*disappointed?*

He rolled off of me, his large frame forcing the mattress to creak as he lay next to me. I couldn't stop crying, though relief did wash over me. Why was he doing this!

He stroked my hair for a long time, touching my face with his fingertips. The bed creaked again as he repositioned his body to massage my back, my arms, and my legs, slowly, gently…practiced. I cried softly into the bed, then not at all as he managed to lull me into an irrational sense of safety. I tensed all over when he lay his body back down over mine. He bade me over and over to relax. He kissed me everywhere, not like before, not angry. And God help me, it shouldn't have made a difference, but somehow it did.

I had never been this close to a man before. I had never known how the heat of his bare body pressed against mine would affect me. I struggled against reflex. My body wanted to curl into him and my mind told me it would be a horrible mistake. What would it be like to touch him the way he touched me? Would he be as thoroughly under my spell as I seemed to be under his?

 Despite my best efforts I lost myself in his gentle caresses, soft moans escaping my lips. His hand palmed my backside, squeezing, gently prying. I didn't fight him. Not even when his fingers followed my crease over the curve of backside and spread the outer lips of my sex. Fear breached, but desire bloomed as he encountered the traitorous little knot hidden therein. I gave a start, but forced myself to settle into his touch. He'd done this to me before, used his fingers against that traitorous aperture to bring me to the heights of ecstasy. And he was right; he'd never asked the same of me. Not once. I needed this. I needed to forget everything, even if for a few minutes. He made me feel good, so good and it was difficult to resist when he'd only force me anyway. He rubbed me endlessly, wrenching the moans from my chest. It was coming, the tingling that led to the explosion.

"Open your legs," he whispered, his throbbing cock rubbing against the outside of my thigh. The thought of it made me moan more loudly than I ever had. I didn't know what was happening to me. I only knew I needed to open my legs. "Wider," he groaned and I obeyed.

I shivered uncontrollably as my orgasm gripped me from deep inside. I tilted my hips back, searching for his fingers, begging without words for a firmer touch. He gave me what I wanted and I clung to my orgasm as long as possible. It barely registered in my mind when he rose up on his knees and took up a position between my wantonly spread thighs.

The moment something came in contact with my ass, I shot up. His hand pressed between my shoulders, "Put your head down." His fingers scooped up the wetness I had created and he adeptly applied it to the tight ring of muscles. I shook uncontrollably. I was very surprised to discover that my fear stemmed in equal parts from deafening embarrassment at being touched in such a secret place as well as the pain involved with being penetrated there. This was not a part of my body meant to be seen. I'd certainly never seen it. When one of his fingers breached my opening and assailed that secret part of me, it became the only part I knew existed. I flexed against the intrusion, but it mattered very little. He pressed in slowly, asking me to relax before he slid out and then in again. It seemed to go on forever and the entire time I felt more focused on not embarrassing myself further than on what he was actually doing to me. Before long, it didn't even hurt anymore. Apparently satisfied, he held me steady by the small of my back.

Something impossibly huge pressed against my opening. I froze. There was no damn way he was going to get that thing inside me. I bucked. Fought the inevitable. "Relax, Kitten. Relax. Take a deep breath… good, now another." I was being split open. My universe flipped upside down. He held me firmly as he pushed his way inside me, all the while coaching me along. I listened intently to his steady words and tried to do exactly as he asked. Whilst the pain outweighed the pleasure, I tried my best to cram the sheets into my mouth. It took a long time before he filled me entirely. He stilled, and laid his head on mine, speaking to me gently, "Don't fight." He caressed my breasts, my belly, kissed my shoulder, once again making me moan with pleasure against my will. *Against your will? Really?* My body relaxed and the enormous size of him settled inside me. His breath warmed the nape of my neck and he let out a grunt. The sound of it, so male, so primal, I marveled at it.

"Please." I whispered, but I didn't know what I was asking him for. He was inside me, in every cell. His penis throbbed inside me and I could feel it. But more than that, I knew he could feel me. Not just my shaking. But me.

Each day I was more vulnerable than the last. Each day he stripped away more of my sense of self. And now he'd taken the last of it, the last of me. But who did that make me? An extension of him? Someone new? I didn't know. Didn't want to know.

He leaned over me, kissing away the tears on the side of my face. And still he didn't move. It wasn't enough to fuck my body, he wanted to mindfuck me as well. It was working. I wanted him to be nice to me. To kiss me. To make it nice for me. I was scared it would hurt, and I once again looked to him for protection. How messed up was that!

Then he fucked me.

In my entire life, I never felt anything like it. Sensation assaulted me, paralyzed me, as if my mind could not possibly keep up with how I should react. My entire body trembled and shook around him as he impaled me over and over again, and yet, there was a sick sort of pleasure also present. It built up inside me and begged to be released. Was it always like this? Would it feel the same if he fucked my...even my thoughts demurred away from the word *pussy*. *Caleb calls it your pussy.* I came. Hard. The force of it stilled him inside me as I pulsed around him. He made a pained sound and pressed his mouth to my shoulder, "God...I knew you'd be like this." Before I had a chance to ask what he meant, he moved inside me and all thought fled.

I came several more times while he fucked me, each time, it reduced me more and more into someone I recognized less and less. Finally, he squeezed and pulled at my ass. "You feel so good. I love your tight little ass." He grunted and slammed into me. He swelled inside me and I couldn't believe it was actually getting *bigger*. He moaned loudly, "Oh fuck!" Moments later he filled me with his semen.

When he no longer pulsated inside me he collapsed on top of me, whispering reassurances in my ear. I whimpered softly under him as he once again became all softness and comfort. He reached for something and placed it underneath me. He pulled out slowly, his cock inching its way out of me and creating an overwhelming panic. Would his semen come running out of me! I clenched without meaning to and he hissed. Again, he had found new ways to humiliate me. Tears streamed down my burning cheeks.

We bathed together for the first time, crammed into the tub, my body between his legs, against a part of him I had yet to see. He held my head on his chest. I wept, indifferent and exhausted against him, all my strength gone. He stroked me, washed me, spoke to me. "What's your name?"

"Kitten," I whispered weakly.

"And mine?" he tensed beneath my fingers.

"Master."

After the bath, he toweled me in silence. I was grateful. I climbed into bed without protest, seeking the oblivion of sleep even as I prayed I wouldn't dream of all that had just transpired. Violation, confusion and more uncertainty. More powerlessness. My prayers, like all of them, were left unanswered. He lay down next to me, and I knew sleep was not an option.

I opened my eyes and stared into the dark. I was numb—heartbroken. Not only was I shocked over what he'd done, but I was more shocked over how he'd managed to turn my body against me. The pain had been intense, and yet at times it was as if that same pain added to the violent shiver that coursed through me when he'd made me come. Shame had overwhelmed me. Part of me had more than enjoyed it. The few times he'd eased off of me just before that shiver, I'd held onto him tighter. *Where am I supposed to go from here?* I lay there, my eyes wide, my breath shallow, my soul defeated, and I stared into nothingness.

He lay next to me, naked and warm, against my skin. I tried not to move, not to think of him, not to think of anything but this dark room that was quickly becoming my entire life. My tears ran across my face, out my right eye, across the bridge of my nose, into my left eye and down onto my pillow. *My pillow, my only friend.* I sobbed, determined to keep my tears private. They were mine, not his. And he wouldn't care anyway. *He doesn't care about* me *anyway.*

"Kitten, that's no way to behave," he said, his voice denoting he was wide awake and ready to torment me. "I know it wasn't all bad for you, you came— more than once." His words cut me and a strong pang of humiliation in my chest made me draw tighter into myself. I wanted to say something vicious, but swallowed it down. I didn't want to open my mouth, if I did, I would just burst into tears and I didn't wish to cry anymore. I was sick to death of crying. He kissed my head and I jerked it away.

I swallowed very hard and took a long slow breath.

"All you want to do is hurt me," I said calmly. A hint of fear laced my words. I expected more violence but didn't give a shit. Instead he shushed me.

"Come here," he said, very gently, sounding so safe. "It's going to be okay."

He grabbed me roughly and turned my face into his chest. Before I had any thought about it, I wrapped my arms around him and held on to him as hard as I could. He was my tormentor and my solace; the creator of the dark and the light within. I didn't care that he would undoubtedly hurt me at any moment; right now, I just needed somebody to hold me, somebody to be kind to me, somebody to tell me exactly those words. *It's going to be okay.* It wasn't, of course, I knew that. But I didn't care. I needed the lie. I needed my books, my movies, and now Caleb's arms.

He held me for what seemed like an eternity and rocked me gently, until all my crying had lulled and I simply rested against him. "Please don't leave me in here. I hate it in here."

His fingers caressed the side of my face and it gave me hope. But then I felt him inch his way out of the bed. Without a word of reassurance, he gathered his clothes and left me.

Lost, I lay back down and pulled my pillows closer. They smelled like him.

EIGHT

The door opened slowly, Caleb's shadow significantly less ominous, haloed by the light of the room behind him. I was, dare I admit it, relieved to see him. *Caleb.* I stopped myself before I said his name and instead took a huge breath. I sat...I waited. He stood by the door, and then leaned against it casually. What looked like a silk nightgown was held almost carelessly in his left hand. I stared at it as he held it out toward me. Weary, I tried to make out his expression in the dark. Was this another fucking game? If so, it was the cruelest yet.

"Well, Kitten? Are you going to put it on or are you finally over your self-indulgent modesty?" I waited for the tease to play out, but he continued to stare at me with a quizzical expression. I walked toward him, and grabbed it from his hand, fully expecting to meet with resistance. When I didn't, I fell forward slightly, my cheek colliding with his chest for a brief moment before I righted myself. He laughed and it was almost...sweet.

The fabric was soft and sensual as it glided through my fingers while I discerned the opening. I had never been this close to the open door and my excitement was palpable. The light filtering in from the room behind him beckoned me sharply. I fumbled with the slippery silk.

Caleb's hands unexpectedly reached out for mine. He held them still, steadying my trembling, overly excited hands. I looked up at him, finally able to make out his features in the glow of the adjoining room. I was strangely excited to see him in the light, to really see him, as plainly as I had that fated day on the street. It seemed a lifetime ago.

His right hand lifted toward my face. It was pure instinct that bade me to close my eyes when his fingers caressed first my brow, then my cheekbone, the curve of my jaw, and finally, his thumb across the bow of my lips. I swayed. My former instincts to fend off his caresses had left me at some point, but I couldn't recall when exactly they had stopped. His touches were expected now. My skin unconsciously eager, waiting for a stroke to feed this new hunger in me. I could suddenly feel his weight at my back, hear his low grunts in my ear as he had taken his pleasure from me. I released the nightgown into his all too capable hands and opened my eyes, expectant but also bemused. I tried, and failed to suppress a shudder when his hands slipped it on over my head. The silk licked my flesh from head to toe, first cool, then warm as it absorbed my heat.

"There," his voice was hoarse. Another caress, this one down my arm. I stared at his chest, the dark buttons against dark cloth. He took my hand and led me out the door. My nipples hardened, pressing against the silk.

He was really going to let me out? "Come," he said, giving a small smile of approval. But I froze. I kept asking myself: is this really happening? And like always, the answer was: yes.

I stepped into the living room as if I stepped into a whole other world. It was one I was strangely frightened to enter. I hesitated, the room felt too big, too cold, and too bright to my sensitive eyes. I squeezed

Caleb's hand, needing to make certain he was close to me, and then stopped. I recognized the ridiculousness of my thought process, but also knew there was no way to change it. What was it called when a hostage took refuge behind her abductor? *Stockholm's?* Did I have it? Could you catch it like the flu? I knew it was stupid to wonder. The simple answer was I didn't want to run into that other guy, the one that took me—that's all. *Yes, yes, of course.* These thoughts soothed me. Caleb hadn't gotten to me, not like that. *Hasn't he?* I shook off the thought and let go of Caleb's hand to emphasize my point. *Take* that *inner monologue.*

My eyes devoured every surface, any object because who knew when I'd be put back in my black box. I looked up at the ceiling, some twelve feet high, and marveled at the thick wooden beams that ran from wall to wall. It was beautiful, old, and grandiose. Beneath my feet were ceramic tiles, large ones, some with flower-like designs. Tapestries and wall sconces lined the large room, accentuating the low antique looking chairs. I felt like I was in an eighteenth century sitting room. Any minute now, a man wearing a cravat and brandishing a stylish, if not useless, walking stick was going to enter the room and offer me tea. Though one look at the arched entrance to a hallway directly opposite my room and I knew the man would probably not be English. This place had a lot of Spanish vibes. Where the hell was I? To the left I spied a type of kitchen area. There was a table at least. And directly across, to my right I finally saw...*a window*.

I think I let out a giddy squeal. I ran to the window, shaking off Caleb's grasp when he tried to stop me, but he didn't pursue me. I gripped the bars, peering out. It was still night! I was hoping it was daylight; I hadn't seen the sun in...in...in? My brain couldn't process anything beyond seeing the *outside world*. I was still trapped. This was a prison within a prison. Still, this was more freedom than I'd had in a long time, a taste, but it would have to be enough to sustain me.

Overwhelmed, I stared out into the night. I reached through the bars, wishing they weren't there, and touched the window, the warmth of the glass. The landscape was muted and hard to make out; the moon, nowhere to be seen. I wondered if this black immutable landscape was why he'd let me out this night—I couldn't tell where the hell I was. I could be three blocks from home, or in an entirely different country. That gnawed at me, Mexico was way too close to California and yet too far away from any expectation of rescue. Caleb's voice invaded my thoughts, "Are you hungry?" he said behind me, way behind me.

I didn't look back at him, absorbed in the darkness outside, and distracted by everything else. I managed a, "Kind of."

"Well, it's 'kind of' a yes or no question. I'd appreciate it if you answered me properly, and face me when I speak to you." I ripped my eyes away from the window and looked at him. He had that big smile on his face again. The same smile he had been using to cause so much inner turmoil. In the dark, it twisted me in knots, in the light—it was almost crippling.

"I'm sorry, Master," I said, regaining my composure. "Yes...I'm hungry." I turned toward the window and squeezed the bars. His words echoed in my head, *"You feel so good. I love your tight little ass."*

"There's chicken and rice, or tamales. Which would you prefer?"

"Um, the rice?" I responded, turning around again. Even this felt like a test, a game. I wasn't feeling all that hungry, but I was afraid if I didn't eat I'd have to go back inside my prison. He grabbed the leftovers from the refrigerator and spooned the contents out onto a plate. How domestic of him.

"I was just getting ready to eat when you decided to have your little...episode." He spoke so casually, as though we were conversing about the color scheme of the room. He carefully and quietly closed the microwave door and set the timer, going about this mundane task. *My episode.* He'd been inside me, deep. I felt a twinge of pain and a flutter of desire at the same time. My stomach clenched. Episode.

What he called an episode I knew was a life changing event. I would never be the same, and it didn't seem to matter to him. I blinked rapidly. *Do not cry, Livvie.*

I must have been unsuccessful in cloaking my emotions because he quickly added, "No more crying, Kitten. No more dark so no more tears." He slipped the spoon he used into his mouth and opened the refrigerator again. I stood there, staring at him like an idiot not sure what I should do. I nodded. It was all I was capable of.

He took two beers out of the fridge and set them on the counter before removing the plate from the microwave. "Here, take this," he handed me the plate, "be careful it's hot. Sit at the table." I held the plate in my hands, still standing and staring before the heat

126

started to burn my hands.

"Shit!" I exclaimed and hurried to set the hot plate down on the table. He laughed under his breath as he put another plate of food in the microwave. I sucked my middle and ring fingers on my left hand, feeling like a moron.

He pulled the other plate from the microwave and set it down on the table. He then picked up one of the beers and walked over to me. He took my left hand and wrapped it around the long hard length of the bottle, my hand under his. The cool wetness felt amazing under our hot fingers. I looked up at him and all of a sudden I couldn't breathe.

"Feel better?" he asked, only I heard something else and I throbbed with it. I pressed my thighs together. His hand suddenly left mine, and I snapped out of my trance. I pulled out my chair to sit.

I hated the fact it was night again, that I'd missed an opportunity to see the sun. No one ever thinks about how lucky they are to see the sun everyday. I certainly never did, not until now. Disappointment shivered through me, pulling me down again. Caleb noticed. When did he *not* notice something?

"What? What could be wrong now?"

I looked at him with eyes that all but yelled, *are you kidding me!*

He shrugged. "I could always put you back inside your room."

I winced at the suggestion. "No. I'm...grateful. I just, I guess I'm just disappointed the sun isn't up. I haven't seen the sun in a long time."

"Hmm," was all he said.

I tried not to look at him; every time I did, all I could think about was the fact that he had been inside me. The way he had been so soft and so gentle and forced my body to feel good, even though I had fought it, and then the way he had been so cruel. I pushed the food around, thinking about things beyond my old life. I wondered if I would ever manage to escape. The thought seemed less and less likely the longer I remained here with Caleb. Though I knew I could never give up hope. I abruptly wondered what would happen to Caleb once I made it home. Would he be brought to justice? The thought gave me mixed emotions. Fuck, maybe I did have Stockholm's.

"I didn't bring you out here to eat with me so you could stare off into your food." I looked up. He smiled again. *Or maybe he's just too pretty for prison.* Thinking of prison only served to remind me of being sodomized.

"So tell me about home, Kitten; brothers, sisters?" I could feel the pin pricks behind my eyes, threatening to burst through in a flood of tears. I set my fork down and put my hands over my face, willing them back. I didn't want to talk about this, not with him; it hurt too much. Yet the logical side of my brain was thinking perhaps if I opened up to him and got him to see me as a human being, he'd treat me differently. Let me out of the dark for good. Maybe even let me go. This was an opportunity. A big one. The tears were beaten back for the moment. I could do this. I had to do this.

"I have five brothers," I refused to tell him anything about my sisters.

He eyed me at length before speaking again. "And you are…?"

"The eldest."

He sat back in his chair and stared at me, tunneling through me with that dark gaze as if he knew something I didn't and was amused by it. "And your parents?"

Why did he suddenly care? "It's just my mom. My dad's been gone for a long time now."

"He died?" he asked, almost thoughtfully.

"No," I said, edgy, "just...*gone*."

"And so your brothers have a different father?"

"Um...fathers." I looked down at my plate again, shifting the food around, trying not to think about him staring at me.

"Your mother had children with more than one man?" he sounded...disapproving. He shook his head slightly, and then, under his breath, he muttered, "The West." His eyes once again bored into mine, "How does it make you feel?"

What are you? My Shrink? "I don't know. I guess I don't care."

"And what does your eldest brother think?" he leaned in. He was actually interested. I was getting a little freaked out.

"My brother?" I asked. I didn't understand; where was he going with this? My brother was fourteen and all he gave a shit about was running the streets with his friends. Mom and the others were my responsibility.

"The burden of caring for you and your mother would naturally fall upon your eldest brother," he said, his tone inquisitive but oddly perplexed.

I scoffed, "Hardly."

My answer seemed to displease him on some level, but he nodded slowly in realization. What rock had he been living under? "Yes, of course. How forgetful of me." His gaze became almost pitying.

Heat crawled up my face and the lump in my throat got harder to swallow and keep at bay. I bit on my lip and looked down at my plate of cooling food.

"With so much responsibility resting upon your shoulders, how is it you're still so innocent, still a trembling little thing needing to be told what to do?"

"I'm not a baby," I stated firmly, but my voice lacked that certain kind of conviction—of confidence.

"Right," he said, a big grin played across his face. It fell quickly, "Do you blame your mother?" Taken aback, I blinked and simply nodded in response. How could he see me so well? I wiped away the tears before they spilled from my eyes.

"Yes!" I cried and succumbed to my tears, head in my hands.

"I don't mean to make you cry, Kitten." He leaned in farther, his hand reaching for mine. *The hell you don't.* I tried to pull my hand away, but his hold was insistent. I dared a look at him. Was that my pain reflected in the pool of his eyes? He swallowed and it was as if he was hiding some powerful emotion. He cleared his throat and when he spoke, he was once again in charge of himself, "Do you think she misses you?" He asked so matter-of-factly, as if the answer was not capable of breaking me inside, but it was, it really was.

I cried so hard the tears spread all over my face and I kept wiping my hands on my nightgown. "Please, stop it. Why are you being so cruel?"

He seemed impatient, "Just answer my question. It's very simple—do you think she misses you? Or do you think it's possible she's already moved on and forgotten you?"

I pulled my hand from under his oppressive grip and pounded the table, "You don't know me! You don't know my family. You don't know a single thing about me. You're just some sick pervert who kidnaps women so you can feel superior! You think I give a fuck about what you say? *I don't.* I hate you!" The moment I finished with my outburst, cold, black, heavy fear took hold of me. He looked pissed. He gently tapped his fork against his plate, but one look at his knuckles, all white with the intensity of his grasp, suggested there was nothing gentle about him just now. I looked into his eyes, keeping his gaze locked onto mine, hoping that his anger would ebb. If I looked away, there was no hope for me.

Suddenly, he burst into a fit of laughter so loud and forceful that I jumped and slapped my hands over my ears. It made me want to scream, just to make him stop laughing. He rose from his chair and came at me with his hands out. I quickly threw my hands up to protect my face. To my surprise, he grabbed my face in his hands and kissed me on the mouth so intensely it made my lips hurt a little. His face lingered close to mine, his breath warm on my mouth.

"I'll let you have that one, Kitten. I'll let you have it because it's told me so much about you already. And I like you; I like your saucy little mouth. I don't want to hurt it. I'd rather kiss it, just like this." He put his mouth on mine again, this time softly, his tongue gently probing my lips, until forced apart. I put my hands on his wrists, gently pushing him back before I turned my head away and wiped my mouth with the back of my hand. He stood upright, grabbing my chin and tilting it upward. We looked at each other again.

"But if you keep this up," he continued, "I will have to teach your saucy mouth a cruel lesson. Do you understand?" I nodded slowly, his hand still holding my chin. He smiled, "Good." He sat back down at his chair, seemingly delighted with himself. So much for his pity.

"My mother *does* miss me," I was adamant. "She'll never stop looking for me; no mother would ever stop looking for her child." But my tone wasn't too convincing, not even to my own ears. For a moment he looked just as stricken as I felt, but only for a moment. Did I want to know why? Was he after more than my misery?

"If you say so," he whispered, expression cooling.

I looked away and chugged on my beer, picked up my fork and stuck a big scoop of food into my mouth. If my mouth was full, I couldn't talk. We sat in silence for several minutes, just the sound of both of us chewing and drinking. I stared at the fork, my *metal* fork and for too long because when I felt watched, I looked up. Caleb just smiled at me. He was daring me to use it as a weapon. It was odd to discover I was learning his various smiles. I think I got a little bit drunk because the world seemed a little, I don't know, wobbly? For reasons unknown to me at the time, I felt compelled to repeat a question...carefully.

He had told me once before he would do whatever he wanted with me, but he'd never told me what that might be. Was what happened between us the worst of it? I was surprisingly hopeful. "Master?" I paused. When he said nothing, I continued. "What happened

132

before…is that all you plan to do with me?" The question didn't seem to surprise him in the least, but it felt like I'd asked him the most important question I could ever ask him.

He continued eating without another look at me. I pushed the food around, drank my beer as the weight of the silence became denser, more obvious he had an answer and didn't want to say anything.

My face grew very warm, though I figured the alcohol was responsible for a little of it. I looked down at my plate again. I had eaten everything; funny, I didn't remember doing that. "Another one?" He pointed at my drink, that smile of his playing on the curve of his lips.

"Um, yeah, I guess." He got up from the table and moved around in the small kitchen. I looked around again, still in mild shock over how it was that I had come to be here. I never believed such a thing could happen to me. I had never imagined my life could take such an outrageous turn, or at least, certainly not for the worst. Not that I ever had any reason to be optimistic. He returned shortly, bottle in hand and opened it before giving it to me.

"Don't drink too much, Kitten. I don't want you to be sick." I drank from the bottle, marveling to myself at just how much like water it tasted now. He sat back down, set on ignoring me while he continued to eat and drink. It was pissing me off.

"And what about you—*Master*?" I provoked. "What about your family?"

"What about them?"

"I assume they aren't all kidnappers."

He actually smiled. Not the usual half smile, the one he always tried to hide. A real smile. God, he was a beautiful son of a bitch. Not fair. "No."

"No sisters?"

"No. What about you?"

"No." Hadn't we covered that? What did he know? "What about your mom?"

Caleb's face went blank. "Dead."

There was a great feeling of loss that swept across the table and despite my better judgment I couldn't help but be deeply touched. If my mother were dead... I would be lost. It didn't matter that she was an impossible woman, or that she still held me responsible for things I knew deep down weren't my fault. I loved her. Nothing else mattered. Not even the feeling that the love may be one sided. "I'm sorry" I whispered and meant it.

"Thank you." He gritted.

"How did she die?" His eyes blazed with a fierceness I had yet to see, but I held my ground. To my chagrin, he broke eye contact first. He stabbed his tamale, and I wondered if he had meant that forceful jab for me. *He has mother issues—figures.* Didn't we all?

"What happened to your mother?" he asked. "Men came in and out of your lives, making promises, taking what they wanted and leaving?"

"Isn't that how it always is?" I sneered. *Or worse.*

"Come here, Kitten." My heart thudded loudly in my ears at the sound of his suddenly baritone voice. I already recognized what that tone meant. My head shook, "*No,*" of its own volition, making my thoughts known to him before I formulated words. "I won't hurt you, Kitten, not unless you make me. Now come here."

134

His voice was soft yet firm and his words pressed upon me with a grave seriousness. I stood up and slowly crossed the distance between us, stopping when I stood directly in front of him. He reached out and put his hands around my forearms, steadying me.

"You see," he sighed, "right now you are so sweet, so docile and meek. You respect me; you respect what I can do to you if I wanted. Just as you are, all I want to do is hold you, protect you, and take away all the distress in your little face. Right now, if *I* made you a promise, I would keep it."

He stood from his chair, still holding my arms. My breath hitched in my chest, my mind reeled from the alcohol and the new anxiety in my chest. I looked down at my feet, refusing to meet his eyes, though I felt them on me. His breathing seemed heavier, his hold more pronounced. He leaned down, my breath non-existent now, and he kissed me, almost tenderly, first on one cheek and then the other. And then he simply walked passed me, calling out behind him, "Put the dishes in the sink. I'll be right back."

I operated as if under a spell, quickly gathering up all the dishes and placing them in the sink, wiping off the table with a sponge I found. Then I returned and sat at the table. My thoughts were all over the place. Were it not for the fact I had watched him open my drink I would have thought maybe he had slipped me something, but no, I guess I was just drunk. It didn't even occur to me that I was alone, that I could be searching for a way to escape until I heard his footsteps making their way toward me. Had he been testing me? I suddenly felt like a trained animal. *Stay, Livvie. Stay.*

Good girl.

"Well, Kitten, that was really fun, but I'm afraid I have some business to attend to; so that means you'll have to return to your room." A cold chill ran up my spine, and I shivered, a little too violently.

"Please, Master," I said, looking him straight in the eyes "I can't go in there, please don't make me go in there." My body began to convulse with dread and panic, but no longer that frantic and angry rush. The alcohol made it nearly impossible to disguise my emotions.

"Kitten, we both know begging won't get you anywhere. I said I have things to do, and I don't have time to baby-sit."

I begged anyway. "You won't have to baby-sit, I promise. I'll stay out of the way, I'll be quiet; I'll be whatever you say. Just please! Don't make me go back into that dark room. I'll go crazy in there." I looked at him, imploring him with everything I had at my disposal. I could not go back in that room. I couldn't go back to the dark, to the loneliness, to the fear within those walls.

He sighed heavily, weighing me silently.

"Tell me, Kitten, what's in it for me?"

NINE

Caleb had been surprised at the lengths to which his captive had agreed to go in order to stay out of "her room." He wondered, not for the first time, what the fuck he was thinking. He knew this was the last thing he should be doing, inviting her into his space. She'd already worked her way much too far into his thoughts. The longer he was near her, the less he seemed capable of trusting himself. Especially now, when every glance at her triggered the memory of her quivering beneath him, wanting more and never realizing it. She had come a long way from the timid girl he'd met on the streets of Los Angeles. What he had done was wrong, somewhere inside him he knew that and still he couldn't say with any sincerity he wouldn't do it again given the chance. Or that he didn't want to do it again. There was just something about her, something he wanted to taste and touch. Something he wanted to claim. This was the first time she had ever offered him anything and he was hard pressed to refuse.

An unexpected shiver ran down his spine and his cock instantly lengthened. While his mind had doubts about what he wanted, his body apparently did not. He closed his eyes, trying to feel what she must be feeling as she stood a few feet away blindfolded and shaking slightly. He felt the cold tile under his bare feet, smelled the crisp scent of the candles in the air, and tasted the slightest trace of sweat on his lip. He wanted to taste *her* sweat. He wanted to do anything to distract him from the debacle at the kitchen table.

It had been a mistake to ask her all those questions. He didn't really want to know. He especially loathed all that talk about mothers. He had said his mother was dead. And she could be for all he knew. Regardless, she was dead in all the ways that mattered. His passion instantly cooled at the memory of her pitying expression. *Fuck pity.* He didn't need it. He didn't need anything from anyone, least of all her. *Liar.*

Caleb potentially had a mother out there, and according to the girl, she might still be missing him. Why couldn't he remember her? He felt, somewhere, very distantly, he had once...loved her? But he felt nothing when he thought of her now. It was... unsettling. Breaking free of his frustrating and perplexing thoughts, Caleb refocused his attention on the girl.

He smiled to himself as he looked at her, standing in the grandeur of the oversized, old-world bathroom. In some countries it could be its own home. She stood a few feet away blindfolded and vulnerable. But this was her choice. Her shapely and tremulous form rekindled his softening erection. She couldn't possibly know the effect she had; his little innocent captive. Her hair was absolutely unruly, having been left to dry on its own after their bath. It was as untamed as the girl, and almost as alluring.

Before entering his room she had become increasingly bashful. He suspected the reason. He had released his pleasure inside her, and then she had eaten a large meal and gotten drunk. It didn't take a genius to figure out why she was suddenly talking her way out of his room, when she had worked so hard to get an invitation. She was very cute when she was drunk. But then, she was always cute, inebriated state aside.

But in the end, she'd gone with him. Trusted him to take care of her as he'd promised.

She gasped at the sound of him snapping the table into place, and he wondered what she thought it could possibly be. He nearly groaned when he spied her nipples tautly pressed against the satin of her nightgown, all but entreating him to take them into his mouth and suckle them until her body succumbed to remorseless shudders. He sighed. What the hell was wrong with him? After leaving Tehran he had glutted himself on women. Done everything he had ever fantasized about doing. He'd been with so many women, yet none of them had ever affected him the way she did.

If the first lesson every slave had to learn was to accept that their wishes did not matter, then the first lesson every master had to learn was not to be a slave to their own desires. The logic was simple, to command a slave, you must command yourself.

Over the last three weeks it had become easier to bend his captive to his will, to make her respond in ways Caleb knew she would. Yet the more her body obeyed, the less her mind seemed to play a part. The less he knew of her thoughts, the more he wanted to get inside her in every way possible. But at every turn he remained locked out, denied, rejected—infuriated. His aggression toward her had escalated, but their dynamic remained the same. It had begun to bother him in ways he could not explain.

He should have been satisfied, relieved in fact. Vladek would have no part of her. In her mind, she would remain safe and untouched by him even as her body would not. Still, the thought of Vladek touching her repulsed him.

"Take off the nightgown," Caleb said softly but firmly. He smiled, taking pleasure in her little startled jump at the sound of his voice. She fidgeted, shifting her weight from one hip to the other, trying to find something to do with her hands.

"Um...?" she hesitated. Her voice was nearly lost in the cavernous tiled bathroom. Caleb moved toward her, as stealthily as possible, wanting to enjoy the obvious tension that coursed through her tender frame. He truly was a sick bastard. She panted ever so softly and then sharply sucked in a breath as Caleb put his hand across her belly, gently forcing her back into the breadth of his chest. She was warm, deliciously warm.

"Are you afraid I'm going to hurt you, Kitten?" he whispered into the shell of her ear, "because that's not what I'm interested in, not in the least. I promised not to hurt you, and I won't, not as long as you keep your promise to do whatever I ask." Her breath was forced and ragged and he suddenly wanted nothing more than to kiss her bottom lip, which she presently used as a chew toy. Instead he stepped back and simply repeated, "Take off the nightgown."

The girl took a deep, but shaky breath, searching no doubt for resolve. Caleb felt both wise and devious for allowing her to partake of a shot of tequila after dinner. He was surprised she didn't sway more on her feet given the fact she was blindfolded. With a trembling hand, she slipped the right strap off her shoulder, shortly followed by the left, exposing her beautiful breasts as the nightgown slipped down to her waist. Caleb had to focus on his breathing, barely able to keep himself rooted in place.

Next she attempted to push the nightgown the rest of the way down, but her ample hips wouldn't allow it. He thought it was all so fucking naïvely sexy. Exhausting the possibility of pushing the fabric down, which would have been more modest, she finally endeavored to pull the fabric over her head. Caleb's body seemed to sway with the motion of her generous breasts.

His cock could not possibly be any harder. He grabbed it and adjusted it into yet another position that didn't leave it so painfully twisted. "Stop," he said huskily. "Just leave it the way it is." He walked over to her and effortlessly hoisted her into his arms and laid her flat on the table he had prepared. She didn't seem to know what to do with her hands, but Caleb wasn't surprised when she instinctively went to cover her exposed breasts. He wanted to stay her hands, to correct her behavior, but he let her have her seductive modesty. Especially since her soft little sobs, barely audible over the rush of the water in the bathtub, let him know that tears undoubtedly hid behind the fur lined blindfold. Warm, salty, delicious tears that he suddenly wanted to feel against his lips.

"Turn over, Kitten."

"What are you going to do?" she gasped.

When she hesitated he added, "I promise not to hurt you." She seemed sated with that and slowly turned onto her stomach. She cried out when Caleb reached for the nightgown and pulled it up to her waist. All at once she scrambled to get up, but he quickly used the weight of his body to pin her still. "This is for your own good, no pain."

Caleb listened to the fear in her voice and though it made him the slightest bit heady, he felt somewhat uncertain. The truth was he hadn't meant to do what he had done earlier, no matter how much he had enjoyed it. She wasn't his to do with as he pleased. But it was that thought alone that had spurred his anger and his lust to begin with.

She had called him Caleb.

She had yelled out his name: in fear, in anger, in need of him and god help him—it had turned him inside out. He had reached the limits of his desire for her, and in his mind there had been no alternative to cure him than to have her. He'd been made weak, just for a moment, for her. The way her body responded to his touch was simply unheard of, not under the circumstances. But her body was just naturally pliant, electric with its need to be touched. So he had hurt her more than he intended and he felt hesitant of his actions. It was a feeling all together new to him.

"Because of...earlier, you might be hurt. I mean to make it better." Her body tensed all over but, she remained silent. "I need you to pull your knees up to your chest and part your legs for me." The intense blush that rose to Kitten's face eluded description, though crimson was as close as Caleb could guess. His smile on the other hand could be easily categorized as brilliant.

Gingerly, she did as he asked, seemingly grateful for Caleb's help. He had noticed when he insisted on helping her she gave in to him more easily. He allowed her the illusion of her defeated resistance and she assented to his mounting demands. Perhaps she felt she was not doing something vulgar of her own free will, but submitting to something that would be done with her consent or without. She made no protest when he locked her wrists to the table and placed a spreader bar between her knees.

"This will help you to stay still," he explained, knowing it was help she would definitely need. She bucked wildly at the first touch of Caleb's fingers touching lubricant to her shy and no doubt very sore bottom.

The bathroom was soon filled with the sound of her tearful sniffles and humiliated sobs. The light echoes, bouncing off the walls, seemed for a moment to reverberate something inside him. He didn't feel guilt very often and she seemed to have an uncanny ability to bring it out of him. The feeling was...alien, unpleasant, and aggravating as hell.

"That's enough! You're crying more out of embarrassment than anything else. Stop. Crying." The sound of his voice filled the room and the girl stilled, obviously frightened. Caleb sighed. "Here, this'll help." Caleb placed a small amount of lubricant onto his finger and gently seized her clit between his thumb and forefinger. She shuddered, paralyzed by his touch, and he knew she was silently willing him to release her sensitive flesh, which, of course, he would not. "You're okay, Kitten. It's okay," he reassured her gently and began to rub the slippery epicenter of her being. And he was practiced, as well he should be, always careful to not rub too hard, and always careful not to rub too softly. He wasn't that much of a tease. He'd do it just right, to make it up to her.

He watched intently as she pressed her lips together, desperately trying to not let the slightest sound escape her. Yet, slowly, her lips opened and her soft little sobs could be heard. Soon those tiny sobs became whimpers, which in turn became rapid little pants that became elongated gravelly moans. Caleb once again marveled at the responsiveness of her flesh, at the way her deeply pink mouth went just a little slack, her kitten tongue darting out ever so often to remoisten the delicate supple tissue of her lips.

She was getting close, she pulled on her restraints, trying to fight off the moment of ultimate release, yet she unconsciously undulated against the back of his fingers searching for what she feared. He backed off just a little, drawing out the moment so he could do what he needed to do. He reached out with his left hand and grabbed the malleable tubing that was required. As he once again brought his beautiful captive to the jagged peaks of ecstasy that had her moaning and crying at the same time, he inserted the tube into her ass. She jerked harshly at the intrusion, but he held her steady. Slowly, thoughtfully, he rubbed her clit until her hands finally unclenched, her knees relaxed, and her breathing became languorous.

Caleb ignored the insistent press of his cock against his zipper, along with the sharp pang of lust mimicking pain in his belly and focused on soothing his pliant slave. Her cheeks were stained a deep pink beneath the russet color of her skin. It was a blush only orgasm could achieve, and Caleb couldn't resist feeling pride over having put it there. He stroked her back, no longer surprised at the way she arched into his touch. He would miss it. This. *Her*. Shaking the thought away, he set about talking her through his actions.

She sobbed quietly while he filled her with water, assuring her the pressure in her belly was normal, not to panic, though she did anyway. Her fingers on her right hand curled tightly around his, those on her left balled into a fist against the vinyl of the table. When he sensed she couldn't possibly hold more water inside her he stopped the flow and forced her to push. She cried in earnest then. She begged him not to press against her belly, embarrassment and shame apparent in her frantic pleas and pained expression. Caleb tried his best to keep her still, promising everything was alright, that she had nothing to fear or be ashamed of, but it was futile to try and calm her. Finally, he resorted to pressing her down with his weight. His face next to hers as over and again he filled her with water and emptied her, not ceasing until he was sure nothing more could be gained by subjecting her to his ministrations.

When it was all over, he took the blindfold off and released her bonds so he could sit her up on her knees on the table. To Caleb's astonishment, she wrapped her arms around his neck and buried her face against his shoulder, refusing to let go. Warmth spread through his limbs wherever her trembling body met his, a feeling as pleasant as letting the sun touch his face.

Unbidden, the memory of her looking up at him on the sidewalk engulfed him. She had been squinting that morning, even as she tried to take him in with her eyes. He had thought her charming, especially when she smiled. He suddenly ached to see her smile up at him like that. Instead, he pressed her back so he might kiss her warm, salty tears from her soft cheeks. She even tasted like sun. Did he prefer her smile or her tears?

Bewildered by his divergent thoughts, he left her to wash her face, instructing her to come into the bedroom when she was finished.

Caleb paced his bedroom slowly. Thinking so many things. Rafiq had informed him transport was in order once they reached Tuxtepec. He had also confirmed their route to Pakistan was free of customs officials and equipped with enough fuel for each leg of the journey. It was all good news, but Caleb had been lackadaisical at best, and outright disgruntled at worst. After twelve years, it suddenly seemed to be happening too quickly. At some point, very soon, he would have to make the girl aware of her fate. He would have to force her to understand that he had made her a whore. Vladek's whore. He couldn't help imagining the look she would give him in that moment. He also knew he would avoid it as long as possible. *Three weeks.*

Suddenly wondering what kept her so long, Caleb considered reentering the bathroom, but then thought the better of it. It was best to allow her to calm down and come out on her own. He looked about the room. No one would ever truly guess at the wealth and opulence hidden inside. The crown jewel of this dusty Mexican city. The plush carpet imported from Turkey, along with the tapestries. The bed was goose down, the sheets the finest Egyptian cotton, marble fireplace from Italy. The fireplace was probably by far the most excessive item in the room. Caleb was sure it never got cold enough to use it. One side of the room was made entirely of reinforced glass, with a hidden slide door leading out onto a terrace.

Caleb sighed and smiled. *She's probably never seen this much opulence in her entire life?* Where would Vladek keep her? His stomach twisted.

He heard the handle being turned and faced the door to watch her reaction. He wasn't disappointed when her hands shot up to her mouth, eyes wide, full of wonder.

"Not what you expected?" Caleb teased.

"N-n-no!" she replied, eyes scrutinizing the room. Caleb laughed heartily and helped her farther inside the room. She wandered around, half in a trance, touching her fingers to everything. "Do you live here? How do you afford this place?" she asked, innocent of any treachery. He knew her question had more to do with curiosity than guile.

He abruptly wished this were his home, so he could answer her admiration in the affirmative. He was struck by his sudden desire to impress her. She was hardly worth impressing, a slave, or so he reminded himself. His home in Pakistan was just as remarkable, if not more so. But she would never see it.

Impulsively, he drew her away from the curtains to face him, wanting her close despite his own objections to his boyish behavior. She stilled, as if just now remembering he was there. How dare she forget him, even for a moment. He attempted to refocus her concentration by gently, but firmly, slipping down the straps of her nightgown.

"What are you doing?" she asked timidly. Caleb looked down at her intently, the corners of his mouth giving just the slightest hint of a smile.

"You made a deal, Kitten, you stay out of your room, and I get an obedient little pet." He bent slowly and kissed her bottom lip, just as he had desired to do. She sucked it in. "You're going to ruin your lip if you keep that up Kitten." He tilted her chin so he could look at her big brown eyes, not at all marred by the puffiness caused from her crying. "I'm not going to fuck you again if that's what you're worried about." She tried to look away, but he held her gaze steady, if he concentrated, he thought he might be able to hear her pulse. He bent again and kissed the shell of her ear, "I'm just going to be a little *selfish*."

"What does that mean?" she asked, unsure. Without saying a word Caleb took her hand and walked over to the king size, cherry wood, four poster bed, a bed with many uses and not all of them easily evident.

"I'll show you," Caleb sat himself on the edge of the bed with his reluctant volunteer standing in front of him. The anxiety coursing through her was obvious to his interested eyes. For what seemed an eternity, neither of them said anything. Caleb simply watched, examined, and made mental notes. When he finally spoke, she started. "Just touch me."

"You want me to touch you? Where?" Caleb really enjoyed that about her, the way she seemed both guarded but curious. It hinted at her bravery, her wily and adventurous nature. All of which, she seemed strangely unaware of. Sometimes it was difficult not to see him in her. It was both endearing and disturbing.

"Wherever you'd like," he smiled. Her brows knit together, as if the answer needed further explanation. It didn't. He wanted her to touch him, anywhere, everywhere, so long as he didn't have to force her.

148

Perhaps because he thought if she touched him, of her own free will, he could stop feeling guilty for pushing her earlier. Or perhaps, he only needed to be touched by her. There had been a time when Caleb despised being touched, by anyone, only knowing cruelty, but now, under the right circumstances, he rather liked it.

"And then what? What are you going to do?" She was almost angry now, annoyed. Caleb understood, he supposed. She had no reason to believe he wouldn't take advantage of her. If he was honest, and he was for the most part, he wasn't sure he wouldn't either. Still, he was a man of his word. Rafiq had made sure of at least that much.

"I'll keep my hands right here," he patted the bed on either side of him, "unless you ask me otherwise." His smile became mischievous and he knew it, but he couldn't help himself. He tried not to laugh outright when she gave a derisive little snort and rolled her eyes. She didn't believe him, not one little bit. *Guarded, but curious.* The room remained silent for several moments, Caleb appraising her with his steady gaze, while she contemplated what to do or say next.

His heart picked up speed, as did his breathing. Was he actually anxious? It was a palpable aphrodisiac. She bit at her lip repeatedly, her little white teeth digging into the supple flesh. His fingers unconsciously pressed into the bedspread. There were places he wanted her mouth, other places he wouldn't mind the feeling of her little teeth pressing into him.

She cleared her throat, rousing Caleb from his devious thoughts. "So, um, if I don't...then I have to go back to my room right?" The way she posed the question was almost leading. Caleb nodded. He noticed her shoulders drop slightly, as if she were more relaxed. She wanted this. She wanted him. He refused to smile. "Okay. I'll do it. But you have to promise to keep your hands on the bed. You promise?" Caleb couldn't fight the smile any longer, he nodded. She hadn't even asked what he would accept as far as the touching went.

Her face was flushed, but her voice was almost confident. Again Caleb marveled at her facets. Shy one moment, a lioness the next. "Close your eyes. I don't think I can do it otherwise." Caleb laughed, especially when she blushed deeply, but reluctantly, he complied.

***

It was late, late enough to almost be early depending on how one looked at it. The girl slept peacefully beside him, her bottom pressed against his groin. It amazed him how easily she had fallen asleep, though he supposed he had put her through a lot. He shut his eyes and breathed in the scent of her hair, her scent beneath it.

He thought of her curious little fingers burrowing through his wavy blond hair. It had been the first thing she went for. His entire scalp had tingled, the sensation coursing down the back of his neck, along his spine and radiating out toward each of his limbs. One simple touch and he already doubted he'd be able to keep his promise. But he had remained still. He had wanted to know how far she'd go.

He had told himself, also, it was part of her training. To allow her to become accustomed to touching and knowing a man's body. Not all men were like him. They derived more pleasure from receiving than giving, and Caleb had only taught Kitten how to submit to his touch, not how to exact her own sense of control by initiating contact. He had admitted to himself, in that moment, he had avoided teaching her this aspect of what was required of her. It made him somewhat vulnerable, not because he was a slave to touch, nothing so insipid as that. All the slaves he had trained had touched him, frequently. But with them he had always remained detached, clinical, informing them what felt good and what needed work along the way.

With her, he wanted…something. And the obscurity of his desires was a distraction he could ill afford. Yet she needed to learn, didn't she? He had to endure it. He didn't have a choice. He had leaned into her touch and she had tightened her grip in his hair. There was a hint of pain, and his cock had leapt at the sensation.

She had roamed his face, her delicate fingertips dancing along his brow, his cheekbones, and his jaw. When she pressed her thumbs across his lips he tensed, thinking she would kiss him. She hadn't. Instead she trailed along his neck and shoulders, even venturing into his shirt by way of the few undone buttons at his throat. He felt her body heat ratchet up a few degrees, the heat of her womb radiating against the inch of space separating her from his straining cock. In the end, he had been the one to put an end to it.

He'd quickly had enough of trying to keep his promise.

He had told her it was enough, to get in bed. His voice had sounded cold, though he felt anything but.

He had secured her left wrist to a gold cord protruding from one of the bedposts. It was thin, but strong, capable of allowing her comfortable sleep without threat of escape. Then he'd gone to take a shower and do something he hadn't needed to do in a very long time. As shiny ribbons of semen spilled across the tile of the shower, he once again asked himself what the fuck he was thinking.

Now he lay in bed next to her, holding her like a lover, smelling her fucking hair and caressing her arm. Worse, he didn't think he could stop. He didn't want to stop. He banded his arm around her waist and pulled her deeper into him. She sighed. The little tart even tilted her head back, her cheek turning onto the fabric of his t-shirt. Did she want him to kiss her? He wasted no time in finding out. He pressed his lips to hers, gently, inquiring. She sighed again, opening her lips, sluggishly, still asleep.

Encouraged, he teased her mouth with the tip of his tongue. He was a masochist. Why else would he torture himself like this? She tasted warm, sweet, to some extent of liquor. A soft moan entered his mouth courtesy of her. Her body turned slightly toward him, her lips now seeking his. He gave her what they both wanted as his tongue ventured gently into her mouth. She was suddenly ravenous. She sucked at his mouth, sloppily, greedily, still asleep. He pulled back and she whimpered, seeking him blindly. He stifled a laugh.

"Mmm, Caleb," she said on a painful sounding sigh. His heart instantly sped up three times. Blood thudded in his ears. She was dreaming of him? Or was she feigning sleep? Did she know he was kissing her, had she willingly reciprocated?

"Yes, Kitten?" he asked, honestly nervous.

"Mmm," she replied. There was a hint of a smile tilting her lips. He wanted to kiss her again, but he didn't. She tried to turn toward him, the cord holding her wrist prevented it. Her brow furrowed, but she didn't wake. Caleb leaned over and let her loose. Instantly she rolled toward him and rested her head on his shoulder. Her newly freed left arm pulled him close. Her left leg pinned his thigh to the mattress. Her hot little pussy pressed against his hip. Was this really fucking happening? Resigned, he placed his left arm around her, the other he rested on his chest, against his still racing heart.

After a while, sleep finally rescued him from his sweet torture.

TEN

It was the same dream, the one I'd been having since the day we met. The one I used to eagerly anticipate before hitting my pillow at night. I didn't want to be having it, but I had no choice. I think perhaps my subconscious was determined to go back and look over the facts, find what I'd missed the first time.

I'm hurrying down the sidewalk, trying to get away from the sinister man in the car behind me when I look up and see him. Perhaps it's his easy stride, or the way his gaze sweeps past me instead of over me, but for whatever reason, he seems safe. I throw my arms about his waist and whisper, "Just play along okay."

Beyond the prison of my dream, I feel real sweat trickling down my neck. Obscurely, I'm aware of my tossing and turning, but I can't put together why I feel so uneasy.

He does and I'm surprised when his arms wrap around me. The moment of danger seems to pass very quickly, but for some reason I don't want to let go. I feel safe in these arms, and I've never really felt safe before. And he smells good, he smells the way I imagine a man should smell, like crisp, clean soap, and warm skin, and a light sweat. I think I'm taking too long to let go, so I release him as though he's burned me. Then I stare up and acknowledge the angel in front of me. My knees almost buckle.

Outside the dream, I can hear myself whimper. Part of me knows why I don't want to keep looking at him, but I can't stop it from happening. I dream in third person. I am a spectator.

He is the most beautiful thing I have ever seen: that includes puppies, babies, rainbows, sunsets, and sunrises. I can't even call him a man—men don't look this good. His skin is beautifully tanned, as if the sun itself took the time to kiss his skin to perfection. His muscled forearms are dusted with the same golden hair of his head. And his eyes mimic the blue-green of the Caribbean Sea I've only seen on movie posters.

He smiles, and I can't help but smile, too. I'm a puppet. He pulls my strings. His smile reveals his beautiful white teeth, but also his sharp canine on the left side. His teeth aren't perfect, and the small imperfection seems to make him more beautiful.

He's saying something to me, something about another girl, but I refuse to listen.

Off in the distance, I hear a familiar voice, my voice. Inside the dream? Outside the dream? I'm unsure. All I know is that I'm begging for the dream to stop. I didn't find what I was looking for—the thing I missed. I should stop. I should stop before I get to the unbearable part, the part that has nothing to do with memory, but fantasy, desire.

I lean in and tilt my head up. I want him to put those full lips to good use, I won't take no for an answer. When his tongue slides across the seam of my lips I feel things between my legs I have never felt before. I feel an aching sort of fullness and abruptly I can feel my heart beating, not only in my chest, but within those secret folds. I moan behind the kiss, and shortly after I hear him moan, too.

I want to touch him every where. I don't care if he takes me right here on the sidewalk, that's how badly I want him. I don't care what my mother will say. For him I'll be a whore. I'm glad I've waited. I'm glad it's him who gets to have me.

His hand has found its way into my hair, and for some reason I sense danger, but I make the feeling go away.

The kiss has turned hungry, ravenous—my lips hurt a little. His hand has become a fist in my hair. The sensation is familiar but distant. I want to keep kissing.

Do I taste beer? It's suddenly all too familiar.

A kiss. A touch.

"Is this what you do when I go to bed, Livvie? You put on your puta *clothes and try to seduce your father?"*

"He's not my dad!" He's the one to blame. Not me.

"Act like a whore and you'll get treated like one."

I hate you.

Without warning I am hit with an overwhelming sense of grief. Something is horribly wrong. I pull back from the kiss and my eyes go wide with horror.

The same youthful face I'd found beautiful beyond all explanation looks back at me with a menacing expression. His eyes still remind me of the sea, but instead of sunny Caribbean beaches, I now see hideous creatures of the deep lurking in the depths of his gaze. No longer an angel, he is the devil I have always feared.

My eyes flew open and I stared into the nothingness surrounding me. My heart pounded, my tears welled, but despite it all—I was shamefully wet between my legs. Old dread threatened to pull me into fresh hell,

156

and I fought hard to keep it from happening.

Caleb slept peacefully beside me, his arm wrapped around me like a vise. I should've been struggling to get up. But truth be told, the press of his muscular body against my back gave me a feeling of comfort I'd been longing for, for weeks. For years. And besides, it was actually cool in his room. It lacked all the hot stickiness that seemed to permeate throughout my room. *My room —that's funny.*

I thought about what had happened before, barely able to wrap my mind around the events that transpired. I think if I'd been watching it in a movie or reading it in a book, I'd have thought it was sexy. But to be living it, to be right there in the flesh...I think it was just scary. *Mostly.* Just thinking about it, my heart pounded even harder and faster in my chest, but it was different than before. Also, I had this heavy, sinking, sort of tingle in my belly. It reminded me of the feeling I used to get as a kid playing hide and go seek in the dark. I didn't want to get caught, but just sitting there, not know whether or not I would be was both exciting and frightening. I had known then it was the rush I enjoyed, not the hiding or the seeking.

Being around Caleb was feeling that all the time. I kept seeing his face, eyes closed, head tilted into my hands, soft masculine flesh beneath my fingers. The whole thing replayed in my mind as a series of flashes, flashes that kept me awake in the dark. I had dreamed of kissing him too, of doing more than kissing him. He was hard against my ass and against all logic I wanted to touch him there. I wanted to see what had been inside me.

157

When he'd asked me to stop last night, I had been mildly disappointed. Perhaps even hurt, thinking maybe I'd done something wrong. His voice had been harsh, distant at first, but then he'd softened and told me I'd been good, too good. For some crazy reason, in addition to being totally embarrassed, I felt, well, I don't know if relieved is the right word, or even proud, but something like it.

Caleb was a strange person, cruel and inhuman; a monster, yet, at other times, he seemed so capable of something like caring. He made me cry and scream and shake with fear, and nearly a split second later he could make me almost believe he wasn't responsible for any of it. He could hold me and make me feel safe. How was that possible? *I guess I'm more gullible than I'd ever thought.*

Slowly, as I stared at the curtains, I witnessed a sight I'd been missing for a long time. Daylight made its big debut, turning the curtains a slightly lighter shade. My heart quickened and anxiety coursed through me. It felt like Christmas morning.

I went slowly for Caleb's hand, gently urging it away from my breast. He grunted, and for a moment I was perfectly still, terrified. He sighed gruffly, and then, to my overwhelming relief, he rolled over. I was free of him. More surprisingly, I was free of the gold cord he'd secured around my wrist. Refusing to give it much thought and perhaps too quickly, I slid out of bed and crawled toward the light.

I pulled back the curtains, just a crack, but when the sunlight hit my eyes it made my head hurt. I shut my eyes tightly. It had been so damn long! I opened my eyes slowly. This time I saw what my soul had been aching to see for *so* long. I saw light; beautiful, warm, safe, light. I could barely keep from tearing up. For a moment I felt as though everything that had happened thus far had been a dream, and now that the sun was up, I could wake from it. I would never fall asleep again. The monsters would never come back. I opened the curtain a bit more, and I could make out a big deck. There was a table with a big umbrella, pots and plants and sun chairs; it was unreal. I pressed the palm of my hand against the glass, feeling the warmth of the sun and the chill of the morning against my skin, but it was all unreal.

I looked back at Caleb's sleeping form, his breathing was heavy. He wouldn't be waking any time soon. My heart thundered in my chest. This was it, my chance to escape. My mind screamed, *if you do this, and he catches you, you're dead! Are you stupid!* But it also said, *If you don't do this now, you may never get another chance.* I made up my mind. I was going to make a break for it.

I closed the curtain behind me and quietly looked around for a way to open the door. I surveyed my surroundings and didn't see much, no buildings, or roads, or people. I didn't let that dissuade me. My fingers touched along the glass, looking for some way to open the window, but I didn't see or feel anything. I did the same along the wall and found nothing. Nervous and agitated, I glanced back into the room. Caleb still slept peacefully. I pushed on the glass, but that didn't much help, *DAMN IT!* I could see that the glass was on tracks, so I knew it had to slide open. *Think! Just think!* I couldn't *see* where the door opened, but it had to open somehow, so maybe...the lock was somewhere I couldn't see. I stared at the top of the door, crushed by the realization I definitely couldn't reach it.

My only chance of opening the door sat in one of the corners, a big leather chair. It looked heavy. I almost screamed. I looked back at Caleb. *How the hell am I going to move that without him waking up!*

I walked silently toward my inanimate nemesis and gave it a hard shove. The chair made a soft scraping noise against the carpet, and I instantly looked at the bed. He continued to sleep. But there was no fucking way I was going to be able to move the chair without waking him.

I glanced around the room and tried not to pass out from the rush of blood draining from my face. Hanging on the door of an armoire was Caleb's suit jacket and peeking out from beneath it, a shoulder holster. Could it be? Oh God, could it *please* fucking be? I reached for the soft fabric and lifted it. It was the biggest damn gun I had ever seen, the *only* one actually— but still. I felt like vomiting. Part of me wanted to forget the whole damn thing and get back in bed. What was the saying: Cowardice is the better part of valor? *Fuck it!* I reached for the gun. The damn thing weighed a ton.

The armoire opened and for a moment I was actually surprised by the amount of pain inflicting instruments hidden inside. Riding crops, whips, chains, and other things I didn't recognize from watching *Real Sex* on HBO while at Nicole's house. Was that a spiky dildo? I almost swooned. Had he planned to use this stuff on me? Sick fuck. And yet....

I spotted a pair of handcuffs, several actually, without fur on them. That meant they were real right?

Cause it could be embarrassing otherwise. I was willing to take a chance. I put Caleb's jacket on, instantly overwhelmed by the size of it. I set the gun on the seat of the chair and began rolling up the sleeves.

"What the hell are you doing," Caleb's angry voice momentarily had me frozen in place. Our eyes met, mine wide and terrified, his cold and venomous. I reached for the gun as he burst out of bed. I was faster. For once.

"Don't fucking move! Not one step," my voice was shrill, almost panicked. I might have shot him out of fear alone, and I think he understood because he instantly halted his approach. My heart was beating too fast, my vision was hazy. *Keep it together, Livvie. Keep it fucking together.*

"Put the gun down, Kitten," he whispered, as if I were more frightened than him. Shit, maybe I was. This probably wasn't the first time he'd had a gun in his face, but it was definitely the first time I'd threatened someone's life. I wanted to cry. I didn't want to have to do this. I didn't want to hurt him. *No choice now, Livvie. It's you or him.* I hated this. I felt like one of those dumb girls in the movies, the one holding the gun on her would-be killer. Her hands are shaking and the killer just keeps stepping closer. She can't fucking kill him. Then she's dead. Then *I'm* dead.

I took a deep breath and held the gun steady, ignoring how heavy it was, ignoring the twitch in my forearms as I tried to keep it level. I especially ignored the sweat in my palms, making the handle slippery. "Please, Caleb," I almost begged, "don't move. Let me go and don't make me kill you, cause I will. I swear to

God, I will."

He was calm, too calm. "No one is going to kill anyone, Kitten. But I can't let you go. Just put it down and I promise I won't do anything to hurt you." I couldn't help but laugh. I was holding the gun, but he was the one holding me hostage. Still, my laugh was hysterical.

My mind went to that special place of mine. And perhaps, inspired by the big damn gun in my hands, conjured Dirty Harry. "'I know what you're thinking, '" I half choked out. "'*Did he fire six shots or only five?* Well, to tell you the truth, in all this excitement I kind of lost track myself. But being as this is a .44 Magnum, the most powerful handgun in the world, and would blow your head clean off, you've got to ask yourself one question: Do I feel lucky? Well, do ya, punk?'" Caleb's expression was priceless, somewhere between deep concern (for my sanity) and anger (at my idiocy).

"Kitten," he began. I cocked the gun, with two hands because I couldn't manage it with one. In the process my finger pressed against the trigger slightly and for the first time I saw real fear skid across my captor's features. He swallowed. I eased my finger off the trigger, relieved I hadn't just done something stupid, or in my case, stupid-*er*. I reached for the handcuffs and threw them in his direction. He caught them without breaking eye contact. "The gun isn't loaded, Kitten."

My heart fluttered. "Bullshit, Caleb. Don't make me find out which one of us is bluffing." He smiled, just a little. If you didn't know him as well as I did, you'd have missed it for what it was. I don't know why, but I looked down at his shorts. The bastard was hard. "Cuff yourself to the bed and don't make me ask again."

This time his smile was broad, even smug. "Kitten, if that's what you wanted, you need only have asked?" Really? Would he have let me cuff him to the bed? *Livvie! Focus.*

"Just shut up and do what I said." I was caustic. He furrowed his brow and, for a moment, I had forgotten who had the upper hand. Heavy metal sliding in my sweaty palm reminded me. "Now!" He walked to the post nearest me, still a few feet away and cuffed his wrists together. "Tighter," I was impatient, nervous. He complied and I breathed a sigh of relief.

I lowered the gun, taking a moment to let the anxiety settle, to allow my vision to clear and the adrenaline to dissipate. "Feel better, Pet?" he whispered, still playful. Possessed, I took two steps closer to him and slapped him so hard my hand stung. Instantly he leapt forward, his hands clutching for my hip and his feet sweeping my ankles. I fell flat on my back, the gun flung behind me. He could no longer reach me with his bound hands, but he was trying to grasp me between his legs. I scrambled backward with all my strength, refusing to be caught. I got free and collided with the chair behind me. "You're going to pay for that," he panted. The right side of his face sported an angry red handprint.

I shook out my hand, "I already have. That was my change."

A few minutes later, I finally had the chair close enough to the window. I stepped up and felt around the edge. *Please let me be right about this.* My heart made a roaring sound in my ears, and I shut my eyes against doubt. Finally, I felt a little switch and my heart stopped all together. I glanced back to see Caleb. The angry expression had left his face though my handprint remained. I said a silent prayer, stepped down, and slid the door open. Caleb's voice came from behind, "Kitten," he sounded worried or sad, "Don't let me find you." Was that a threat? I wasn't going to stick around to find out.

I didn't look back. I ran with all the force my legs could muster. My lungs burned as my bare feet thudded heavily against the dust of the ground. It was still early, the ground not warm yet. I wanted to scream for help, but wasn't sure if I was far enough away to keep Caleb from hearing me, so I just ran. Up ahead I saw a man in an apron, pushing a dolly of crates into a building.

"Help me!" The man looked in my direction, his expression one of confusion and distress. As I reached him, I all but flew into his arms trying to push the both of us inside.

"*Que pasa? Que te paso?*" he asked in Spanish.

I shoved him harder until we both nearly fell over the dolly on our way inside the building. My breath came in gasps while I tried to slow down and explain in Spanish that I was an American citizen who had been kidnapped and held against my will. I told him I escaped but that my captor was not far and I needed the police right away.

"Who is this man?" he asked "Who is the man who took you?" he seemed just as frantic as I was and he opened the door to look in the direction I had come from.

"Get away from the door!" I yelled. "Caleb! His name is Caleb. Please, just call the police. Where the fuck am I?" Finally, the man quickly shut the door and bolted the lock.

"Mexico."

"Mexico!"

"Sí, Mexico," the man was exasperated. *Fucking Mexico. I* knew *it!*

"Shit yeah, you are," came a man's gravelly voice from the corner. The man, who I assumed was the bartender, and I looked in his direction. He appeared dirty; not the kind of dirty that came from poverty or sloth, but the kind of dirty that came from an obnoxious lifestyle. It was early in the morning, and here he was already in a bar, an American biker. He stared at me intently, took a drink of his beer and licked the foam from his mustache. Suddenly, I became aware of my clothing. I was nearly naked under Caleb's coat. I crossed my arms and took a step behind the edge of the bar.

"Can you help me, please? I need to get to the police." He took another drink as he shook his head.

"You don't want to go to the police darlin', trust me on that. Those dirty Mexicans are crooked as hell. They'd just sell you back to whoever you're running from. Best thing you can do is try to get back over the border and let our guys help you out." I looked at the bartender.

"*Es la verdad,*" he said. *It's the truth.*

Exasperated, I yelled, "Well can you help me get to the fucking border then!" The bartender jumped and anxiously hustled to the back room. The biker stood, grabbed his beer and drank it down before slamming the glass on the table and wiping his mouth with the back of his hand.

"Well, damn, honey, you ain't got to be nasty about it." He walked over to me, tracing his hand along the bar, purposely eyeing me inappropriately. "I'm sure we can work something out."

"Fuck you," I said and looked at him with disgust.

He chuckled. "I was thinking of some other arrangement baby doll, a ransom maybe. A finder's fee?" He looked me up and down again. "Of course, I'm always willin' to compromise."

Just then a loud bang came from the door and whoever stood on the other side wasn't happy. The biker looked at me, saw my instant panic, and pushed me down behind the bar. "Get the fuck down there and don't breathe a single breath if you want to live through this!" Acting on instinct alone, I curled up in the fetal position under the cash register. The biker ran into the back room and returned quickly with a few crates of alcohol. Before I knew what he was up to, he stacked them on the ground and pushed them under the bar next to me. Meanwhile, the thunderous banging continued at the door of the bar.

"Don't move," he said one last time. He grabbed a glass from the counter and began filling it with beer when a loud bang splintered the wood of the door. I nearly urinated.

"Whoa!" said the biker, laughing loudly. My heart pounded hard in my chest, my eyes shut tightly as I worked to imagine myself somewhere else.

"Where the fuck is she?" Caleb demanded, calm and inhuman.

"Where's who, man?"

"Don't play dumb right now, fuckface, or I'll blow your goddamn head off!"

"Well that don't sound too good. Look man, I'm just here watching Javier's bar."

"And where's Javier?"

"He had some problem at home with his old lady, fuck if I know or care. I'm just enjoying the free beer while he's gone."

"What's with the dropped crates outside?"

"You ain't ever left someplace in a hurry?" A deafening silence filled the room. "Besides, if you're in here looking for him with a damn shotgun, he probably had a real good reason to leave in a hurry." He said with an obnoxious chuckle. More silence. Caleb's footsteps made a slow steady sound as they came near the bar. I did urinate a little at that point. Not my finest moment, I assure you.

"What did you say your name is?" asked Caleb.

"I didn't; but you can call me Tiny."

Caleb let out a short, stern laugh.

"Tiny, huh? Well, Tiny," I heard the distinct sound of Caleb cocking the shotgun. "I'm going to ask you this, one, fucking, time, and then I'm going to blow a hole in your chest. Where's the girl?"

Tiny cleared his throat loudly, "Alright man look… seems to me you lost somebody important to you, and I swear that if I had any fucking idea where that person might be I would tell you, but I don't. I was just here having a beer, and Javier had to leave in a hurry. I figured what the fuck, I'll stick around. I don't know nothing about your bitch. So kindly," I heard him pull out a gun and cock it. "Get that fucking gun outta my face before I redecorate Javier's bar with yours!"

The silence that followed crushed the air around

me. Sweat dripped down my face, burning my tightly shut eyes. My fingernails sunk into the skin of my arms. I was positive that someone would die while I hid behind crates of piss-warm beer. Suddenly, Caleb erupted into laughter. I bit down hard on my lip to keep from screaming. Tiny soon joined in on the joke and I worried he had given me away.

"Alright, Mr. Tiny, tell you what. I'll take you at your word that you don't know what I'm talking about, and trust that if you happen to run into a half naked girl telling wild stories, that I'll be the first person you get in touch with. It's the big house up the road. Ask for Caleb. No one else."

"You got it man. Can we put these down now?" It was quiet. For a few moments I heard nothing. Then I heard Caleb's feet moving farther and farther away from the bar. Before I could feel relieved, Caleb's voice called out from a distance a few feet away, "But if I find out you lied to me, I *will* find you. And if I find out you've done something to my property— I'll kill you." And then he was gone.

ELEVEN

"Where is she, Caleb?" Rafiq's tone was anger tempered with restraint. Caleb knew it well. It was the tone Rafiq had adopted whenever he spoke to Caleb in the beginning, when he had been a difficult boy. He didn't like it, not one bit.

It was early evening and the girl was still missing. She could be hundreds of miles away by now. *Why the fuck had he let her go?* It wasn't like him to be so impulsive, or stupid. Though lately, he wasn't so sure. First he had failed to secure his weapon. Then he'd let her loose in the middle of the night. And now, he'd set unknown factors into play.

"I don't know where she is Rafiq. If I knew, I would be collecting her now."

"Would you?" The question held very strong implications. When had Rafiq started to doubt him? When had Caleb ever given him cause? The answer to both questions was of course *now*. So Caleb replied with the same tempered anger and restraint, "I understand how important she is, Rafiq. I know why I'm here."

To destroy Vladek. He felt mildly detached. Where and when had he lost that objective? When had his focus wavered? Strangely, he didn't feel guilty. Already, he was thinking, they could find another way to Vladek. Necessity was the master of invention. Still, he didn't know why he'd let her go. He'd known she was nearby, perhaps hiding with the bartender, the biker's body language had told him as much. So, why? Why was he suddenly risking so much when he stood to gain nothing and lose everything?

"I would *usually* agree Caleb," Rafiq said softly. "But you're also not in the habit of making mistakes, let alone of this magnitude. Have you forgotten so easily what I've done for you? I found you. I took you in. I helped you become the man your enemies fear. Do you need to be reminded of where you would be without my interference?" Caleb's jaw clenched hard.

"No, of course not." It was also impossible for Caleb to forget that Rafiq was so fond of reminding him. "May I also remind you that it is *me* who kills for you?" He had meant it to sound like a threat, but it came off as a strange plea. As if from a child to a parent. There was a long silence on the other end of the line and the longer it stretched on, the more uneasy Caleb became. "I've failed you Rafiq. I'll make it right." Somehow he'd *find* a way.

"I'm sorry I doubted you *khoya*," Rafiq replied, voice softening, "I know how much you have sacrificed. It is only…"

"I understand Rafiq." He paused, briefly. "I'll let you know the moment I find her." Caleb hung up before anything else could be said. He needed to think, and the longer he spoke to Rafiq, the more he thought about the wrong things, though he had no clue what the right things would be. He'd never been one to grapple with slight differences.

Caleb pressed his fingers to his forehead and tried to alleviate some of the pressure there. Was he betraying the one person he trusted? The heavy reality was finally settling in. Who was he all of a sudden? Certainly not a man of his word.

Anger rose like bile within his chest. It was her. Ever since he had laid eyes on her she had caused him nothing but confusion and conflict. He had allowed himself to feel...something. And she had repaid him by pointing his own gun at his face. His fingers touched upon the left side of his face. It still stung, in more ways than one. He pushed at his cheek, wanting to feel the tight, itchy burn just beneath the surface. He should find her. Bring her back. Take control of her and, in the process, himself. *Is that the only reason you want her back?* He thought of her soft supple body pressed against his, her arm wrapped around his midsection.

He'd let her go, he'd done it through his own stupidity, but he'd let her go. And all he could think about was that she hadn't even looked back. She'd just run away...from him.

He almost didn't want to find her, but he couldn't stop until he did. He wasn't going to fail again.

Focus and objectivity replaced the unease and confusion. It was time to pay a visit to the bartender.

***

After Caleb had left the bar, I had refused to move from my hiding space beneath the counter for over an hour. At least I thought it had been that long, my sense of time was probably way off. What had to amount to weeks of being held hostage in a dark room would do that. Finally, the behemoth of a man who called himself *Tiny* had hoisted me up by my arm and shook me until I stopped my hysterics.

When I'd calmed down, I'd asked, "Why are you

helping me?"

He just frowned at me. "Because you look like you could use a lot of help. And you're American."

He'd led me outside where the bartender, Javier, was waiting in an old, rusted, baby blue pickup of indeterminate origin. I was scared to get in the truck. I didn't know where they planned on taking me, or what they planned to do with me once they had me where they wanted me. I only knew Tiny had told me I'd be safe and he'd help me. If there'd been more options I would've gotten as far away from the dirty biker as possible. The fact was this: I didn't have better options, and he knew that. So I got in the truck

We only drove for about fifteen minutes before we pulled up to a small concrete shack. *Shit*. My fear never subsided, it even went up a few notches but as I looked around, I forced myself to keep looking, watching. Ready to run. Chicken wire surrounded the structure and indeed a few chickens were walking about, pecking at random feed strewn across the dirt. The air was thick with the smell of heat and animal excrement. Still, there was a 'homey' feeling to old run-down building. There was a child's tricycle lying on its side next to the house, one of the chickens was pecking at the torn seat.

"What are we doing here?" I asked. I felt stupid, but hopeful. Hopeful we'd be leaving for the border soon. For a miracle or an intervention by God. I'd settle for a phone. I was hoping on a lot, and on a stranger. I was tired of meeting new people.

"We need to get you a change of clothes. Plus Javier has a phone we can use to make our arrangements."

I felt triumphant over the existence of a phone, but

172

then the rest of his words had set in, "What arrangements?" The sense of unease I felt—doubled. Dread quickly sunk in.

Tiny snorted, "Like they say darlin': ass, grass, or cash, no one rides for free. And since you ain't got no grass and I prefer cash to ass...I think you know where I'm going with this."

My heart jumped into overdrive, thumping loud staccato beats in my ear, *boom-boom-boom.* "How much cash are we talking about?" I didn't want to confess how fucking broke my family was. I certainly didn't want to have to pay in ass.

"Pretty little thing like you? I'd say you're worth at least a hundred grand to somebody." I almost threw up from the sharp twist in my stomach at his words. My family didn't have anywhere near that kind of money. The only person I knew who could possibly have that kind of cash was Nicole, but it wasn't hers to give was it? It belonged to her parents, and I hardly knew them. Nicole was always alone in that big house. Despair, cut through me. To escape, only for this. I stared at Tiny. I felt things snapping loose, snapping in. Fight or flight. I was going to do both.

"And if I'm not?" I whispered under my breath, not really wanting to know the answer but having to ask the question because it was a likely outcome. "Worth that much to anybody?"

He looked down at me and smiled, "Oh, I'm sure you're worth at least that much to your boy Caleb." He looked me up and down, slow, leering, then smiled widely at me. "Aren't you darlin'?" I swallowed the bile that time. Where was the bartender? Where had he gone? Did it matter?

He grabbed me, my arm engulfed by one meaty, sweaty hand and he dragged me behind him as I struggled out of his grasp. I was going to make this difficult. He laughed at me the whole way and I knew I'd done more harm to myself, than him.

The house was better kept on the inside than it was on the outside. There were even pictures secured to the concrete walls, mostly religious paintings. Right in front of me, over the small, plastic covered sofa was a picture of Christ on the cross, his expression pained, blood tears running down his face as he stared toward heaven asking why God had forsaken him. I could ask the same question. I'd left the Devil I knew for one I didn't and it was going to cost me—hopefully a hundred grand, but potentially so much more.

"Where's the phone?" My voice was hoarse, on the verge of tears. I sucked in desperation and hot air. I prayed Nicole's family would help me. I wasn't sure how huge of a long shot it was, if they'd believe me, let alone help me. Would they call the police? Hang up on me?

Tiny pointed to the end of the sofa where an old rotary phone, my lifeline, waited for me to make the most important call of my life.

***

It hadn't been too difficult to find out where the bartender lived, a simple matter of waiting for the regulars to arrive at the bar and then waiving large American bills. All citizens of dusty countries understood the value of the dollar. American money represented an American life, a chance to pursue a future deserved rather than destined. It was a future

174

worthy of stealing, killing, and selling one's soul. Caleb couldn't help but scoff at how easy it had been to find her. He had told her not to be found and he had meant it. Once again, she had not listened.

Instead, Caleb had successfully honed in on his target. There was, within him, a sense of victory. But there was something else, too. Conflict. Always conflict when it came to her. What would he do when he saw her? Beat her? Scream at her? Spank her until she wept and begged for mercy or cover her in kisses that would cause the same? He never knew with her, not until the moment took over him, controlled him.

He walked back to the plantation, in no rush to collect his prize. Victory and anger aside, he did not relish any of the things he might have to do next. He hoped the bartender didn't have a family. He hoped his Kitten would come without added agitation. He hoped there would be no one to kill. Still, he doubted each of these scenarios. So he walked. No rush.

As he listened to the warm dirt crunching under his boots, he stared out at the landscape of the village. Not far beyond, lay the city. She was out there, beneath one of those many homes made of sand, clay and lime, sweating under a rusted tin roof. There were hundreds of them, sprawling out before him on into the horizon, but it didn't matter. The city could appear large, but it was very small in every way that mattered. Poverty bred despair and despair bred corruption and corruption would guarantee him safe haven. No matter what happened this night, Caleb would return and not empty-handed.

The heel of his boot hit the ground with a hard

crack. *She never turned back. Not once.* She'd just run away from him. His ire rose. "'Do I feel lucky?' Yes, Kitten, I feel very lucky." He picked up his pace. It was best to strike while his anger was hot and his passion ice cold.

***

The sun beat down on my shoulders, though it was early evening. Dust covered my body from head to toe and filled my mouth as we tore up the road on Tiny's motorcycle. Javier had provided me with one of his wife's dresses to wear. Unfortunately, she was a somewhat larger woman and the dress did little better than the nightgown. But it was black and that was good. I put it on over the nightgown and put on Caleb's jacket. It was cold comfort compared to what could now happen to me.

Nicole had come through. Or at least she'd promised she would. The moment I heard her voice I had burst into tears of relief and pure joy. She'd cried, too. Through the grainy connection I listened to her strained voice explain how she'd never thought I'd run away, not without her. She also made it clear my mother had no such faith in me.

In fact, she held Nicole completely responsible for my disappearance, demanding that the police pull her in for questioning and force her to give up my whereabouts. When that didn't work, because there was no indication of foul play—my books were never discovered—and I was eighteen, she had gathered up all my stuff and dumped it on Nicole's front lawn. My mother had yelled at Nicole, called her a whore and self-serving rich girl. She had called me worse. My heart sunk into my stomach, extinguishing some of my joy. Maybe Caleb had been right. Still, Nicole reassured me she would make everything right, call my mother and explain. I told her not to bother. She hadn't given a damn about me. In some ways, right now, I fucking didn't care. I wanted to *live*. I wanted out of this hell.

What I needed was cash, lots of it. A hundred grand to be exact. "Holy shit Livvie! How am I supposed to get that kind of money? My parents are on a cruise right now." Not what I needed to hear. I had looked up at Tiny and Javier, one of them looked expectant, the other worried his eye on the door. I wish it had been only Javier at the bar, he seemed more malleable, but then again, he also left me there to be captured.

"I need that money, Nick. Please," I said, my voice high and almost screeching. "I don't know what he'll do to me." That quieted her and she was in the middle of telling me something when Tiny took the receiver and made it very clear what would happen to me if she didn't come through. Everywhere I turned these days I was someone's property.

He looked down at me. *I should have called the cops* But I knew since my own mother had failed to help me, it was all too likely the cops would care even less. Especially in a poor, drug-run country like Mexico. I had a choice between bad, worse and excruciating. It was no choice at all.

"We're leaving—now."

I didn't bother asking where. We drove, too fast for me to consider jumping off, but I still had a small sliver of hope that this fucked up plan would work, and I'd be free. As Tiny's bike slowed down, my heart sped up.

We were headed toward Chihuahua. Nicole would

meet us there tomorrow night with the money. How she was going to do it I had no idea. Worse, I didn't know if she *could* do it. I only knew she had told Tiny she'd be there with the money. If she was bluffing, it didn't matter, she was buying me time. But first we had to make a stop and pick up the rest of Tiny's "gang." I was not at all excited to meet more people like Tiny, but as usual, I had no choice and no say. I pulled Caleb's jacket closer to my body.

Traveling more slowly, his scent wafted up to my nostrils, pulling my thoughts toward him. What would happen now? Was he looking for me? And why did the idea fill me with both a sense of dread and hope? Hope for what? For a moment I wished I had just lain in the bed next to him, given him a chance to be kind. Perhaps he would have let me go eventually. I blinked, hard. *You did the right thing, Livvie. This can work, it can.*

As we pulled up to the run-down house I heard several voices laughing, shouting, or making chatter as loud rock music filled the air. I wobbled and nearly fell when I got off the bike. Tiny laughed as he walked to the door.

"Watch yourself little girl, you don't want that bike fallin' down on you." I didn't think it was too damn funny.

He opened the door to the house and let out the only thing more overwhelming than the music: the smell of Marijuana. I stood outside, lamenting every decision I had ever made to lead me here, and then I stepped through the doorway. All conversation came to a halt. Nine bikers, one of them a young woman, turned to stare at me. I tensed at their blatant scrutiny, most of them confused, and some of them seemingly aroused.

178

"Everybody, this is Jessica," Tiny introduced me, sounding happy and counting his cash in his head most likely. I decided to use a fake name, for no other reason than I didn't want anyone to know my real one. "Nobody fuck with her," he looked at me lasciviously, "unless she wants to be fucked with." Still silence, except for the long version of "November Rain" blasting through crappy boom box speakers. I shrank further inside Caleb's coat, another comforting whiff of him, another regretted decision. This whole fucking thing was twisted irony. Tiny turned to me, finishing the introductions, "Jessica, this is Joker, Smokey, Casanova, Stinky, Boston, Abe, Hog, Kid, and his bitch, Nancy."

Who the fuck cared? I sure didn't. I just stared blankly at all of them, at none of them.

Nancy just gave a snide look, as if I called her a bitch as a greeting.

I said nothing. Growing up poor and in LA taught me something. You can't look weak, but you can't look too defiant or someone could take it as a challenge. And fuck with me. I flicked my gaze around, holding only a few of the eyes briefly before just staring off, not responding and just giving an indifferent and vague nod of acknowledgment. I wish Caleb had taught me something more valuable than how to withstand a strong hand on my ass. I almost laughed, feeling hysterical for a moment, and bit down on my tongue. I was not going to freak out, not when I needed to be aware.

"Nancy, why don't you take Jessica here and get her something to eat before we pack up and ride out. I want to make it to Chihuahua by night fall."

Nancy rolled her eyes at Tiny and then looked at me for a moment before saying, "Well come on then."

Nancy and I went down a small hallway into another little room. Inside, a few dirty airbeds and small piles of clothes that seemed to also serve as sheets and pillows lined the floor. She angrily kicked at the clothes in her way and headed toward the corner of the room to the bed covered in clothes, make-up, hairspray and individually wrapped condoms. I looked away, saying nothing.

"Listen here, girl. You better either pay me for this food or replace it cause I don't have money to throw away on anyone." I didn't say anything, just a tad shocked. So much for us females sticking together or some sympathy. Then I realized that was asking for way too much. Caleb had taught me not to expect sympathy, even if he'd shown me some from time to time. Or at least what passed for it, considering the source. I had to stop thinking about the son of a bitch.

She picked up a pair of cut-off jean shorts and a skimpy leather top that laced up the front. I couldn't help it, I winced at the whore-ware. Suddenly my chest suffered a direct hit and a small pile of snack foods dropped to my feet. I gritted my teeth. She responded with a sneer. *Bitch.* I picked up the bag of chips and two protein bars. Yeah, I'd be sure to reimburse her for these delicacies. She continued to give a stiff upper lip as she kicked more clothes into a corner.

"Well, are you gonna just stand there or are you gonna sit down and eat?"

I looked at her, incredulous. Then loud voices drifted in from the other room.

"Are you fucking *crazy*!"

Eruption of a lot of voices arose.

"Bringing that bitch in here is a mistake, man," said someone.

"Jesus Christ, Tiny, you should give her back while you can," said another.

"When did you become such a pussy?" said Tiny.

"What's going on?" Nancy shot daggers at me with her eyes. I cast my eyes toward the floor. She grabbed me by the elbow, squeezed, and easily pushed me out of the room before she left to join the argument. As Tiny told the real story, the shouting escalated. It went back and forth for about forty-five minutes, and then most of the guys decided to leave and avoid "The Shitstorm."

Nancy returned, livid. I found a corner to hide in while they packed, not wanting anyone to see me and start yelling at me. They packed pretty quickly, most of them just throwing a few handfuls of clothes in a backpack—obviously all they came with. I watched, not feeling anything, just learning names I didn't care about. I was just so tired and scared. I wanted…I wasn't sure what I wanted. The fear and terror drained me, took my energy and hope. Despair in, hope out. Repeat. Repeat.

"Come on, Kid, let's just go." I heard Nancy. I lifted my gaze toward the fighting twosome. The way she was clinging to him, I was assuming he was the boyfriend.

"You know I can't do that, I'm not leaving Tiny alone. Besides, I ain't afraid of no fucking pervert. Let him come, Tiny'll put that fucker down for good."

They argued. "Baby, please, let's just *go*."

A few tense moments later Kid replied, "No."

"*Fine*," she said lowly, seething. And then she stormed out of the room.

When it was all said and done, only Joker, Nancy, Abe, and Kid stayed to keep Tiny and me company. I had to admit, they didn't seem like the nicest guys, and Nancy, I already knew, was a huge bitch. But at least I was headed home in the morning. They decided we would spend the night.

It was late, I didn't know the time, but it was dark. I stayed in my corner a long time while they all sat around drinking beer and laughing loudly. I think I sat there for so many hours that they may have forgotten I was there. No one slept, and I couldn't stomach anything.

I just waited for night to fall and sat in my corner, listening to the time tick away. But toward what, I had no idea.

***

Ransomed. She'd been ransomed. Javier's family huddled in a corner, Javier himself just a limp body, barely breathing but still alive. The motherfucker was going to get a cut of the ransom if he helped smuggle what was *his*.

He chanced a glance in the direction of Javier's family and instantly recognized the pitiful pleading expression on the woman's face. Kitten would look at him like that when she was terrified of what he'd do next. In some ways, he imagined that look had softened. As he kept staring at the woman, Javier's wife, something inside him twisted and he *had* to look away. It was a good thing he had decided to come alone. It was also a good thing Javier's wife and child were at home with him. They were the reason Javier would live after tonight. He would never kill a man in front of his child, but Jair and the rest would do so with too much pleasure.

Caleb walked toward a coffee table and picked up a short pencil and a pad of paper resting near a phone. Kitten had used that phone, today. She had touched all these things, but there was no sign of her now. He thought of her smell, still embedded in the pillow on his bed, some of her hair too. At the time he had felt anger, now....

He dropped the pencil and pad next to Javier. "*Direcciones. ¡Ahora!*" Directions. Now. Javier sputtered and wept, bloody drool dripping from his quivering lip as he forced himself to write. Caleb looked on dispassionately. *Ransomed.* If they were holding her for ransom, if they didn't care about the law, about getting back to the U.S., then what else could they be doing to her at this very moment? Rage ripped through him, and he fought the strong urge to kick Javier. Emotions were only useful to control, survive and succeed. He was apparently re-learning the lesson he thought he'd mastered.

Caleb collected the piece of bloody paper. The biker's weren't too far away, but he also knew he couldn't go in alone. He would have to return to the house and gather Jair and a few more men along with weapons. The bikers were armed. To his shock, it wasn't his own safety he was concerned with. That girl, that damn stupid girl. He had to get her back.

Caleb couldn't wait until he saw the bikers.

***

I got up and ran to the bathroom to throw up. I heard their laughter in the background and Kid saying they were assholes. My arms wrapped around the top of the toilet, and probably touched piss, but with no food in my stomach and getting high off the heavy pot fumes, I couldn't really do too much about it.

They laughed at me. Assholes. I should never have let my guard down. I should never have trusted anyone. I should have run away from Tiny, and I definitely should not have fallen asleep in the bathroom. But the gagging and dry heaving had worn me out further and I was exhausted. And high.

It started out simply at first, my skin felt warmer and that was nice. Little tingles spread throughout my body and I stretched out. My thoughts felt liquid and surreal, like nothing was what it was, like I was falling, but it was okay to fall, and so I did. I felt enveloped. Then the softness became rougher and the warmth hot and uncomfortable. I jerked, my body confused. *My buzzing head.* My eyes began to flutter, but I couldn't open them all the way and suddenly I had the odd sensation my nipples were being tugged through my dress by something blunt but firm.

Instinctively, I pushed at the pressure, of hands. When I realized it was someone, I pushed with my sluggish and weak arms and then I attempted to protest, scream bloody murder but my head felt huge and my tongue felt dead in my mouth. When I felt a mouth on my breast, sucking harder, a yelp escaped my lips. I finally broke through the haze. And I woke up.

"Shhh, you don't want to wake everybody up." The voice was feminine—Nancy's. What the…fuck…was going on? I tried to scream and a hand covered my mouth. Too heavy and large to belong to Nancy. I tried to scream louder, beyond the hand. And still, I heard another voice. Three. But who? It was too dark to tell.

"Hurry up man, she's wakin' up." I swung my arms wildly, surprised when feminine hands grabbed them and held them down. Fabric ripped and my chest was suddenly bare. The man on top of me wasted no time in sucking my breast into his mouth, scratching me with the stubble of his beard. With his free hand he pulled at my dress, trying to raise it up. I kicked wildly, but he forced his way between my legs and his naked chest lay on mine.

"Don't be shy baby, I know what you are. You're a whore aren't you?" And then he let out the shrill laughter that finally gave away his identity—Joker.

"Flip her over," said the other man.

"I can't man, if I move my hand she's gonna start screaming."

"Don't be such a fucking pussy dude, I'll let you go first, pass her here."

Eyes wide and somewhat adjusted to the dark, I watched in horror as Joker grabbed his shirt that was lying nearby and shoved it into my mouth as Abe pushed me forward onto Joker's chest, so that I straddled him. My arms, posing no seeming struggle, were pinned high on my back. I cried and screamed pitifully, my cries falling on uncaring ears.

"Why are you letting them do this?" I screamed at Nancy who despite the shirt in my mouth could probably understand me. She looked panicked, but it seemed to stem from anger or excitement. Her eyes were wild, frenzied. She was enjoying this as much as the men.

Joker lay back onto the floor and held my arms as I was bent into an impossibly uncomfortable position. My mind sober, flashed with horrific scenarios which did nothing to formulate a way out of the situation. Behind me Abe pulled down his pants and pressed his penis against me, searching for any way in.

"Oh my god, you feel good, baby." I pulled as far away from him as I could and strained my arms so that they almost came out of their sockets. My struggle only served to bend me more impossibly.

Finally, I worked the cloth out of my mouth and in one quick movement bit into Joker's shoulder so hard his blood seemed to squirt into my mouth. He howled and it rocked my head. The next moment I flew through the air, my ribs landing across the toilet.

"What the fuck? What the fuck? What the fuck?" Abe yelled over and over as Joker continued to scream and curse.

"You fucking, bitch!" Joker yelled. He grabbed my hair and I heard the awful crunch of his fist connecting with my face. I choked on both my blood and his.

"Oh my god, man, what the hell are you doing!" Nancy finally yelled.

But she could do nothing to stop her associate from kicking me repeatedly in the ribs. My breath protested and all I heard was *Crack. Crack. Crack.*

The yells and screams coming from the bathroom must have scared everyone in the house, because the door burst open.

"Oh my god!" Kid yelled.

"You fucking idiot, what did you do!" hollered Tiny. Then I remember nothing because my body was

186

shaking, and I was drifting away.

TWELVE

*Blood. Lots of it. It mixed with the fine dust of the
ground and created a mixture inside the boy's mouth.
He cried. He'd never been hit so hard. Above him the
strange man was yelling again, but he didn't
understand. The words were too fast for him to piece
together, and even if they weren't, he'd never heard
those kinds of words before. He wanted to go home.*

*He closed his eyes, and for a moment, he was there.
He was drawn up in his mother's arms and she was
kissing his neck, making him giggle. He was her
"Handsome Little Man." His small legs flailed as he
squealed with laughter, but his mother held him tight,
she wouldn't let him fall. Tears burned his eyes.
Everything burned.*

*"Sukat!" said the man. The boy knew that word, it
was what the man always said when he cried or
screamed. The boy forced his mouth shut, trying to
breathe through his nose and swallowing all the blood
that drained into the back of his throat because of it.
He was no longer hungry. His belly was full of blood
now.*

*His hunger had led to this. Every morning Narweh
placed a scarce amount of unleavened bread and water
on a small table in the room, eyeing the boys wickedly
as he left. There were six of them in all; two English
boys, one Spaniard, two Arabs, and the boy.*

*At first they shared it in equal measure, but as the
days wore on and hunger set in, it became a battle that
ended in a full belly for one or two, and a bloody nose*

for those that challenged. The boy was often the victor in such battles, but on more than one occasion the collective strength of the others was used to rob him of his spoils. Such had been the case that day.

When he'd smelled the food, he hadn't been able to help it. It had been two days since his last won meal. The water had been hot and the bread cold, but he'd savored it all too quickly. Not enough. The plate on the table had lots of things, and he thought he smelled chicken. He was still young enough that all meat was "chicken" to him. He sat at the small table and picked up the meat. It burned his mouth, but he didn't care, the tingling tickle infusing his lips, tongue and throat wasn't enough to overpower the deliciousness of his stolen meal.

The boy hadn't seen the blow coming. One moment his mouth was filled with delicious chicken and the next, blood and dirt. He didn't even know what he'd been hit with. He didn't really know why he'd deserve it, just that he wouldn't do it again.

"Ghabi! Kéleb!"

Something hot and wet collided with the side of his face. His eyes were really on fire now. His small hands rubbed at his eyes but it only made matters worse. He screamed, gurgling sounds bubbling out of his blood filled throat. Still, in the grips of his agony, he could taste the savory food sliding into his mouth. He swallowed. Eyes tightly shut against the burning pain of the spices he dragged the food out of his hair and across his face into his mouth. It burned twice as much as before because there were open cuts in his mouth. But he was, apparently, still too hungry to care.

Kéleb, the man continued to call him, then grabbed him by the nape and dragged him across the floor while he struggled to crawl on hands and knees.

The boy cried.

Screamed.

Begged for his mother.

She never came. He hated her.

***

The air was thick. Tangible. Filled with an all-consuming excitement for things to come. She wasn't far. His fingers curled tighter around the steering wheel of the SUV. *Stroke her or strangle her?* He still didn't know. He only knew he wanted his hands on her. He gripped the wheel tighter and pressed farther down on the gas pedal. Jair gave him a bemused look from the passenger seat. *Fuck him.*

"How did she get away?" Jair accused. Caleb shot him a look he hoped could murder him where he sat. Jair only smiled. "She must be good. I look forward to having a taste after Rafiq learns she's ruined."

Caleb said nothing, focused instead on controlling the rage running rampant through his veins. This time was critical. He still didn't know Rafiq's purpose in Jair and reacting would only lend credence to things that weren't true. Caleb's loyalties remained intact, even if his resolve had wavered for a fraction of a moment. "Touch her and I'll cut off your hands," he grated. *Stupid.* "We're here."

Caleb parked the SUV some distance from their intended target. The house hadn't been difficult to spot. It was the only house with any lights on and the only one blaring music. Still, he didn't want to risk losing the element of surprise. *"Attack him where he is*

190

unprepared, appear where you are not expected." One of the very first lessons in Sun Tzu's, *The Art of War*.

The second car containing Jair's cousins pulled up behind them and cut the engine. The three men exited the vehicle and immediately headed toward the rear of the SUV to retrieve their weapons. Caleb's hand sought his S&W Model 29 revolver with its powerful .44 magnum cartridges; it was enough to blow a hole through a door. Or a face. Whatever. He looked at Jair, resisting the urge to shoot him in the head and just be done with it, but he managed to restrain himself. Jair still had *some* uses.

Caleb looked at the revolver. He hadn't fired it in quite some time, but already a familiar feeling was making its way through his fingers, up his arm, spreading through his chest and forcing his heart to speed. His head swam with adrenaline, and three feet below that he grew semi-erect at the thought of killing and taking back what was rightfully his.

Jair checked his AK-47 and Caleb observed how he stroked the weapon. He understood Jair in ways he rarely did. Blood lust and shared understanding that there was any commonality between them made him feel nothing but disgust. Jair snorted and spat on the ground near Caleb's feet. Caleb drew his weapon, checking its functionality and watching Jair. Both their fingers curved around the trigger of their weapons. "Well?" Jair challenged, when Caleb said nothing Jair continued, "Let's go retrieve your little whore."

He wasn't afraid. Fear was reserved for those who had something to live for. Caleb was long over fear. As his gaze swept from Jair to his cousins, he let them see.

He let them see there was nothing inside, and each man looked away, hiding his own fear. Jair sneered. Caleb turned his back on them, his way of letting them know who was in complete control and to follow.

The trunk was closed with a soft click, but to Caleb it'd exploded, a feeling cutting through him. He didn't look back. Jair and his men eventually followed. Their steps crunching against the dusty, pebbled ground resonated in the stark stillness of pre-dawn. Up ahead the lights grew brighter, the music louder and finally Caleb heard voices. Loud, angry, hysterical voices. Something was wrong. Something was very wrong and again, that foreign sensation—it stirred and bloomed. His heart stuttered. His steps faltered and he paused to regain control. A deep, calm breath. Another. And another. A sound, feminine and angry traveled down the distance. Before he knew it—he ran. The men followed quietly behind.

Caleb pulled up short as he neared so none inside would even realize they were there. He took cover beneath a small window.

"You are such a dumb fuck! What the hell are we supposed to do with her now?" a man yelled inside. Caleb's heart slammed in his chest ,and he was rendered nearly deaf by the sound thundering in his ears. He fought to control his breathing. What had they done to her?

"The fucking bitch bit me, what did you *want* me to do!" another man replied. Caleb carefully lifted his head and looked through the window. He recognized the biker from the bar, the one who called himself Tiny. He was a big sonofabitch and he only looked more so as he paced the small living room in his clunky biker

192

boots. He pushed his hand through his long, greasy hair and spoke again, "What the fuck were you assholes doing in there to begin with? I told you not to fuck with her."

A petite blonde appeared from an area behind the two arguing men. Street trash, Caleb thought, too much makeup and too little clothing, and hungry, always starving for something. And unpredictable. "We were just messing around Tiny. She's the one who got crazy."

Tiny pointed—nothing but menace in his eyes. "You stay out of this, *bitch*. I *know* what you were doing there."

Caleb tried to assess how many combatants were in the house by sight and sound. It wasn't a large house but big enough and sounds carried in a bare space. And where was the girl? It took every ounce of self-control for Caleb to remain where he was. He needed to know what he was up against. If the girl was still alive, he needed to make sure he could get to her before the shooting started. *If. If she's alive…if.* He pressed against the trigger of his weapon. One thing he was certain of, *if* any of them had hurt her….

The one with the lanky black hair had done something to her. He had hurt her, possibly raped her… killed her. Caleb swallowed past the dryness in his mouth. He was going to kill that motherfucker and he was going to make the blonde watch, giving her a preview of things to come.

"Fuck you, Tiny," the blonde retorted, "Blame Abe and Joker, they're the ones who couldn't keep their dicks in their pants. Not. Me."

Caleb bit the inside of his mouth until he tasted blood. The men behind him shifted their feet in the dirt as they waited for Caleb to give the signal.

"This is the only entrance," Jair whispered, breaking through his murderous thoughts. "How many inside?"

"Two men and a woman in the living room, at least one more in the back. There could be others." It was time. The girl could be dead or dying and Caleb didn't have time to wait for the rest of the gang to emerge.

"There's five bikes out here," Jair pointed out.

Caleb gave a nod. "Two missing. Jair, Dani, the two of you bust in the door and the rest of us will come in behind you. I'll head toward the back with Khalid and find the girl." He glanced over at Jair and the man smiled. "When it begins, make them feel it. I don't want it to be quick."

"For once, you and I agree." The smile grew even broader. "I like this side of you, Caleb."

***

Narweh's English consisted only of simple words and phrases – yes, no, eat, sleep, come, and sex. His main form of communication was using a stick to beat understanding into the boys, though sometimes, he did much worse.

There were other things that went on, things Kéleb *forced himself not to think about. When he was pliant he was often rewarded with food, clothing, or gifts from different men, and though he loathed what he did to get such rewards, he'd done his best to endure. When he refused, the beatings that took place were more than some grown men could withstand.*

Eventually, Kéleb *grew in years, height, and*

194

beauty. Armed with all these, his arrogance and quick wit were soon to follow. He knew more Arabic than English, though the English boys helped him retain a rudimentary knowledge. He soon chose his tormentors, pitting them against one another with the promise of true affection, though he was incapable of giving it. Still a child in the eyes of many and treated with little more than cruelty, he understood only one thing—survival.

Each night, as he huddled close to his partners in suffering on the dirty floor of the brothel they were held in he remembered less and less the boy he had been. Worse, he no longer cared. He was Dog. *It was all he had ever been. Instinct. Hunger.*

He was always hungry. For food, for shelter, for power, for more...constantly more. He even learned to crave the pain. It meant he was still alive, still surviving. If he could handle the pain, control his reaction to it, make it work for *him instead of against him, then he was free. And more than anything,* Kéleb *was hungry for freedom.*

Narweh knew this. Had always somehow known. It was the reason the other girls and boys were called by alluring names to entice the patrons while he was called Dog. *It was meant to demean him, to drag him to a place where he was no longer human. To make him feel* less *than human. It didn't work. When Narweh looked into his eyes,* Kéleb *refused to lower them. And one day Narweh had had enough.*

Kéleb *knew he was about to be punished. He knelt on the ground and was unafraid. Narweh loved to beat him and he no longer struggled against it. He had too much pride for that.*

He gritted his teeth when asked to undress. "It's to be rape then?" he said in perfect Arabic, "Do your friends know how much you love fucking dogs." Kéleb's *face throbbed with the slap he received, but he bore it in silence, fists clenched at his sides. He was free, he reminded himself.*

Raising his calm and steady eyes to meet Narweh's frenzied ones, he removed his thobe. *Narweh's eyes remained venomous, but now lust swirled behind the rage.* Kéleb *nearly smiled. Yes, he* was *a beautiful animal. Another slap and* Kéleb *forced himself to look away, but not toward the ground, never that.*

There was noise behind him, he wanted to look but would not give the son of a bitch the satisfaction of piquing his curiosity. It didn't matter, the mystery was soon revealed. A mirror. Narweh placed a mirror directly in front of him. In it he saw his bearing waver. This was too much, he couldn't possibly watch this. And yet, he refused to stare at the floor.

"What's the matter?" Narweh taunted, "Don't you like looking at how beautiful you are? Vanity; it's the plague of your entire race. It's the reason you think you deserve everything when you deserve nothing, less than nothing. Death is all you deserve."

Kéleb *strained against every impulse rushing through his body. He willed himself to remain still, he could handle this. He could handle anything.*

Narweh knelt behind him and Kéleb *ceased to breathe.* Anything but this. Please. Anything. *He closed his eyes. "Shut them and I will make it so you never can again." For the first time in a long time,* Kéleb *almost whimpered.*

Lifting his thobe *and spitting into his hand Narweh prepared to enter him and there was not a thing to be done. It was this or death.* Kéleb *dug deep into the part of him determined to be free. He took a deep breath and held it as he was entered savagely, refusing to make the slightest sound. But the mirror...the mirror forced him to see what he tried to pretend wasn't real. He wasn't free. Behind the boy, in the glass, Narweh smiled at him.* Kéleb *looked at the ground.*

It wasn't over quickly. Narweh did not simply wish to use him as he had in the past, throwing him to the ground and rutting against him like a savage beast, punching and slapping him. He took his time. He wanted Kéleb *to feel every moment of the urge to fight back, and the moment after it when he realized he couldn't. A sob finally broke through, and he was forced to look up at the boy in the mirror. He was... broken.*

Kéleb *hated the boy, hated his weakness. In a rage he struck out at the mirror, shattering it and tossing it to the ground. He lunged for the shards of broken glass, extricating himself as he turned on his tormentor. Narweh laughed, loudly.* Kéleb *flew toward him, fingers bleeding as they gripped the broken mirror.*

For all his size, Kéleb *was still a boy, still lanky and awkward. His strength meant nothing against Narweh. As he lunged toward him, Narweh planted his foot firmly into his stomach and tossed him over his head and onto the ground. His vision blurred and his breath left him.*

Narweh stood quickly, taking swift advantage. His foot collided repeatedly with Kéleb's *ribs, genitals and chest.* Kéleb *rolled onto his side groping for air and Narweh's foot. Neither aim was achieved, and he blacked out as the darkness encroached around him.*

The next time he opened his eyes it was to expel a silent scream as his skin was split open. Before he knew what was happening, he was struck again and again. He tried to move his limbs, to run, to fight, but he was tied down. Wet fire danced along his back and he instantly knew he would die that night. The whip landed again, another tearing of flesh. This time Kéleb *managed to scream.*

***

A rush unlike any Caleb had ever felt raced through his veins as the sound of angry gunfire and splintering wood erupted. *Rat-tat-tat-tat. Creak. BOOM.* The door was kicked in. Racing footsteps—theirs. Startled yelps and angry shouts—from inside.

Jair was the first one in, his warrior cry stunning their prey even further. By the time Tiny thought to act, he was cracked across the face with the butt of Jair's weapon. Blood sprayed across the wall behind Tiny as he fell to the ground. First blood, but not the last.

The woman screamed and darted toward the hallway, screaming for someone named Kid. Caleb rushed in after her. Behind him two of Jair's cousins were beating the other biker in the living room with Tiny.

The woman was screaming at someone. There were two doors ahead of Caleb. One to the right with a light on, the other directly ahead, door shut. Caleb fired two shots at the door in front of him. The door swung open and Caleb hit the ground. *Shuck-Shuck-Boom!* The shotgun blast rang out in the narrow space of the hallway. "Come get some motherfucker!" the man at the end of the hall yelled. *Shuck-Shuck.*

Caleb lifted his head and aimed for the biker's pelvic area. He wanted to avoid center mass, but he couldn't risk aiming for the knee and missing. He fired. The biker wailed in agony as the bullet hit. He dropped the cocked shotgun and clutched at his lower abdomen, blood already covered his quaking fingers and shock distorted the man's features. Behind Caleb, Khalid laughed uproariously as he leapt over Caleb's splayed legs to cover the second door. Caleb let out a breath. He needed to steel himself for what he might find.

He lifted himself into a crouch and hugged the wall nearest the door. "This can be very simple," he called out. "Your friends can't help you." He paused, letting that sink in. "We just want the girl."

"Fuck you!" It was the woman who spoke. She was hysterical. Unpredictable. "I'll kill this fucking bitch, I swear to god I will." Caleb's heart tripped all over itself. *She's alive.*

"Make her say something!" Caleb shouted back. Heavy breathing, resistance. Panicked squeals.

"I-I," a male voice now, faltering, "I think she's in shock or something. Look man, we didn't have anything to do with it. I swear." The man's voice cracked with panic as he spoke. "Just…go and we'll leave her here for you."

Caleb looked at Khalid. He was poised to strike, anticipating the kill. Any second now, this could get complicated and it wouldn't matter to Khalid if the girl was dead or alive. It only mattered to Caleb. In fact, for Jair, dead would be better. Rafiq would blame Caleb and Jair and his cousins would savor the ensuing confrontation.

Caleb thought quickly what his options were. What were the chances the two were armed? The door at the end of the hall was a bedroom and the house wasn't very big at all. Who carried a weapon into the bathroom? Caleb took decisive action.

Everything moved in slow motion. Khalid's footsteps as he went for the shotgun lying next to the bleeding biker. The curdled scream of the blonde as Caleb's weapon rounded the corner of the door. The young man's panicked yell as he clutched a bloody mass to his chest and scrambled toward the farthest corner of the small bathroom. The blonde threw herself at Caleb, clutching at his hair and clothes as she shouted like a banshee in his ear. One hard shove and she sprawled over the toilet, gasping for breath as the impact forced the air from her lungs.

Caleb knew he should shoot her, just put her down, but he was too numb to do anything. The sight in front of him took him to places he had long since tried to forget. *Tehran. Blood. Whip. Rape. Blood. Whip. Rape.* Staccato visions raced through his memory. *His clenched fists gripping the sheets. His wails. The blood. So much blood.* He could almost hear the whip cracking against his flesh, a crisp, wet sound as it landed on fresh blood. *His screams pierced the air and for a moment he believed he would finally die. Finally. Then the whip fell again. And again.*

"What. Happened." His body shook with a fury he had not felt since the night he finally murdered Narweh. Caleb met the eyes of the trembling boy holding Kitten to his chest, who was trying to speak but couldn't.

200

"Who are you?"

"Kid," the boy managed to get out.

Kid made sounds, but none of them coherent. Caleb lifted his gun and waited. "What…happened?" he asked again, through gritted teeth.

"Please," Kid begged and his blue eyes gave away too much emotion, "it wasn't me, I tried to stop them… they…" The kid swallowed and held Kitten closer. Caleb's finger almost squeezed the trigger. He didn't want to look at her. If he looked at her….

"They what!"

Kid flinched. The gun was still aimed squarely at the boy's head. "They tried to rape her, okay! They tried. But, b-b-b-but they didn't. She fought and… and…" Tears fell from Kid's eyes. Fear. Fear he was about die. Kid looked away and held his arms toward Caleb. "Please." Kid whispered.

Caleb eyed the boy. *Kid.* The name fit. His face was baby smooth, his lips a little too full, like his own. Something perverse took root inside him. He would let this one live, the girl too. Though they would soon wish he hadn't. Caleb finally looked at Kitten. Her face was a bruised and bloody mess. Her eyes were closed, but her lips were moving, trembling violently as was the rest of her body. Her head hung awkwardly to the left, her arms straight out over Kid's arms. Lower, her splayed legs showed bruises and boot marks where she had obviously been stomped on. Caleb swallowed. "Khalid," Caleb's voice was steady, "get a blanket and put it over the girl. She's in shock. Then bring these two out to me."

As Caleb turned, Dani was standing with Khalid in

the hallway. The two men entered as he left and already Caleb could hear the blonde struggling against them. Caleb allowed the old memories to wash over him as he approached the living room, spliced together with images of Kitten beaten and shaking on the bathroom floor. They were all the fuel he needed for what he was about to do.

As he entered the living room he saw Jair standing over Tiny, who lay face down on the floor with his arms tied behind his back. Caleb pushed Jair back and grabbed hold of the biker's greasy hair and pulled. For a moment, it seemed as though Jair might push Caleb back, but once their eyes met it was obvious Caleb was not to be fucked with and that Tiny was about to learn the same. "Jair. Knife."

Tiny struggled and cursed so that Caleb had to straddle his back to keep the man steady. The moment the knife landed in Caleb's palm a rush of endorphins and rage poured down his spine. "I warned you, you motherfucker!" He was blind. Bloodlust consumed his vision. He raised the knife at a forty-five degree angle and plunged in straight into the base of Tiny's neck where it met his right shoulder. Tiny let out an inhuman scream and more endorphins released inside Caleb. He pulled the knife out and blood sprayed across his arm, chest, and neck. His head swam and his nostrils flared. He brought the knife down again, this time toward the back of the neck to separate the spinal cord.

Tiny's accomplice screamed and screamed and screamed, making Caleb drunk with power and pure male satisfaction. Jair and his men yelled and cheered, wanting their turn. In the background the woman was making shrill incoherent sounds as she begged for

Caleb to stop. Caleb lifted the knife and once again plunged it deep. Tiny no longer made sounds. He just bled and ripped apart under Caleb's knife.

As Tiny's body sagged in Caleb's grasp, his head holding up his body by only a few inches of muscle, bone and sinew, Caleb's thoughts slowly began to clear. As he took in the sight of the blood covered room and screams of those who were about to suffer, Caleb's thoughts returned to Kitten. She was hurt. She needed him. Caleb let go of Tiny and watched as he fell to the ground a lifeless lump of meat.

He stood, drenched in Tiny's blood holding the gore covered knife. His eyes found those of the whimpering boy they called Kid and he slowly approached. Kid began screaming even before Caleb ever reached him. He pressed the tip of the knife under his baby smooth chin, "Kid. I'm going to take you and that little bitch over there with me and when Kitten wakes up she's going to tell me what happened. And if either of you had anything to do with it I'm going to do you worse. Understand?" Kid shut his eyes and tears streamed down his face. Caleb almost let the knife run through the boy. Something about his features, his youth, and his weepiness made Caleb want to slap him to the ground, so he did.

"Jair," Caleb's voice was cold, "take this little pussy and the girl alive. Kill the rest and burn the house down." Caleb dropped the knife and didn't look back as he made his way toward the bathroom.

The man from earlier was still bleeding and writhing on the floor of the hallway, but as he saw Caleb approach he worked to remain still, become invisible. Caleb's fury rose up again. This was one of the men who had hurt her. He wanted to go back for the knife and play a little game of poke the rapist, but he didn't have time. Kitten needed a hospital.

He approached her quivering body slowly, suddenly wishing he wasn't covered in blood. She whimpered and cried as he gathered her into his arms. His heart lurched and he fought hard not to squeeze her to his chest.

He lifted her and walked as efficiently as possible out of the house and out into the light. He looked down at her, watching as the sun lit her bloodied face. Her trembling stilled somewhat and her brows knitted slightly. For a moment he saw her as he had that day, a shy young girl looking up at him with awe. Her savior. *I've failed you.*

Caleb kissed her forehead and whispered into her ear, "Don't worry, Kitten, I promise I'm going to make it better."

THIRTEEN

I was sinking, falling. I struggled to open my eyes but my world was a blur, a mirage. Not real.

Could it be real?

All around me there was blaring light and muffled voices, but I couldn't lift my head to see where they came from. A man wearing a white coat came into view and spoke. *Mulder?* I was in an episode of *The X-files*. No, that didn't make sense. Scientist? Doctor? Madman with a scalpel? I couldn't make out what he said, but his face seemed full of reassurances, false promises, empty words in a tone meant to pacify me. Then there was a tunnel of soft blue light surrounding me. I wanted to say something, or get up, but the pain was too intense. My eyes closed in their heaviness, and I sunk back into myself.

There were other moments of time when I drifted in and out of consciousness, but I couldn't remember them clearly. Time was irrelevant. It was not now, or then, or later.

There was only pain. More pain. Less pain. It was the only constant.

I'm sinking.

Down.

Down.

Down.

No bottom, only down—forever.

I'm crying? I can't be sure.

It must be because I'm burning.

I'm sinking and I'm burning.

Mother was right. I'm going to hell.

Can a person make such a huge mistake they can never be forgiven?

I guess so.

I don't want to burn. I don't want to fall into forever, dragged down.

Forever—it's unimaginable.

There has to be an end to the suffering. I don't deserve this.

"It wasn't all my fault!"

I trusted him, too. He said it would be okay. A kiss. A touch. A few more kisses. A few more touches. I didn't know what to do. I didn't know what to say. It wasn't all my fault!

Forgive me.

Forgive me.

You bitch...forgive me.

I'm sinking. Still burning.

Forever.

I opened my eyes. For certain this time. Dark. Just a low lamp in the corner. Startled, I tried to move all at once, and my entire body contracted in pain with the effort. For a moment I thought I might still be dreaming. My body burned. I placed a hand on my ribs and felt the bandages surrounding my midsection. It hurt to breathe. I kept hearing a low buzz in my ears, and I realized it was coming from inside me. I saw pinpricks of dots every time I moved my head and the light hurt. My fingers and gaze followed the pattern of damage. My left arm was in a sling across my neck, and my nose was covered in a type of tape. My eyes were puffy and blinking felt like a chore, an exercise in futility but a necessary one. Gently, I touched my face again, carefully removing the cakiness around my eyes.

There was a shadow, man-shaped, sitting quietly and unmoving in the corner. I squinted and leaned forward. Fuck the pain. Caleb, sitting eerily unmoving and in the dark with me.

"Try not to move," he said just above a whisper. He leaned into the light. The initial impulse was to move but the pain stopped me, and Caleb, his appearance disarming. He looked rough, like he'd been to hell and back. *Me too.* Pieces floated to me, some sharp, others vague. Every second of that moment played again, in fast forward, then slow motion, then fast again.

So he'd gotten me back.

That realization echoed through me. Did I feel relieved? Terrified? I couldn't muster any emotion one way or another. I was just…numb. Empty and buzzing.

He rose from the chair and came toward me. "Don't be afraid. You'll be all right now." I wasn't afraid. I wasn't all right and never would be. "Your face is bruised, but nothing's broken. Your shoulder was dislocated and you have a few cracked ribs, not broken. You'll heal, but I'm afraid all I have to offer you is rest and medicine for the pain." His words made no difference to me. I was still alive. And still with Caleb. When he got up, I didn't flinch but just watched as he came toward me. What was left to be afraid of? What did I have left to lose?

"Where am I?" I hardly recognized my own voice. It was hoarse and gravelly, as dry and brittle as my throat felt.

"Somewhere different," he said. Vague. Typical.

He sat next to me on the bed. Nice bed, nice room, I thought, focusing on the easy stuff my witless brain could handle. *I really don't give a fuck.* He reached for my hand. My fingers recoiled, just a slight clench and tension. He nodded and withdrew.

Did he have blood in his hair? *Blood. Everywhere.* I shut my eyes and blocked it out. I wanted to stay numb. Get this over with. I was ready for whatever malicious words he had prepared for me. Ready for him to tell me how stupid I had been to think I'd get away from him. *Jokes on you, asshole, I already know.* Ready for him to threaten me with rape or death. *Get it over with. Please.*

"I'm sorry, Kitten," he whispered. *He* was sorry? Coming from Caleb, guilt was highly unlikely and the last thing I had anticipated. My face did some weird snort-scoff-laugh-cry thing. It hurt, but I almost laughed. Would have, if it didn't hurt to breathe. "For what they did to you."

Right, he was sorry, but not for taking me from home. "Good." *Home. My family.* All this because I had wanted to get back to my worthless mother. *Even if she doesn't want me there. Never did. No matter how many times I said I was sorry.* My eyes were stinging. I couldn't believe I still had tears for her. I hated her. I *hated* her, because I loved her so fucking much and she obviously didn't feel the same way.

Caleb cleared his throat and swallowed. "I made them pay."

Them. A group of them that was, possibly, worse than Caleb. I felt shaky all over again, but hearing those words from Caleb's lips was somewhat satisfying. "Yeah, well," I said, hollowly, "you're into that." A hint of a smile touched his lips, and for some reason it cut through me in an essential way. My life was a joke, to him, to my mother, to those asshole bikers! A cruel, heartbreaking joke, and I was more than ready for the punchline. Ready for my life, the joke, to be over. Right now, I just needed *someone*. I needed to not feel so discarded and alone. I choked back words I knew I'd regret later, and only said, "Caleb..."

"What?"

I stared at him, not sure, wondering what the next step was, and as terrified as ever. He continued to look at me, inquisitive, his face a twisted mask of indecision. If that mask was real, I almost pitied him. It was better than feeling sorry for myself, but I wanted to be stronger, even as I just wanted to crawl into a hole. *Get it over with.* "I don't know what you have planned for me. I know...I know it..." I paused, taking a moment to collect myself as much as my thoughts but the words in me had to be spoken. If not now, then never. I let the sparks of pain encourage me. "...I know it can't be good. Whatever it is you're planning. But if you could do me one favor?"

"Oh?"

I blinked once, "If it's anywhere near as bad as what those assholes did to me.... I'm tired of living through this shit just to step into deeper fucking shit. So if all you have planned for me is more torture, I think I'd rather die. Just do me one favor and don't...I don't want to die slow."

He reared back as if I had slapped him. Or not. I had slapped him twice before and he had never looked the way he did now. He suddenly wasn't so inquisitive or indecisive—he looked pissed! But also...offended. "Is that what you think?" he said, his voice strained and tight. "You think I would..." He stood up and paced. I could do nothing but stare.

"What do you want me to think, Caleb?" I said harshly. My face was hot and my nose hurt and felt stuffy. Breathing hurt. "You kidnap me, you beat me, you do...unspeakable things to me." The burning in my chest felt like it was spreading, and it was all the anger and my despair that had been coiling within me, now oozing to the surface. "What am I to expect from you?" I did a lackluster imitation of his abnormal accent "'Don't let me find you.' Isn't that what you said?"

Finally, he stopped in the center of the room, his eyes flashing then cooling. "You are a stupid, stupid girl, Kitten." I did laugh this time. Loudly, hysterically, laughing through the pain even as it ripped through every fiber of my being. He had never said anything more true. I *was* a stupid, stupid girl! Stupid to think my mother would ever forgive me. Stupid to think I could be something other than what I was. What had that filthy fucking biker called me? *Whore!* The label followed me everywhere. And what had I done to earn it? Not enough! Still virgin territory. A whore fighting her nature. For what? Yes, I was a stupid, stupid girl. I laughed and laughed and laughed until finally...I cracked. My laughter devolved into wails of pure loss, grief, and black despair.

Eventually, I found him at my side, his arms engulfing me. I let him. I was always seeking shelter in the people who hurt me the most. My mother. My father. Caleb. Like a battered dog begging for love from a malicious master. It was all I knew. And still his arms felt safe, warm, meant for me to seek sanctuary within.

The cycle of damage would never end because I couldn't tell the difference until it was too late.

"I made them pay." He whispered again, his tone cold and final, but his words meant nothing to me, though I suspected they meant a great deal to him. Only his arms mattered, only the tangible feel of hard, sturdy flesh surrounding mine. His embrace said all the things his lips could not or would not, they said, *you're safe and I will protect you*, maybe even some semblance of caring about me, however fucked up, but everything was fucked up. Through it all, his lips only repeated, "I made them pay," and I felt something different that still felt oddly real to me, more real than anything.

I hated him, but I didn't either. And I didn't understand anything anymore, least of all myself.

I cried for a while, taking solace in the comforting lie of his embrace. The illusion, the fantasy, it helped. I never wanted to leave. I wanted to stay here forever, held tight to his chest, his fingers stroking my hair, his heart beating against my ear: you're-safe, trust-me, love-you. *Love.* Did I want him to love me? Yes. I wanted *someone* to love me. And what was love if not someone risking their lives to save you? Caleb had saved me. Did it mean he loved me? A part of me wanted to think so. To believe in a romantic ideal that didn't exist. I wanted to believe the lie. But more than that—I wanted it not to *be* a lie.

After a while, I forced myself to pull away. The longer I stayed, the more I doubted I could keep my resolve to escape, and that was dangerous. I was torn, constantly, between emotions that continued to fight each other. Caleb was dangerous. And not just because he was bigger, stronger, and more sadistic than I cared to think about. "Can I see a mirror?" I asked warily, sniffling. It wasn't about vanity. I needed to see just how close I'd come to losing my life, and I wanted it to mean something real for me. A harsh dose of reality to shake me free of all my stupid fantasies.

He was very slow, dare I say, reluctant, to release me. Even as I tried to put distance between us, his fingertips wiped gently at the corners of my swollen eyes and the look on his face said the hurt, pain and superficiality didn't matter. His words echoed the sentiments I read on his face. "It's not necessary. The damage isn't permanent."

"That bad, huh?" I asked, but the look in his eyes shifted, turning harder, colder and it told me all I needed to know. Those sons-of-bitches had done a number on me. *My arm bent behind my back. Pain. Laughter. A cock pushing against me, looking for a way in.*

"It's not necessary," he repeated firmly. "The damage isn't permanent." He paused, the hesitation odd in his otherwise firm and confident demeanor. "I made them pay." Caleb was not a man who hesitated or questioned anything. And yet, I felt him doing so at that moment. There were things he wanted to say and wasn't. "I know you've been through more than enough." He reached out and tilted my chin gently, meeting my eyes, "But promise me you'll never do it again." I turned my head slightly away. He was telling me, not asking me, to never run away from him again. Without saying it, he was chastising me, letting me know that by taking matters into my own hands, I'd just

212

gotten into deeper trouble and all on my own. It was a bitter pill to swallow...because he was right.

"Yes, Caleb." I paused, "Yes, Master," I whispered dully, feeling hollow again. Caleb frowned but nodded. I didn't know what was more frightening, that in that moment I meant it or that Caleb had expected it.

His fingers continued to play softly across my jaw. He was tentative, pensive, and wary of causing me any pain or discomfort. I couldn't stand it. There was always confusion when he was near. A conflict over what I should do and what I wanted to do.

I thought about my life, the history of my existence, a past that revolved around my mother who'd ushered me in this world. About the way my wants had led to this moment. Just the same way her wants had led her to hers. As hard as I'd tried to not be like her, I felt like I was becoming exactly like her. It was so unfair, and as I stared at Caleb, and his fingers danced across my lips so delicately and intimately, I reaffirmed that life was anything but fair.

I pushed his hand away, not roughly, but firmly issuing my denial of his touch, and oddly, I knew, in the corner of my mind, that it was my denial, too.

There was a flicker of something primal in his eyes before he schooled his features into an impassive mask. He sat up straight with his back against the headboard. The foot of space between us may as well have been an ocean. Our silence an uneasy calm before an impending storm. He did have a plan for me. And he still wasn't telling me what it was.

"Caleb..."

"It wasn't, you know." He must have read the confusion on my face and expected it because he pressed forward seamlessly, "In your sleep. You said it wasn't all your fault, and it isn't—none of it is your fault. It's…. It just isn't."

There was a hard knot in my throat. No matter how hard I tried, I couldn't swallow it down. It was just stuck there, choking me. Caleb's fingers slid across the bedspread toward my leg, then faltered and returned to his own personal space. Why couldn't he just keep being an evil, soulless bastard so I knew what his role was and I knew mine? Why did he have to continually switch back from cold and unforgiving, to comforting and warm?

"What did they do to you, Kitten? Can you tell me?" His eyes slid closed and I wondered at what he was hiding. Was this about me? It hardly made sense. He had tortured me, kept me prisoner, beat me, forced me into situations beyond my imagination. And now, *now* he felt...something for me?

A voice in my head reminded me that despite everything he'd done to me, there had always been some semblance of mercy. Yes, I was still alive, and he hadn't tried to do what those animals had tried. I had not been a person to them. I understood the fine line between what Caleb was doing with me, and what he could have done so easily *to* me. He was always in control of himself. Had always explained why he was doing one thing or another. He kissed and caressed me, brought me ecstasy.

I was as real to him as he was to me and it struck me just then that I meant something to him. In whatever capacity he was able, I meant something. The irony of

214

that epiphany made my gut twist. Now that I knew what real horror felt like, I knew I had never felt it with Caleb. Even when he hurt me, when he made me feel shame, he was there to massage me, hold me—take responsibility for me. He would never do the things those motherfuckers had done. I knew that. But did any of it matter? I didn't know. Perhaps nothing really mattered.

I had tried so hard to be something, someone. I had tried to make my life mean something. But, sitting here at this moment, desolate, empty and still held hostage, I knew I was never going to write a screenplay, or a book, or direct a movie. I felt like I was never going to be anything more than what everyone presumed I would be. Nothing I did mattered. Never did. Never would. And I'd been completely naïve in assuming otherwise, but hoping and dreaming had never seemed such a bad thing.

I finally answered his question. "It doesn't matter anymore Caleb." I sounded brittle, tired. "Nothing does."

He was quiet for a few seconds, but I could tell he was angry. But so was I. Even in my numbness, I was seething. I watched him. Subtle changes I wouldn't have noticed in the beginning were completely visible to me. What window did I now have into him? Did he know I saw him? Worse, could he really see into me? "You and I both know the truth. What they did to you matters." There was no anger in his voice, only certainty. "Everything matters. Everything is very personal. You know that just as I do. Don't act so defeated, we both know it isn't like you."

I laughed, but it died in my throat and it came out as a ragged choke. "How would you know?" He had never answered me fully before and his words often smacked of half truths, but in some odd way, I sensed it was because he didn't know *how* to answer. In other words, he *wanted* to answer me. "You don't know me. Not the simplest things, not even my name."

More silence. I stared at him intently, waiting for his rage, *wanting it*. I needed to pick a fight with someone I knew wouldn't really hurt me. I needed to rail. In that moment, I knew Caleb was right, giving up wasn't like me, no matter how much I wanted it to be. He remained calm, kept his eyes closed. His beautiful golden hair was tinged reddish brown, there was blood caked in his hairline. I shuddered. *I made them pay.* Delicious, beautiful words, something I'd never hear from anyone but a man like Caleb.

There was a shift in his body, muscles in play but he remained utterly still. His expression was cold, stark but it wasn't directed at me. "You're right. I don't know your real name. But I don't know mine either, and it's never stopped me from knowing who I am or taking what I want."

His words were the last I was expecting. I sat dumbfounded and confused. He was telling me something important, but I wasn't sure what to do with it or if it'd ease my pain. I understood it was something few people knew and by his expression, it mattered to him greatly. It made my heart speed up to know he'd just opened up to me in some way. I realized I wanted to know how he'd become the person sitting next to me. *Caleb.* It wasn't his real name. He didn't *know* his real name.

What happened to you Caleb? Who did this to you? And why are you now doing this to me? I watched his face, the lines hard but not cultivated to project his usual demeanor. I felt it then.

There is a moment, in all my studying of movies and scripts, that I'd realized something elemental about human beings and why I'd been attracted to that imaginary world. Each piece of work was attempting to describe the human condition, in all its good, bad and ugly glory. At first, it'd been an extension of my own life, strangely mirrored in this world of "fiction."

Each story wanted, no—*needed*—to reveal a human fragility, a human bondage which tied people to the things they did and to be the person they held in their heads. Those stories were something true and sometimes horrific, but people were people and the parts didn't just tell the whole story. I'd seen parts of this man, Caleb. What was the whole man, unshielded, and vulnerable? Who was this man that could do this to me, to anyone, and live with himself? And what type of person was I, to see some light in him that was somehow redeemable? Why did I try? But then, more importantly, why did he?

He waited. I waited. I wanted to press him, to dig for more, but I knew it would only push him away. He had thrown down a gauntlet. He would only give as well as he got, and if I wanted to know more, then it would be up to me to make him beholden to me. Perhaps the more we knew about one another, the closer we would become, and maybe, possibly, I could convince him to stop hurting me.

Surrender, he had once said. He had wanted me to surrender. Not just my body. My mind. I would try. I would try for him. Not for the sadistic, confusing man sitting next to me, not for Caleb. I would try for the handsome stranger underneath. The one I had met on the sidewalk that fated day—the one with no name. I was willing to try and understand him, piecemeal, and what came of it, I'd let fate decide. I made the first move because he wouldn't. Maybe he couldn't.

"Part of me thinks I'm actually glad—to be away from my old life." I could tell he was surprised by the detour of our conversation, and it felt nice to surprise him for a change. "Not that this is much better, but at least you wanted me back...I don't think my mother would." I licked my dry lips and forced myself to continue. "She thinks I did all this to myself. That I ran away...that I'm a whore. But she's always thought that." The lump in my throat moved down instead of up. Surprisingly, my muscles loosened. It felt good to say things out loud. I had said things about my past to Nicole, but this was different. Caleb was strong. He wouldn't flinch. Somehow I knew he could bear the weight, and not feel the burden and uncomfortable unease associated with it, like Nicole had. "She hates herself, and I'm a part of her, manifested."

Caleb's eyes opened slowly, his brows furrowed, intent on listening. I continued, "When I was thirteen my mother caught her boyfriend kissing me. Or rather, she caught us kissing. He was younger than her, an immigrant looking for a green card. My mom was looking for a man who couldn't leave her.

"His name was Paulo.

"I never meant to cause my mother any problems. I just wanted to be like other girls, wear things they did, do things they did. But she was too strict.

"I kind of...," tears spilled from my eyes, "I kind of...liked the way he looked at me. Boys at school didn't really look at me, you know? I was always wearing these long, ugly dresses. But Paulo...he looked at me like I was the most beautiful thing he'd ever seen."

Across the bed spread, Caleb's fingers drifted slowly toward mine. Before he could pull back, I hesitantly placed my open palm, face-up on the bed. Without a word, his fingers intertwined with mine. "What happened next?" His voice was rough, edged with some emotion I couldn't discern.

"My mother was sleeping. I was out in the living room watching television. There was this movie on *Cinemax* starring Shannon Tweed." Caleb didn't recognize the name of the most infamous soft-core skin flick actress of all time. It almost made me smile. There was something sweetly innocent about it. Something innocent beneath the façade of *Caleb*.

He squeezed my hand, urging me on. I felt like I had someone who was on my side and the irony of it didn't escape me. My mother hadn't believed me, but I knew, *I knew*, Caleb would. Because *I* said it was the truth.

"There was this...sex scene. I was alone, so I... started touching my breasts. I knew it was wrong to be watching it, but...everything I did was wrong." I squeezed Caleb's strong hand in my own as my anxiety grew and old shame threatened to rip what was left of me apart.

"Paulo caught me. He was wearing this bikini underwear, and I could see he was really hard. I'd never seen that before. They never showed that in the movies." More tears ran down my face, I was blind with them. My vision swimming in a water-color of memories.

"I tried to get up and go to bed, but he stopped me. He was drunk. I could smell beer on his breath when he pressed me back down into the couch. He put his hand over my tank-top. I told him to stop. But…he said if I didn't kiss him he would tell my mom what I'd been doing." Without meaning to, I sobbed.

"It's okay, Kitten, you don't have to tell me anymore." Caleb's body was close to mine, his warmth pressed against my side, but he only held my hand.

"No! I just have to say what happened…why she doesn't love me anymore." I squeezed my eyes tight, blasting myself with both physical and emotional pain. I wanted him to know this about me. I wanted him to do what he always did after I was wrung out. I wanted him to take the pain away.

"He kissed me. It was my first kiss. He tasted like beer, but that wasn't such a bad thing. For some reason, I've always liked the smell of liquor. He kissed me and my head swam. When he told me to open my mouth…I did. It was different after that. I didn't like it anymore. His tongue was slimy and he kept moving it in my mouth like a snake, in and out. It was gross. I tried to pull away, but he wouldn't really let me."

"My mom walked in on us. Paulo jumped up. His horrible fucking erection pressing against his ridiculous underwear. But she wasn't mad at him. She was mad at me. She looked at the TV and back at us. I tried to explain but she just said, 'Is this what you do when I go to bed, Livvie? You put on your *puta* clothes and try to seduce your father?'"

"'He's not my dad.' I said, but that wasn't the point. I tried to explain how he was the one who kissed me. I didn't ask him to. I didn't want him to, not really. Paulo didn't say anything. It was like he knew the entire thing was about us, about me and my mom."

"'Act like a whore and you'll get treated like one.' That's all she had to say to me."

I cried for a while after I repeated my mother's words. They were the words that echoed through my head whenever I thought about rebelling against my mother in the years after that night. Caleb sat silently. His hand loosely holding mine. I wanted to look at him but I didn't dare. I couldn't bear the look of disgust he might be giving me. Or the look of pity.

"Paulo got deported. But my mom never forgave me. She stopped paying attention to me, focusing on my other brothers and sisters...especially my brothers. It was like I was a ghost in my mother's house. There, but not really."

"I tried to get back into her good graces. I was the perfect fucking child. I didn't date, I didn't go out. I got good grades. I wore the most unflattering clothes I could find. But..."

Caleb's voice broke through my memories, "But she blamed you for ruining her happiness."

I nodded. My numbness had finally returned.

I felt my arm being lifted slowly and then I felt Caleb's soft lips pressing against the back of my hand. "For what it's worth, Livvie, I never thought of you as a whore. And you *are*...the most beautiful thing I've ever seen."

I lifted my face to his. God he was beautiful. So beautiful because, for the first time, I was seeing him, and however long this moment lasted, I'd take it for what it was. He smiled gently and I knew he was disguising so many things. My face was a hideous mess and he still thought me beautiful. "Well...maybe that's my problem then...too pretty." His smile fell and I wish I'd kept my mouth shut. I struggled to make it right, "Hey, you know my name now."

He smiled thinly and slowly withdrew his hand from mine. The warmth between us was quickly dissipating. Tears welled in my eyes again as he stood, "You'll always be Kitten to me...Livvie."

It was my turn to smile weakly. His words, as ever, could be a double entendre.

He circled the bed and made his way to my left side. He leaned toward the nightstand and opened the top drawer. "This is for the pain." He held up a syringe and pulled the cap off.

"What is it?" I asked, dreading the needle.

"I've told you already."

"What if I don't want it?"

He looked slightly amused now. "In a little while, when the last dose fades, you'll want it."

"Will it make me sleep? I don't want to sleep."

"No." I had the distinct impression he was lying. "It just makes the pain easier to deal with."

"And you?" I was suddenly anxious. And shy.

"What about me?"

"Are you just going to leave me here alone?"

The long silence had me wondering how much I'd imagined the past few minutes. "If you want, I'll stay."

Caleb stared, but I said nothing. I couldn't bring myself to admit how vulnerable I was feeling. My mother had let me go. I was free of her, but not free.

"Kitten?" His voice was calm, his blue eyes filled with emotion I couldn't put into words but his gaze and tone had taken on a faraway look. He shook his head abruptly, waking from his brief daze. *Where did* he *go?*

After a moment of hesitation, I said hoarsely, "I don't want to be alone."

"I'll stay," he said softly.

My face felt like it had been hit with a bag of hammers. But he was here. Taking care of me. Because he knew I needed him to. He pulled back the sheet gently and watched me as he lifted the nightgown I wore to just above my hip. I gasped. My legs were covered in bruises, some of them in the shape of boot soles. "Eyes on me, Kitten." Our eyes met just as I felt the prick of the needle.

Moments later my lids were heavy, and I was flying, free falling, and then flying again. I didn't dream, I just flew toward the horizon neither black nor white.

Caleb could and would hurt me. Not today, but maybe tomorrow or the next day. Still, for the first time I knew he could not destroy me. It would matter to him if I didn't exist. And no matter what happened, I'd land on my feet because Caleb had shown me I had it in me. It was a strange gift, from an unexpected source.

FOURTEEN

There was a reason I didn't want to sleep. I didn't want to dream. I didn't want to think about my mother, or Paulo, or my brothers and sisters. Or everything that followed between Caleb and me.

I especially didn't want to envision Nicole, beautiful Nicole, lost and wandering around Mexico looking for me. I would never forgive myself if something happened to her. I tossed and turned as anger, sadness, and worry turned my mind inside out. The pain in my shoulder didn't help and my tossing and turning had created a dull ache that felt like it was part of the bone.

And then there was the inevitable. The hushed voices. The memory of being held down as they pulled my clothes off. The way they ignored my screams as they sucked and pulled at me. I felt it all over again—that horrible beating.

Against the strength of the drugs I forced my eyes open and screamed. I sucked air into my burning lungs and tried to focus my eyes.

Caleb's body jerked from the chair he'd been sitting in, and he turned on the light.

Realization hit.

I'm safe. I'm here. Caleb's here. He's not going to hurt me.

I gasped. My voice was laced with unshed tears and thick with emotion. "It was so real. It was like they were…" Caleb sat next to me, and I went to him, seeking comfort, solace, anything. I didn't need to say anymore.

"It's alright. They can't hurt you anymore." His words were perfect. So right and comforting. I reached around him with my right arm and pulled him closer.

For long, blissful seconds there was only the feel of his arms, the hard plane of his chest, his heartbeat pulling me away from the horror of my dream. I inhaled. "You smell like soap," I whispered weakly into his shirt. I didn't like the thought he had left me alone. I didn't want to be left alone in the dark, not ever again. His fingers sifted through my sweaty hair.

"I waited until you fell asleep. It didn't take long." That surprised me some. I was so accustomed to Caleb's snide comments. I had been expecting something more like, 'My, my, Kitten, what a big nose you have.'

Were things so different now? Were *we* different? In some ways, I knew the answer.

"You didn't have to sleep in the chair."

"*Really?*" Caleb's voice was slightly mocking but lacking harshness or condescension. I realized he was teasing me.

"Asshole."

He held me a little tighter, "You always have a retort."

It was his tone that caught me off guard. "Is that suddenly a good thing?"

"It means you're not broken." He laughed softly, and it made me want to do the same. But I didn't have a laugh in me just yet. So I sighed contentedly.

It had been that strange, morbid humor that could only exist between Caleb and me at that very instant in time. We both tried to hold on to it, but it faded just as quickly as it had come on. And then we were just quiet. Holding each other and knowing there were a million things that needed to be said, or asked, or explained and knowing neither of us was looking forward to it.

"We have to leave this place today." Caleb whispered the words, as if by doing so he could lessen their impact. Sweat bloomed anew across my body, but still, I couldn't let him go. *I should really get up.*

Right the fuck now.

But I didn't want to move. Not while Caleb's lips rested near my temple and not while the feel of his lean and muscular body wrapped around mine gave me a sense of security and belonging I'd yearned for all my life. But, in the end, it was too dangerous to stay.

I obviously felt things for Caleb. Some feelings were clear, but others weren't. If I let myself trust him, with my safety, my comfort, my life, or...my heart, I was going to end up hurt.

Again!

I winced at the internal reminder.

It had always seemed to me as though I were split into two people, but not equally. One of us, the less dominant, was strong, confident, snarky, and not to be fucked with. She was the one who told Caleb to go to hell, she was the one who threw elbows and bit through shoulders. She was the one who forced me to keep going.

I was the other one. I was the one who needed love and validation. I was the one who didn't want to let Caleb go because I was convinced he was important to me in some irrational, irrevocable way. I was feeling things I'd never felt before, and in other ways, I felt Caleb was more damaged than me. Not in some tragic sense, but in a fundamental way that bridged the vast distances between us.

But my other half didn't think any of that mattered. *He kidnapped you for a reason,* she reminded. *Don't trust him. Don't be like your mother, stop falling for his bullshit. He doesn't care about you!*

I pulled back, but unlike before, his arms released me easily. Deep, Caribbean-blue eyes looked down at me. At first they seemed to want to express so much, but then…nothing. I was tired of nothing. I wanted *something.* I *needed* something.

"What is it?" he asked, his tone carefully veiled. "Tell me."

"I think I'm done trying to run, but I'm also done with not knowing what horrible thing is going to happen to me next. I'd rather know Caleb. Please, just tell me and give me the time…" Sitting there, I didn't really understand what I was saying, but the part of me that was wising up, really did. *Brace yourself…*

Caleb's blond hair, usually groomed, now fell into his eyes. I resisted the sudden urge to brush it away from his face. As we sat in pregnant silence, I watched him stare into his own lap. His jaw was tense, his lips tight, but I wasn't afraid. I was done being frightened of Caleb. If he were going to hurt me, he'd have done it already. He wanted to tell me. I only had to wait.

I remained silent, waiting for his words I craved, my heart jammed into my throat as I willed him to continue. "If only I'd never laid eyes on you, never met you…" His wistful words suddenly caused a deep ache in my chest though I knew they shouldn't. "I have obligations, Kitten." He swallowed deeply. His brows knitted together to instantly let me know he was feeling sadness, anger, and disgust all at once. The desire to touch him was almost too much, but then I realized I should be worried about what the hell his words would mean to *me* and less about what they did to *him*. "There's a man who needs to die. I needed you…*need* —" He paused. "If I don't do this now then I'll never be free. I can't walk away until it's done. Until he pays for what he did to Rafiq's mother, to his sister, until he pays for what he did to me." Caleb stood abruptly, his chest heaving. He ran angry fingers through his hair and fisted his hands at his nape. "Until everything he loves is gone, until he—*feels* it. Then I can let it go. I'll have repaid my debt. Then, perhaps…maybe."

"Rafiq?" I'd heard the name before, but the importance of that name eluded me. Why was he so important? Did he have more say in what happened to me than Caleb?

Caleb's eyes returned to mine. He had been far away again as though his words had not truly been meant for me. He was back in control now, the impassive mask he wore so easily slipped over his face. My guard went up. The past few moments when he seemed almost human, evaporated. "I'm going to sell you as a pleasure slave to a man I despise."

A wave of nausea slammed the pit of my stomach and pushed bile into my throat. His words hit me in harsh staccato slaps, and as each word made contact I flinched.

Sell. Pleasure. Slave.

The reality hit me hard, knocking the air out of me. I felt like I was going to throw up and felt my stomach heaving and throat working.

No more movie references. No more fictional characters to relate to. This was real. It was destiny. I was…a thing, a commodity.

He's made you a whore, Livvie, a fucking whore.

Caleb was still speaking, but I hardly heard him.

With difficulty, I stopped myself from retching and cleared my throat, "Pleasure means sex, right? A sex slave?"

Caleb stopped in the middle of another sentence and gave a tight nod. His head was slung low, his hair hung in his eyes. This time I had no urge to brush it out of his eyes, in fact, it felt like a manipulation. His every move was calculated. He knew just how to knit his brows to portray sadness. How to tumble his perfect hair into his even more beautiful eyes and seem vulnerable and trustworthy. Well, I wasn't going to fall for it anymore. Whatever I might have been feeling, it was dying, and the numbness was left in its wake. "And…that day. The day we met, that's why you were there. Did you know the asshole in the car?"

Caleb's eyes flashed with anger, and then cooled just as quickly. He was too fucking good at hiding his emotions. *Why are you like this? Why the fuck do you care, Livvie? He's made you the one thing you swore never to be.* "Does it really matter–"

"No, I guess it fucking doesn't," I cut in sharply. He wished he'd never met *me?* Well, the feeling was definitely fucking mutual. An old anger flared through me. My life just kept getting better and better. I was finally going to get out of one worthless existence, to prove to everyone I wasn't worthless and my scholarship had been my ticket out, and then Caleb happened to me. I was finally…. "I was finally going to show her she was wrong about me…"

"You don't need her approval," he said, correctly guessing who I was referring to. I looked up at him.

"You know *shit* about what I need. I've been dealing with your mindfucks for I don't know how long now, trying to figure out why someone like you would kidnap me. Despite what you've done to me, I've had these thoughts—"

"Thoughts, or fantasies, Kitten?" he broke in softly, his expression still cloaked.

"Both, I suppose," I admitted. It didn't matter what I said, not really. "I told myself you couldn't help yourself, that something happened to you to make you this way, to make you as fucked up as me, but you're even more fucked up than I am. And in the strangest corners of my mind I thought…"

"That you could fix me? What's more, that I could fix you? Well, sorry, Pet, I don't want to be fixed. Whatever your little school-girl brain told you about men is absurdly wrong. This isn't a romance. You're not a damsel in distress, and I'm not the handsome prince come to save you. You ran. I went to collect my property. End of story.

"In two years, maybe less, I'll have what I want— revenge. After that, I'll make sure you get your freedom. Fuck, I'll even send you on your way with enough money to go wherever you want. To *do whatever* you want. Until then…."

I wanted to cry. But crying hadn't done me a bit of good before, and it certainly wouldn't do me any good now. "How much?"

"Excuse me?"

"Afterward. When I'm done being your whore, how much will you pay me? Whores get paid, don't they?"

Caleb stared at me for what seemed an eternity, then, "What would you like?"

"My freedom. But in lieu of that…a million dollars?" It came out as a question instead of a firm demand. The reality was he didn't have to offer me anything. I had nothing to bargain with. He could take whatever he wanted.

"A million dollars? A bit much don't you think?"

"Fuck you."

Caleb smiled, the self indulgent little shit. "My apologies," he mocked with a slight forward bow, "What I meant to say is: no pussy's that good. Though yours does come close."

Now he was back to trying to shock me, and perhaps if I were still the naïve school girl he'd met all those weeks ago it might have worked. But I wasn't her right now and I liked it. I was powerful. Perhaps the calculating, angry, fighter version of me would take over completely, and I'd never be weak again. "How close?"

His smile was wry, "Half."

Outside, I was a placid lake. Inside, I was a raging ocean, "What exactly do I have to do?"

"Obey."

"You?"

"Yes. But also—"

"The man you're selling me to." My stomach rolled but I met his eyes. I'd survived this man. I could survive anything, I hoped. "Who is he?"

When Caleb spoke his tone was softer, but what did that mean to me now? Nothing. "His name is Demitri Balk. He's a billionaire who deals in guns, drugs, diamonds—anything that deals in misery and money."

And this was the man he intended to sell me to, had always intended. My heart sank lower. *You're not a damsel in distress and I'm not the handsome prince come to save you.* No. He wasn't. In real life you had to save yourself.

"He won't have you forever," Caleb said softly. "But you're a means to an end for others much more powerful than me. In a way, we're both chess pieces. I simply have a larger role to play, and it's a game I've invested my entire life in. If I could give you any hope, it's that I will do all within my power to ensure an end where you and I come out of this with the things we need." His tone said he had no doubt of his words, and I could tell it was important to him I believe him, too.

"Two years is a long time Caleb? Anything could happen." Something in me wanted to give way and break. I refused that inclination. I had to be strong, not for anyone but myself. "Then what?"

He was silent for a long time. "Slaves—" he began, and stopped as he registered my shock over the use of the word. "You'd be worth a lot to him. So long as you were obedient, there would be no need to harm you. You'd be…kept."

I gave a derisive laugh. "Just what every girl dreams of, a billionaire." I swallowed hard, sounding wooden and not myself. "Maybe I'll be ridiculously happy and we'll never have to think of each other again."

"Perhaps."

"Is he handsome, this Demitri? As handsome as you?" I said dully, softly and numb all over. Caleb visibly flinched. Good. That felt good, inflicting pain in him. I looked at Caleb. He was an example of what I could become if I let myself become hard, unforgiving, consumed with rage and vengeance. I couldn't be like that. I didn't want to be like him. "Will he make me come half as well as you do? Tell me, Caleb, tell me all of it. Tell me so I know what I'm getting into, and then tell me how I have no possible way out. It'll be better this way. Clean, and I can depend on myself—no need for the prince charming to rescue the damsel in distress."

Caleb turned his back on me, fists clenched at his sides. I couldn't imagine what the hell had made him angry this time. "You should try and get some sleep."

My eyes were stinging, but this was not the time to cry, not here and not with him being witness. I was tired of crying, of being feeble and in no control of my own life "I'd rather not sleep. I don't want to dream." I ran my hand through my sweat caked hair, something in me turning ice-cold and resolute. "I could use a shower though."

Caleb turned and I noticed immediately his face had altered to a stalemate. The argument was over, and I think we were both relieved to avoid the inevitable for now. He had told me what I wanted to know, and he didn't have to, but it didn't give me any relief, not the way I thought it would. I had thought that if I knew what to expect I could prepare myself for the horror to come. But—

That's not why you're upset. He doesn't care about you. Everything he's done has been to manipulate you into doing what he wants. Every touch, every kiss, him saying you're beautiful—it's all been a lie. And you fell for it.

"I'll help you." I looked up from my thoughts, and stared at Caleb's outstretched hand. I wanted to say what a joke his words were, not only these but every word he'd spoken and whatever words would follow, but I was afraid my voice would fail me, betray all the girlish feelings inside me.

Slowly, I used my good arm to peel the blankets away from my body and stood. My head swooned and I felt my body follow. For a split second my panic was mirrored on Caleb's face, but then relief swept through his features as he caught me. "Livvie," he said softly as his hands held my trembling shoulders, "let me help you."

My eyes remained glued to my lap as my face went both pale and red at the same time. Caleb stared too and I couldn't help but feel as though I had lost ground with him. *Did he just call me Livvie?*

Considering all that had transpired between us, I wasn't sure what I felt one second to the next, each moment laced with a different kind of suspicion and distrust but under all that, a shallow yearning. Caleb wasn't my prince charming, but it didn't mean I had to settle for anything less.

He held out a hand for me to take, and I did so. We walked into the bathroom together, and though this was not an unusual occurrence anymore, the fact that I was so broken, both inside and out made it different—more humiliating. My resolve was cracking under the weight of my tumultuous emotions.

"What's wrong?" Caleb asked, but I only shook my head in response and continued to stare at the ground. He stood in front of me and simply watched me for a moment.

"If I survive this, I can't go back. I'll have to move forward and I don't know what that means." I paused, feeling anesthetized. I would yield because I must, but I had to find a way to keep from breaking. "Do you?"

Caleb said nothing, which didn't mean anything.

He put his arms around me, as he had done so many times before and held me close for a moment. I knew his embrace was nothing more than a comforting lie. There was an end coming. An end to these moments between him and me when the lie felt like anything but. It was all I had left. My loose arm hung at my side, the other in its sling, but it still felt nice to be held, even if I wasn't an active participant. He went to pull away, but I wasn't ready to see his face just yet, and so I stepped closer, asking him in my silent way to wait a little longer. He held me a heartbeat longer and gave me a chaste kiss on the top of my head.

"How long do I have, Caleb? How long before you leave me?" Caleb cleared his throat a few times before he spoke and when he did, his voice cracked.

"A few months." He rushed to say the rest before I could get excited about the length of my reprieve. "You were only supposed to be with me for six weeks and a little over half that time has passed. We won't be alone much longer." He pressed himself against me, and I let him. He was actually talking, and I wanted him to continue. I thought for a moment about what all of this meant. I'd been away from home about three and a half weeks. Over three weeks. I couldn't put it into words – the deep loneliness at realizing I'd been missing for almost a month. Isolated with one other human being. No one really looking for me—not anymore.

"Is there any way—"

"No."

I paused. His tone was absolute. But I wondered if it was because he had considered it, considered keeping me from this fate. I had to believe he had. I had to hope he cared enough about me to ponder it. I had to; it was the only hope I had of seeing myself out of this situation but a part of me reserved itself for the truth.

"Will you miss me, Caleb?" I let my arm circle his waist. I don't know what prompted it and instantly I tried to pull away. He held me still.

"Yes," he said simply. The moment I tried to look up at him, he pulled away and turned his back to me, "But it doesn't change a single thing." I could tell he believed what he said.

He was closed to me again, I could tell in the way his shoulders squared as he turned to face me again. Caleb lifted the sling from around my neck, and the tingle of pain in my shoulder and collarbone brought me back to the moment, but I still stood there in a trance. After the sling came off, he lifted my nightgown over my head, careful to maneuver around my shoulder. He threw it in the wastebasket. I stood in front of him, wearing only bandages. Tonight he didn't really look at me the way he did on other nights. There was nothing *sexy* about me. Tonight he looked at me and there was hardly anything behind his eyes.

He walked back to me. "What's wrong?" he asked again, but he sounded distracted or dismissive, I didn't know which—maybe both.

"Nothing," I said again, solemnly, but I doubted he heard me. He was undoing the bandages around my mid-section, telling me I didn't really need the bandages to heal my ribs, but that having them in place would remind me not to sit in certain positions or make certain movements. He would replace them when I was done showering. Yes, I thought bitterly, the last thing I wanted was for my ribs to heal improperly.

He put his arms around me as he unwound the bandages, but though my breasts were only inches from his face, his eyes didn't register that he even noticed. In a strange way, this added to my embarrassment. Apparently, since everything was out in the open between us, there was no need for him to pretend to feel things for me he didn't. *But he said he would miss me. That has to mean something. Doesn't it?*

Once the bandages were off, we stared at one another for a moment, as if we both tried to figure out what the other was thinking. Then he walked over to the shower in the corner of the room and turned it on.

He never ran the shower, always the bath, though this was a simple thing for me to understand. I didn't exactly want to sit in my bath water at the moment either. What I didn't understand was how he was going to be able to help me wash myself if I was in the shower. I couldn't really raise my arm above my head to wash my hair, and moving around in general was painful because of my ribs. If this meant he was going to be in the shower with me, I didn't like the thought of it.

He tested the water and seemed satisfied. I felt his eyes staring me up and down and heat crept up into my face, my entire body blushed. He cleared his throat.

"Why don't you go ahead and get in this water. I'll get you the things you need. If you want me, call out for me. I'll be in the room."

I nodded as he walked past me, and I stood still until he left the room and the door shut behind him.

The water was warm, and clean, and reassuring on my skin. The shower had multiple heads at varying heights so no part of my body was left open to the air but the pressure wasn't so hard that it made me wince, but soft and gentle. I let it run all over me, I breathed in the steam and it seemed easier to take in air. I stood for several minutes before I lathered myself up, or at least the parts I could reach.

As I stood, I got lost in thought, alone in the shower for the first time in over three weeks. I knew once I stepped out of the shower, I would begin the hardest journey of my entire life. I would have to save myself. I would have to be strong and smart and brave. I would have to let the other side of me, the ruthless side, take over and this me…would cease to exist.

"Make him love you," Ruthless Me whispered. "Make it so he can't live without you. The devil you know." I felt her growing inside me, bringing with her the insane idea I actually wielded power with Caleb. I had never tried to "use my feminine wiles" before, but I had certainly been accused of it. What would happen if I actually tried?

The idea of trying to seduce Caleb frightened me, terrified me to the point of physical ache, but also…I wondered if I could. And that positively thrilled me. I wondered if I could bring that bastard to his knees with desire for me. I knew now why he had never fucked me in any conventional way; he needed a virgin.

And if he needed a virgin, then I needed to be anything but that.

Before I could stop myself, I leaned on the shower wall and cried, and cried, and cried.

Just for old time's sake.

FIFTEEN

It was out now—the truth. He would never forget the look in her eyes when he told her about his plan to sell her into sexual slavery. What had he expected? That she would understand? Revenge was his purpose. She could not understand that, not yet. It would haunt him forever. One more memory among hundreds that always haunted him. Except, he had always been the victim in those memories. Always the boy and never the man. Now, the kind of man he'd become would haunt him, too. Caleb slumped against the bathroom door. He needed a minute, to breathe, to keep from retching, and to deal with the jumble of thoughts tearing him apart. For the first time in recent memory, Caleb wanted something other than revenge. He wanted the girl. He wanted Livvie.

He knew her name now, but it was the least of what he now knew. He knew all kinds of things about her— too much maybe. She wore shapeless clothing to school because she wanted her mother to love her. Her eyes were sad because she knew her mother didn't.

She had brothers *and* sisters. She felt responsible for them and jealous of them.

She was funny, and shy, but also fierce and brave. Her first kiss had been a disaster.

She'd grown up without anyone to protect her.

And no one but Caleb had brought her physical pleasure.

Livvie was a survivor. That much he'd known, but what he hadn't known was *what* she'd had to survive. She deserved better. Better than them and certainly better than him.

He'd seen it in her eyes and her manner, but he had tried not to know why. He had wanted her nameless. He wanted to forget she had ever had a past, a history, dreams and hopes and all of those other things that made her...Livvie.

He could hear her crying through the bathroom door, and it nearly ripped his heart from his chest. He had done that. He had caused each and every one of her tears, and to his complete consternation, they did not make him hard, they made him... profoundly sad. Sadness was an emotion he had not felt in a very, very long time. And back then, he only felt it for himself; he'd never had pity for anyone else, not even the other boys.

Why now? Why her?

An image of her bloody and limp body in that young man's arms flashed across his mind and he doubled over. She could have died. And Caleb knew he would never forgive himself if that had come to pass. Whatever the reason, he felt something for the girl, something he'd never felt before and couldn't put into words. He just didn't know if it mattered. He had told her everything mattered, that everything was very personal, but what did it mean in the grand scheme of everything?

She could no sooner forgive him than he could forgive Narweh. She would never be able to see beyond everything he had done to her. So, in the end, what did it matter? He could never have the girl, so why not his vengeance? Didn't he deserve it?

Narweh is dead! You killed him. What more could you gain by destroying a man you've never seen?

Caleb shook the thoughts away. Rafiq had rescued him. He had put a roof over his head, food in his stomach and women in his bed. Caleb owed him everything, his very life. If Rafiq wanted Vladek dead, then Caleb owed him the man's head.

Rafiq wanted more that Vladek's life. He wanted him to suffer unspeakably. He wanted everything the man had ever loved to disintegrate like ash in his hands. It wouldn't bring his mother back, or his sister, but it seemed...right. It had always felt right to Caleb. He truly was Rafiq's loyal disciple, and it was the only thing that had given his life meaning. Without Rafiq, without their quest...what else did he have?

He could hardly sacrifice twelve years and his debt to Rafiq over three weeks and a girl who could never.... He'd almost thought the word love. *Love.* What the hell did that word even mean? It got tossed around so flippantly, by everyone. What did it really mean? After all this time and everything that had happened, was he even capable?

No. He didn't think so.

His phone rang. At this hour of the night, it could only be one person and wasn't it only too fitting.

"Yes?"

"How is she?" Rafiq's tone was cold and detached.

"Some cracked ribs and a dislocated shoulder." Caleb ran a hand through his still slightly damp hair and made a fist. He didn't want to have this conversation now. "I don't think three weeks will be enough time for

242

her to sufficiently heal. The journey might be too much." There was a long pause and for a moment Caleb thought the line had gone dead.

"Jair says you've taken hostages. He also says you made quite the spectacle of yourself in retrieving the girl...what do you think of that?" Caleb's hackles rose. This conversation was not going anywhere good.

"There was a man and a woman there. They could have answers I need. I don't know who else knows about the girl or about me, there could be witnesses. I don't know if she was able to contact anyone in the States. I'm covering our asses Rafiq. And since when do you get your information from Jair instead of me?" Caleb just barely stopped himself from shouting. He didn't want to scare Kitten...Livvie.

"I get my information from whoever is useful, and lately that hasn't been you." Rafiq spoke so matter-of-factly, as though his words were not deeply insulting. "You've made a mess, Caleb. The girl is injured, there are potential witnesses, no doubt the authorities there will wonder about that fucking fire you set. And now I assume you've taken the girl to a hospital, where there are even more potential loose ends. Sloppy, Caleb."

Caleb sighed heavily; weary down to his very soul. Still, his anger pushed to the fore, "Despite what you and your new friend Jair might think; I'm not a fool. This territory is run by the cartels; I doubt there will be any problems we can't buy our way out of. The house is cleared out by now and we'll be on our way to your contact's home in the morning. The girl will be fine, give me some time and some credit."

"Where are you now?"

"None of your concern." Caleb hung up before it could escalate. Damn it! He just wanted to be left in peace. *Livvie needs you.*

He let out a slow breath and exited the bedroom. He could hear the doctor and his wife whispering angrily in the kitchen. The woman was blaming her husband for their predicament and trying to convince him to loosen her tape so they could leave everything behind and escape. He told her to be quiet and to trust him. *Idiot.*

If the good doctor had any sense he would listen to his wife. Caleb was a killer. If he wanted to, he could kill them both while they were taped to the dining room chairs and walk away. It would certainly be the smartest and most efficient thing to do, but Caleb wasn't much for killing innocent people. Especially after they'd helped him.

Caleb stepped into the kitchen and all conversation abruptly ended. The woman eyed him guardedly, while her husband simply looked at him with raised eyebrows and a question in his eyes. Maybe that was why he was a doctor. Perhaps he was among the few truly altruistic doctors in the world. It would be a shame to kill him.

"Where do you keep your clothes?" He addressed the wife and she stared at him blankly. She obviously didn't speak any English. The doctor did speak some English, but still seemed oddly perplexed.

Caleb shook his head and muddled through his Spanish until the wife's eyebrows shot up. She turned to her husband and told him where he could locate what he needed.

"I understand you. It's just been a long time since I've had to speak." She stared at him with another blank expression. No, she didn't understand a word.

Caleb turned and trudged down the couple's hallway toward their bedroom. Apparently doctors did well for themselves, even here in Mexico. The room was very nicely decorated, warm colors and white furniture, very modern. Their wedding photo sat on their dresser in a crystal frame. They looked happy, presumably...in love.

You're thinking like a woman.

Caleb smiled to himself; *there* was a thought he'd never had. But then, he never waxed philosophically on the topic of love before.

I killed for her. Held a doctor at gun-point in a hospital for her, and then followed the poor bastard home to keep her safe. Even now, I'm searching for things to make her more comfortable. Isn't that what love is?

You'd better hope not.

Caleb's smile faded. This line of thinking could only bring about more tragedy. Even if he wanted... things. What was he supposed to do? Explain it to Rafiq? As if he would understand. As if he would care. He'd probably put a bullet in them both—or at least her. And then he'd *have* to shoot Caleb, because there was no way he would ever allow him to hurt her. This thought instantly shocked him. He had already admitted he would miss her, something he should never have said, and now...he presumed to risk his life for her with Rafiq. He pushed the idea away firmly.

It was better to keep things on course. The girl would heal. Rafiq would get what he wanted and then Caleb would be free of his obligations. He would set the girl free and cut his losses. Yes, he nodded; it was the best thing for all of them, even the girl. *Livvie.*

No. Her name is Kitten.

Caleb found what he was looking for, clothes for Kitten. As he headed back toward his procured bedroom, he passed his hostages in the kitchen. Again, their conversation halted. The wife had been crying, but her manner was stoic. She was a brave one. "We will leave in the morning. I promise no harm will come to either of you, but I must tell you that my mercy is conditional. If you tell anyone we were here, or what happened to you—"

"You have my word!" The doctor was adamant. He'd seen Caleb covered in blood, knew it was arterial, perhaps even knew what Caleb had done. He didn't doubt the doctors' sincerity. While the doctor stared into his wife's tear-filled eyes, Caleb glimpsed the depth of their love for one another. They would live together or they would die together, but either way, they would do anything to protect each other.

It was a strange thing to witness. It was an even stranger thing to feel envious of his hostages. No one had ever looked at him that way, as if life were insignificant without him and he'd never valued anyone more than he valued himself. Whatever love was, it was a concept he could not grasp.

On his way back to Kitten, he spied the linen closet and grabbed a set of fresh sheets for the bed. The air felt different once he entered the room again. The bathroom door was slightly open, steam drifting into the bedroom. Caleb placed the clothes and sheets on the bed and went inside.

246

She had found the mirror. Every bathroom had one and he hadn't thought to cover it in his haste to get away from Livvie and her emotionally charged questions. He stood watching her, trying to discern his next action.

"They really did a number on me didn't they?" She winced as she poked at the large bruise covering most of her cheek and eye.

"It'll fade." Caleb said, trying to imitate her nonchalant tone. They both knew there was nothing casual about the situation, but he was willing to pretend if she was.

"Will I still be pretty enough for Demitri?" Her voice was cold and hard as he'd never heard it. She had meant the words to cut him and with great surprise, Caleb accepted that they had.

"In a few weeks," he said just as harshly and regretted it instantly when he saw sadness break through her façade of calm. She was strange to be around at the moment. A bomb waiting to explode. He couldn't possibly predict any of her actions and it made them both erratic.

She turned, facing him fully nude. Her body may have been marred with bruises, but she was still beautiful. Still…the girl he wanted. There was something in her demeanor that made him want to take a step back, but he fought against that instinct. He would never back down from anyone, especially not her.

She was…stalking him. Like a panther or a lioness, and it was odd to think in that moment that he had given her such an appropriate moniker. Though, she was not truly a kitten at the moment. Kittens didn't approach you with their eyes fixed and their heads lowered in such a manner to evoke images of a huntress eyeing a meal.

She stopped just short of Caleb's chest and so close he could almost feel her nipples brush against him. He shouldn't want her, not when she looked like this. But he did. Perhaps he even wanted her more. She had been beaten and bruised, but she had survived! She had looked those sons of whores in their eyes and she had drawn the first blood. There was a fighter and a killer in there somewhere. And there was just something sexy about that. He'd thought so even while she had pointed his gun at him.

"Caleb," she whispered. Caleb could only make a non-committal sound and stare at her. "So much has happened. I've been so powerless."

Bullshit, Caleb thought.

"If I could just…have *one* thing for myself." Caleb's urge to step back was nearly overwhelming, but he held his ground and nodded.

Livvie looked up at him with pleading and hungry eyes. "Make love to me," she said, so softly Caleb thought she'd only said it in his mind. Then he realized her small hand had slipped under his shirt. "I want to choose this one thing for myself. I'll do what you ask of me. I won't try to run away, but I want this one thing, this one choice…to be mine."

Caleb wanted to say something, anything, but his every thought revolved around being inside her. There was an easy answer for why she might try this. *If she's not a virgin….* He didn't care. He just didn't fucking

248

care. He'd deal with it later. So instead of *no*, he simply said, "I don't want to hurt you."

"You won't. I know you won't."

He couldn't stop himself from leaning down and putting his lips to hers. She shook slightly, more like the kitten he remembered. His heart raced and his cock swelled and pulsed. Her tongue darted out shyly, and he opened his mouth to her, letting her take things where she wanted them to go.

He didn't trust himself to touch her quite yet, so strong was the urgency he felt, so he finally took that step back and rest his hands against the door jam while she pressed forward and kissed him more assuredly and aggressively.

Her mouth tasted of mint, which he figured was toothpaste, and salt from her tears. He didn't want her to cry. Not right now, not for any reason. He pulled away slowly, "Stop." She stared up at him with a startled and vulnerable look on her face.

"Did I do something wrong?" she asked, and the words lanced something deep inside him.

"God, no. You're perfect. I just…I don't want to hurt you. And the way I feel right now…" If he ever blushed in his life, he might have blushed right then. "I know I'll hurt you."

He nearly groaned when she blushed, smiled, and looked away. "So, what then?"

"So come with me." He took her hand, careful of which hand it was and led her to the bed. Slowly, he guided her onto it. She was far more timid now than she had been a few moments ago, but she didn't hesitate. He kissed her lips softly as he lay next to her and coaxed her legs slightly apart. In a maneuver he had practiced with her many times, he kissed his way down her neck, chest, breasts, and stomach.

"Oh!" She whimpered as soon as his lips touched the soft, damp, hair between her thighs. He hadn't even licked her yet and he could feel her coiled tension. He kissed the top of her pussy in the hopes of soothing some of her fear. This wasn't going to hurt one. Little. Bit. He was going to make her feel good. He was going to make her feel the way she deserved to feel.

When he felt her thighs slowly open, giving him room to move, he dipped his head and let the tip of his tongue slide from the very bottom of her slit to the hard pebble of her clit in one slow, steady motion that had her mewling and opening for him further. "Do you want me to stop?" he whispered against her wet lips, and with no intention of doing any such thing.

"Fuck no. I'd kill you." She said with such sincerity that Caleb couldn't help but chuckle against her thigh.

"Where'd you learn to talk like that?" he mocked gently. She responded by rocking her hips up slightly. She winced a little and they both remembered how hurt she was. He didn't want to make her ask again. He caressed her leg and delved his tongue a little deeper, probing, sucking her deep, pink folds into his mouth.

Unconsciously, she attempted to pull away from him. Not because she wasn't enjoying it, he knew, but because the sensation of being licked and sucked simultaneously was nearly too much sensation to bear. His mind entertained a fantasy of his cock being sucked into her mouth, the tip licked by her soft tongue and he groaned against her. His hips rocked hard into the bed, but he remained focused on her pleasure. He let up a

250

little, allowing her to adjust and then he pulled her in tight and did it again.

She gasped and moaned and rocked her little pussy on the tip of his eager tongue, and this time there was no thought of pain. There was only pleasure.

His fingers found her and spread her open. Within her wet folds he found the tiny opening to her body. He licked it and she shivered. He slicked the tip his finger against her clit, loving the way she whimpered and writhed. She moaned. "Caleb," and then her hands were in the way, pressing his fingers to her flesh in a plea for something she didn't fully understand yet. Her hand clutched at his, "It feels…oh god. I think…" And the rest went unsaid as he moved his hand against her clit and his mouth sucked her fingers.

He felt her pussy pulse beneath his hand and he wished he could see it, those tiny muscles contracting. Her pussy leaking wetness onto the bed. He'd lick that up too. But this wasn't about him.

For a long time, he rested his cheek against her thigh, panting and breathless, even as she was also panting and breathless. Her hand moved slowly, and he nearly sighed when she ran her fingers through his hair. Despite the fact his dick felt like it had been punched in the eye, he wished this moment could last for a very long time. He couldn't be certain of her motives for trying to have sex with him, especially after all that had transpired between them and in the hours before he was able to reach her, but he could not deny it had changed something in him, irrevocably. He had underestimated her in some way, and she had found a way to affect him. At the moment, he couldn't bring himself to care, but soon it would matter very much.

"What about you?" The words were sluggish and he suspected she was only being polite and had no real intention of moving, let alone helping him finish.

He smiled. "Don't worry about me. I'm not prone to acts of selflessness, so let's just both enjoy this moment." He looked up in time to see her smile to herself and then she gently nodded off to sleep.

He lifted himself off the bed as stealthily as possible and grabbed the clean sheets he had brought. The comforter was clean, so he didn't bother moving her, he just covered her up and climbed in next to her, clothes and all. He indulged himself for several minutes, simply looking at her, beyond the bruises.

An annoying beep pulled him away from his thoughts. He wanted to kiss her. He wanted to remove his clothes and rub his dick across her soft skin. He wanted inside of her.

He shook himself and got up to pick up his phone from the floor. He had received a text:

R: I'M FLYING IN. SEE YOU SOON.

He felt dizzy, then angry, then like yelling and throwing things around the room, and then...a deep, deep loss. He thought about the three and a half weeks with Livvie and the time that was now lost to them. All the debt piled high above his head. He stared at the text, feeling...nothing at all. He watched Livvie sleep and the rage that had always coiled and seethed, floated away.

Rafiq, he thought, *Rafiq*. Things had just become

more complicated than he had ever dreamed. As he looked at the sleeping girl on the bed, only one thought entered his mind. *Be strong.* Whether he meant the thought for himself or the girl, he had no energy to guess. He only knew he wanted to get back in bed with her and pretend the last few minutes never happened.

A Note to the Reader

I have a very love/hate relationship with series. I love to read them, but I hate to wait! So when it was suggested to me that I make *Dark* into a trilogy, I fought very hard against it. However, after giving it some very serious thought I have come to the conclusion that this story is best told in TWO parts.

The journey that lies ahead for Olivia and Caleb is wrought with discovery, intrigue and of course – passion. *Lots*, of passion. Cramming all of it into one novel would not have done it justice. So, at the risk of losing a fan, I ask you to please be patient and savor the tension. It'll be worth the wait.

In the meantime, I would love to hear what you thought of *Captive in the Dark*. Please feel free to email me at AuthorCJRoberts@gmail.com Who knows, there could be some sneak-peeks of *Seduced in the Dark* in it for you.

Keep Reading,
CJ

About the Author

CJ Roberts sucks at referring to herself in the third person, but she will try.

She was born and raised in Southern California. Following high school, she joined the U.S. Air Force in 1998, served ten years and traveled the world. Her favorite part of traveling is seeking out the seedy underbelly of the city.

She is married to an amazing and talented man who never stops impressing her; they have one beautiful daughter.

She has also self-published one short story on Amazon, entitled *Manwich*, under the name Jennifer Roberts.

Follow her on Twitter @AuthorCJRoberts
www.aboutcjroberts.com

COMING
9/1/2012

Seduced
In the Dark

By: CJ Roberts

Printed in Great Britain
by Amazon.co.uk, Ltd.,
Marston Gate.